RISING
FROM
THE *ashes*

A PICKING UP THE PIECES NOVEL

XOXO -
Jessica Prince

JESSICA PRINCE

D1714269

dedication

To Brittany,

Every snarky one-liner or clever joke Savannah said came from you.
I love you so much, Seester!

contents

prologue

Savannah

PAST: WINTER 2006

"I don't understand. Things have been great between us."

I couldn't bring myself to look into Jeremy's chocolate brown eyes as I ripped both of our hearts to shreds. I was being a total coward, and I knew it, but I reasoned that at least I wasn't doing it through text or email. Not that it was any consolation at all. I hated myself for what I was doing.

"Things have been strained for a while, Jeremy, you know that," I replied in a weak voice. How was I ever going to convince him this was what I really wanted when I couldn't even convince myself?

"That's bullshit, and you know it, Savannah!"

I recoiled, his tone harsh and louder than I'd ever heard it before. The anger burning in his eyes took me completely by surprise. Jeremy wasn't an angry person by nature. I'd never seen him the slightest bit violent in all the years that I'd known him. Hell, the man practically never raised his voice a day in his life. Seeing him react with so much emotion was a hard hit on my already shaky resolve.

"Jer," I whispered, "ever since Emmy—"

He cut me off, slicing his hand through the air. "Don't." His voice, low and cold, caused goose bumps to spread over my arms. "Don't you use what happened to Emmy as a reason to end us. What happened to her was terrible, and my heart broke for her, but that's not us, Savvy. That wasn't our loss, so it shouldn't put a strain on our relationship."

That wasn't exactly true. Emmy losing her baby was definitely part of the reason I was ending my relationship with the guy I'd loved since I was fourteen years old. There was no way I could let him know just how I'd let things snowball out of control after watching my friend hit rock bottom. Jeremy would hate me until the day he died if he knew the truth. That was why I had to end things.

It had been two months since I made the decision that ultimately destroyed everything I held dear, and looking at myself in the mirror was getting harder and harder with every passing day. I knew if Jeremy found out what I'd done, he would be as disgusted with me as I already was. That wasn't a risk I was willing to take. Like I said before, I was a coward.

I made the decision to end things because I couldn't handle the guilt of what I'd done, and the longer I stayed in the relationship, the harder it was to keep it from Jeremy. This was going to hurt him. I knew that because I was already dying inside. But he'd eventually get over it, and hopefully, we'd be able to be friends again. Breaking up with him was the only way I could keep him in my life without running the risk of him finding out and hating me forever.

I honestly thought that I'd be able to get past what I had done. I knew it would be hard for a while, but I never expected it to effect me so strongly. Every day I woke up, the first thing I wished for was to go back and do everything differently. But that was why people say hindsight is twenty-twenty, wasn't it?

I sucked in a deep breath and tried to steel myself for what I had to do next. I was about to drive the final nail into the coffin that was our relationship. If I drug it out any longer it would become impossible for me to stick to my decision.

"I can't do this anymore, Jeremy. Watching what Emmy went through showed me how short life really is. It got me thinking that you're the only person I've ever been with." I squeezed my eyes shut tightly, swallowing past the lump forming in my throat. Hurting Jeremy was the last thing I ever wanted to do, but it was inevitable.

"We've been together since we were fourteen. I want to see what else is out there. I want to be able to date other guys. We shouldn't have to tie ourselves down to one person at nineteen, Jer. We're too damn young. There's too much that we haven't experienced yet. I just feel like we're holding each other back."

If the expression on his face could physically maim, I would have been dead on the floor.

"So, let me get this straight," he hissed out, his jaw ticking from the strain of trying to stay composed. "You're breaking up with me because you wanna fuck other dudes. Am I getting this right?"

"It's not like that." I hated how he'd basically broken down my carefully constructed reason. Deep down, I knew there was no other guy. I didn't want anyone but Jeremy, but because of my actions, I couldn't allow myself to have him anymore.

"AM I FUCKING RIGHT OR NOT?" he roared.

Tears instantly started streaming down my face, unchecked. What I was about to say would do irreparable damage. Worrying about keeping my tears at bay wasn't even a consideration.

"Yes," I whispered in a hoarse, broken voice.

One word.

One word was all it took for Jeremy to look at me like I was a stranger, someone he didn't know anymore.

One word, and I had crushed all hope at having the future I truly wanted.

One word was all it took for him to turn and walk away without looking back.

One word, and I'd lost the only person I ever loved.

CHAPTER
one

PRESENT

"Come on, you fucking piece of shit...WORK!"

It was five o'clock on Friday evening, and my computer had decided it wanted to freeze up before I got the chance to back up all my work. I was determined to beat the stupid excuse for electronic machinery into submission if it was the last thing I did.

I was supposed to be meeting my friends at our local hangout, Colt 45's, for an impromptu engagement party for Gavin and Stacia, but if my fossil of a computer decided to crap out on me, I was going to be stuck drafting deposition designations all weekend long. I wasn't exactly ecstatic about attending an engagement party, not with the way things had been going in my personal life lately, but I wanted to be stuck at the office on a Friday night even less.

I knew I had been acting like a total bitch, and I hated that I couldn't control it. I really *was* happy for Gavin and Stacia. They were two of my best friends and were an adorable couple who had been together forever. It was just that being around all that happiness and love and wedding talk brought my nonexistent love life to the forefront of my mind, shining like a bright red beacon to spinsterhood.

It was like the freaking love bug had bitten everyone I knew—well, everyone but me. Gavin and Stacia had just gotten engaged. Emmy and Luke were back together after an eight-year hiatus, and they were living a life of bliss and sex. But the topper on the romantic crap cake was Jeremy, my ex-boyfriend and the man I was doomed to love for the rest of my pathetic life.

A few months ago, Emmy had hired a new waitress at her diner, Virgie May's. *Charlotte.* Just saying her name was like a curse word for me. I absolutely *hated* that girl. She had everyone fooled into thinking she was this disgustingly sweet, innocent little Southern belle, but I totally knew better. She was a freaking viper just waiting to strike.

Jeremy had taken one look at the delicate little flower and was totally sprung. The two of them were practically sewn together at the hip, and it was enough to make me want to hurl.

Honestly, I wanted nothing more than for Jeremy to be happy. I was still completely in love with the guy, and always would be, but it was my own actions that had driven us apart and kept us that way for all these years. I knew that one day he'd meet someone who would take him away from me for good.

I just didn't want it to be *her.* I just knew there was something shady about Charlotte, the Southern Sweetie. It wasn't like I had any tangible proof that she was a raving bitch or anything. It was more of a gut feeling that had absolutely *nothing* to do with the fact that she was dating Jeremy…really.

When she had first been hired on last summer, things started off pretty well between us. I'd had a sneaking suspicion that she wasn't all that she seemed to be, but I'd just brushed it off as no big deal. When she and Jeremy had started to hang out, I'll admit that it had chapped my ass a little, but I'd tried to pull an Emmy and be the bigger person. I never realized how hard that was going to be.

About a week into her and Jeremy's relationship, she had turned straight-up frosty toward me. One night when we had all gone to Colt's, Lizzy had gotten a little sauced and spilled the beans about my relationship with Jeremy, but it wasn't as if I'd been actively trying to break them up. In my opinion, I'd done a pretty excellent job at faking a crapload of happiness for them. But once she found out that Jeremy and I had a past, she cut off any advances I had tried to make toward friendship.

When we were out as a group, she'd do her best to keep Jeremy away from me. It wasn't out-and-out obvious to the rest of the group, of course. She would be sneaky about it. She'd stay to one side of the group and that always happened to be the opposite side of wherever I was. Considering she was Jeremy's new girlfriend, it didn't take a genius to figure he'd follow her wherever she went.

If an opportunity ever arose where Jeremy and I were able to actually have a conversation, she always had an excuse to leave, or she'd need his help with something so that he'd have to walk away from me. And I never missed the evil little smirks she shot at me when the others weren't watching.

Jeremy having a girlfriend hurt like a son of a bitch, but as long as we remained friends, I knew I'd just have to suck it up. I'd made my own bed, and I was willing to lie in it.

Charlotte trying to take him away from me *completely* was not going to fly though. I needed to figure out a way to out her as the devious little skank she really was without making it obvious to all of my friends. I just hadn't figured out how to pull that one off yet.

Channeling all my frustrations into my piece of shit computer, I hauled my leg back and kicked the living hell out of the unit under my desk. "Ha-ha!" I cried out as the damn thing started back up. I quickly hit the Save button before the computer decided it hated me again and lost all my hard work.

"You sure showed it, didn't you?" came a voice from behind me.

I let out a startled squeak and spun around to see who was in the doorway of my office. Standing in all of his six-one, lean muscled, GQ cover model glory in a three-piece suit was the newest attorney hired on at Pruett & Carter, Attorneys at Law—Benjamin Bennett III.

Growing up in a house with a lawyer as a father had made me swear up and down that I would never be involved in the legal field in any way, shape, or form. But when my best friend, Emmy, had started having complications with her pregnancy and Luke hadn't been in the picture, I couldn't imagine leaving her to deal with things alone, so I'd packed up after graduation and moved back home to help her.

From spending summers helping out at my father's firm, I'd picked up a thing or two, so it hadn't been difficult to get a job. But imagine his shock when I'd turned down a well-paying paralegal position at Morgan & Carls LLP in Houston to take one for half the salary at Pruett & Carter, but I'd had my reasons. First, P&C was located in Cloverleaf, so I was never too far away from Emmy if she ever needed anything. Second was because I'd spent my entire life being *Robert Morgan's daughter*, and I would be damned if I was going to spend one more day of my life stuck under that man's thumb.

The money hadn't mattered to me. I'd gotten a hefty inheritance from my grandmother on my dad's side when she passed away, so I was set financially. What mattered to me was my pride and self-worth. I'd managed to come out of the Morgan household relatively unscathed despite my mother's efforts to shoot my confidence down at every turn, and I was going to make damn sure I stayed that way.

I loved my life and my friends, and they loved me. *They* were what mattered, and after a childhood where everything was conditional, finding a group of friends who loved me unconditionally was all I needed.

So, I took the job at P&C, working directly for Mr. Pruett, and I couldn't have been happier with my decision. Bradford Pruett was in his late sixties and had the disposition of Santa Claus—and the belly to go along with it. He treated me as an equal, not a slave, and he showed all his employees the same amount of respect he would expect in return.

I truly believed I had the best boss in the world—until that moment when my computer breathed its last breath, let out a creepy groan, and died on me completely.

Thank God I saved that shit first.

Mr. Pruett really needed to invest in new computers.

"I think you killed it," Benjamin said as he tried to hide his smile.

My cheeks grew red at having the attention of such a fine specimen. I knew I was relatively attractive with my honey blonde hair and eyes that almost matched. I never really lacked for dates, but the only man who I ever really paid any attention to was Jeremy. And while I found Benjamin to be at least mildly attractive, he was night to Jeremy's day.

Jeremy was all manly man with grease under his nails from working on cars, and big, brawny muscles from a lifetime of manual labor. It was obvious Benjamin hadn't worked with his hands a day in his life.

Jeremy would never be caught dead in a three-piece suit. If it wasn't ripped jeans and a flannel or T-shirt, he wasn't going to bother with it. His carefree attitude about his appearance was only one of the many things that I loved about him.

But Benjamin was the type of man my parents always wanted me to bring home—well mannered, highly educated, and pedigreed. I wasn't used to attracting attention from men like him. My mouth had a tendency to run them off before they got the chance to get to know my sparkling personality.

"Um...yeah. I think it's safe to say there's no bringing this one back," I said as I waved my hand at the computer I'd just murdered. "I think it might be time for the firm to upgrade."

I tried to smile back at him, but I was suddenly embarrassed that I'd been caught taking my anger out on my PC.

His face finally broke into a full-blown smile, showing his perfectly straight, brilliant white teeth. "Yeah, that has to be it. It couldn't possibly be because you went Ali on it."

Is he flirting with me? He couldn't be. There was no way a man like him looked at a woman like me. I might have grown up in a country club household, but I was so far from the typical white-collar persona that it wasn't even funny.

"Sorry about that, Mr. Bennett. I know it wasn't very professional—"

He held up his hand to cut me off. "Please, just call me Ben. Mr. Bennett makes me feel like my old man. And as far as the computer killing goes, I'm right there with you. I wanted to throw mine out the window earlier."

I smiled up at him, feeling some of my embarrassment melt away. "Yeah, well, welcome to P&C where the people are fun to work with, but the electronics are one step up from DOS."

He leaned against the doorjamb to my office and crossed his arms over his chest. I couldn't help but think that he was wrinkling his expensive suit. But damn, if he didn't look good while doing it. The stance made his sleeves pull tightly across his well defined biceps, and I felt the ridiculous need to reach out and squeeze them.

"Yeah, I'm quickly discovering that the people make this a wonderful place to work," he replied with a mouthwatering grin.

Yep, he's flirting.

I sat frozen in my swivel chair as Ben's eyes roamed over my body. It wasn't in that creepy, stalkerish way that made a woman feel violated, but it was still obvious that he was checking me out.

I started to feel that tingly, excited sensation that happens when a woman notices how attractive a man really is. I was normally known for my quick and cutting responses, but for some reason, Ben had me tongue-tied. I couldn't find my footing when he looked at me like that.

"Um…thanks, I guess?" *Fucking brilliant, Savannah!*

He let out a low, rumbling chuckle that I felt deep down in my belly.

"So, you have any big plans for the evening?" he asked casually.

We'd never had a conversation that lasted longer than it took us both to say good morning or good night. Feeling out of sorts from the change in our usual interaction, I turned back to my desk and started packing my stuff up for the evening. I needed to find something to do other than stare at him with my mouth hanging open. And there was a strong possibility that I might have drooled—just a little bit.

"I have to attend an engagement party for a couple of friends tonight. You?" I felt like a total dillhole sitting there, making small talk with one of the firm's attorneys while picturing him naked. Man, I was really off my game.

"No big plans," he responded.

He rubbed his palms on his pant legs, and if I didn't know better, I would have thought he was slightly uncomfortable. But it didn't make sense for him to be uncomfortable around me. I was just a lowly old paralegal. He didn't have any reason to be uncomfortable.

"I was thinking about checking out all that Cloverleaf has to offer. I haven't really had time to do much more than work since I got here."

I slung my purse over my arm and took a step toward him. "Well, I'd give you a tour, but this *is* Cloverleaf. Everything worth seeing is basically in a four block radius. You can stand in the middle of Main Street and turn in a circle to see it all."

He gave me an awkward smile, and it finally dawned on me what he was doing. I felt like a complete moron for not catching on. Ben had only been in town for a few weeks. Having come from Austin, he didn't have any family in Cloverleaf, and with the hours he had been putting in, I couldn't imagine him really having much time to make any friends. The poor guy had to be lonely. I felt horrible for not noticing sooner.

"Hey, if you get a chance, you should stop by Colt's for a drink or two."

"Oh, I don't want to crash your friends' engagement party."

I could tell by the way his eyes widened slightly that the idea of coming for a drink appealed to him, but he was still unsure.

"It's not like that, Ben. We didn't buy out the bar or anything. It's just a group of friends having a drink at our local hangout to congratulate the couple on their engagement. It'll be really laid back, I promise."

11

He finally loosened up a little bit, and his smile became more genuine. "I might take you up on that," he said. "Colt's?"

I forgot that he wouldn't know our bar as Colt's since he wasn't a local. "Sorry, Colt 45's on Walker. You can't miss it. It's one of the only decent bars in town."

"All right, I might just do that."

His eyes scanned me up and down again. How he managed to do that without coming off as perverted was beyond me. The dude had mad skill.

"Well, I hope to see you there, Ben. Have a good evening." He side stepped, allowing me to pass by, before following me out of my office. I pulled the door closed and headed to the elevator.

I was nowhere near being over Jeremy, but he'd moved on, and it was time I did too. I didn't plan on moving on with a coworker. That would be way too messy. But at least I was opening myself up to the idea.

CHAPTER
two

By the time I walked into Colt's, the party was in full swing.

"Savvy!" was yelled by my friends from different directions of the bar.

I made my way to the happy couple and gave them both hugs and congratulations before pushing my way to the bar for a tequila shot and beer chaser. I already knew it was going to be a hard liquor kind of night.

Emmy pushed up next to me and wrapped an arm around my waist. "Almost thought you weren't gonna make it, Savvy."

I hugged her back and let out an exhausted sigh. "I got held up at work."

She gave me a concerned look and asked, "You doing okay?"

It was a standard question she had started asking when Charlotte and Jeremy got together. I was getting so tired of hearing it, but I knew she couldn't help but be concerned.

I downed my shot and smiled up at her. "I'm good now," I replied. Being five-three and having a best friend who was five-seven could be a little challenging on my neck at times, but I wouldn't pick a different BFF for all the money in the world. I grabbed my beer and spun around, holding it in the air. "To the happy couple!" I shouted.

"To the happy couple!" everyone repeated.

If I'd learned anything in the past few months, it was that in order to get the spotlight off of myself, I needed to direct it onto someone else. Since it was Gavin and Stacia's night, who better to point it at than them?

Emmy gave me a look that told me she knew what I was doing, but she let it go anyway. We both knew it wasn't the time or the place to discuss anything the slightest bit upsetting.

Two of our best friends were getting married, and I was going to be my normal, smart-ass, perky self if it killed me.

Stacia stumbled over to the bar where Lizzy had just joined Emmy and me.

"I'm getting married, bitches!" she hollered as she threw her arms in the air, spilling her drink on the floor in the process.

Clearly, Stacia was taking this as her opportunity to get completely annihilated.

"Hey, drunky. How ya doin'?" I asked.

She wrapped her arms around my neck and squeezed me so tight that I thought my bones were going to start cracking. She started petting my hair and rubbing my cheeks. "I lub you so mush, Savvy," she slurred. "You're gonna be a brisemain."

"I'm gonna be a what?" I asked with a laugh, not able to understand a damn drunk word coming out of her mouth.

"A brisemain...a birdman...*damn it!* A bridesmaid!" She finally got the word out on the third try, but she had to drag it out several syllables longer than she needed to.

I did a little hop and wrapped my arms around her as well. "Ah, yay! I'd love to be a bridesmaid!"

"Yay!" she shouted back about five times louder than was necessary, even for the crowded bar.

Everyone turned to look at our exchange before laughing at Stacia's drunken happy dance. Out of the corner of my eye, I caught a glimpse of Charlotte scowling at me. Of course she managed to do it when everyone had turned their attention elsewhere. I decided not to let her ruin my night, and I turned away from her.

"So, who all is in the wedding?" I asked Emmy and Lizzy.

Since there was no way Stacia could form a sentence to answer me, Emmy did. "Well, it's me, you, Lizzy, and Stacia's cousin Mickey on her side, and Luke, Brett, Jeremy, and Trevor on Gavin's."

I smiled at the thought of all my closest friends standing together for Gavin and Stacia's big day. When I looked back over at Charlotte, she was standing slightly behind everyone else, pouting. The only reason I could figure for her sulking was that she was mad she hadn't been included in the wedding party.

Well, too bad, bitch. These are my friends.

It might have been childish, but I couldn't help from thinking that way when it came to her. She was already trying to take Jeremy away. I wasn't going to allow her to take any other friends from me.

Jealousy wasn't an emotion I was familiar with, and I couldn't stand what it was turning me into. I hated the uneasy, anxious feeling that boiled inside of me every time I was around Charlotte. That mixed with the hatred I was carrying around made me feel like I was going crazy most of the time. I'd only felt this miserable once in my life, and I liked it as much now as I had back then.

I looked at Gavin as he stared at his fiancée with a goofy, love-struck smile on his face, and I did my best to soak up some of his happiness.

"I'm so happy for you both, Gavin," I said after he made his way to the bar to stand next to me. I couldn't stop all the mushy feelings coursing through me as I stared into his eyes. There was just so much happiness there. I wrapped him in another hug.

"Thanks, Savvy. I'm just glad all of you are gonna be a part of our big day."

"Me too."

"Shots!" Stacia hollered from the bar a few feet away.

Gavin pulled from my embrace to go stop her from potential alcohol poisoning.

As the night wore on, more drinks were consumed, and everyone was in a celebratory mood—well, everyone except for me. I was mad at myself for not being able to fully enjoy my friends' happiness. I always prided myself on being a hundred percent supportive at all times, but I couldn't, and that just wasn't like me at all.

I was sitting at the bar, watching Luke and Emmy dancing to a slow song, when the bar stool next to me was pulled out. I didn't have to look over to know who was sitting next to me. He affected me so greatly, and I was so in tune with everything about him that I always knew where he was in a room without having to look. I could sense him.

"I feel like I haven't talked to you all night," Jeremy said as he leaned forward and propped both elbows on the bar. I quickly diverted my eyes from the sight of his biceps straining against the fabric of his shirt before I started to drool into my drink. He waved to the bartender with his empty beer bottle, indicating he wanted another.

"That's because you haven't," I responded, instantly regretting the snarky tone of my voice.

Jeremy hadn't done anything other than start a relationship with another woman. I had no right to be mad at him, but the resentment was still there, churning in my gut. I felt like I'd been placed on a back burner when it came to him. We might not be a couple, but we were still supposed to be friends. I thought I was more important than that.

He let out an exhausted sigh and scrubbed his hands over his face. "I know, Savannah, and I'm sorry. It seems like we haven't really talked in a while, doesn't it?"

The tone of his voice echoed exactly how I felt, and I gave him a small, sad smile.

"Yeah, things have been kinda strained, haven't they?"

It was weird, but I needed him to confirm that he was feeling the same way I was. It helped to know that he wasn't ignorant to the fact that our relationship had changed, and it was comforting to know that he wasn't okay with it either.

"They really have...and I hate it."

I felt a sense of relief come over me. I let out a sigh and gave him a real smile. "Me too," I whispered.

He opened his mouth to respond, but a deep voice cut him off. "Savannah?"

I turned around to see Ben standing directly behind me. He'd removed his suit jacket and tie, and he was only in his dress shirt and slacks. The top two buttons of his shirt were undone, and the sleeves were folded almost to his elbows, showing off his thick, corded forearms.

I'd never seen him so casual before. It brought out just how handsome he really was. His face was sporting a little bit of scruff from not having shaved since the morning, and while he still looked GQ, it added a ruggedness to his appearance.

"Ben...hi." I turned to see Jeremy furrow his brows as he took Ben in from the top of his well-styled hair to the bottom of his expensive-as-hell dress shoes.

"I'm not too late, am I?" Ben asked, looking concerned. "Are you about to leave?"

I tucked a loose strand of hair behind my ear and struggled to pull my eyes off of Jeremy and concentrate on Ben standing in front of me. I wanted to continue our conversation, but I also didn't want to be rude to Ben. After all, he was new in town and didn't know anyone.

"Oh no, I'm not leaving yet." I turned back to Jeremy and started introductions. "Jeremy, this is Benjamin Bennett. He's an attorney at P&C." I turned back to Ben. "Ben, this is one of my best friends, Jeremy Matthews."

Ben reached out and shot Jeremy a friendly smile. "It's nice to meet you."

Still looking a little skeptical, Jeremy shook Ben's hand. "Yeah," Jeremy replied sullenly. "You new to P&C or something? I've never heard Savvy talk about you."

It shocked me to hear something so snarky come out of Jeremy's mouth. I swung back around, wide-eyed. Jeremy was one of the nicest, most even-tempered men I'd ever met. By his standards, hearing him say that to Ben was beyond rude.

Ben removed his hand and uncomfortably ran it through his hair. He obviously caught on to the vibe Jeremy was throwing out. "Uh...yeah, I just started a few weeks ago."

Before Jeremy had a chance to say anything in return, Charlotte came sauntering up and glued herself to Jeremy's side. He instinctively threw his arm over her shoulder, and the relief I'd felt earlier deteriorated.

"Jeremy, I'm ready to go," Charlotte whined. "I have a headache."

"Oh, okay." It seemed like Jeremy wasn't thrilled with the idea of leaving, but he decided not to put up much of a fight.

That just disappointed me even more.

Charlotte turned away from Jeremy and finally noticed Ben standing next to me. Being the polite gentleman he was, he extended his hand to Charlotte, and I had to refrain from snatching it back.

"Hi, I'm Ben."

She pasted on a fake ass, sugar sweet smile as she shook his hand. "Charlotte Burton. I'm Jeremy's girlfriend," she replied, looking up at Jeremy and batting her lashes before turning back to Ben. "It's so nice to meet you."

I wanted to hurl. What? Did she not have her own identity?

She turned back to Jer and poked her bottom lip out. "Can we go now, honeybunch?"

Honeybunch? Are you fucking kidding me? I think I just threw up a little.

Jeremy looked at me and then back to her. "Yeah, baby, let's go." He gave me an uncomfortable hug and inclined his head to Ben. "Nice meeting you, man. Y'all have a good night."

Before I could respond, Charlotte pulled Jeremy away and out the door.

CHAPTER
three

Jeremy

Who the hell was that mega douche grinning at Savannah like a moron? I'd never even heard her mention the guy's name before, and he just came strutting up like he's known her forever. What the hell? And who wears a suit to Colt's, for Christ's sake? The dude stood out like a sore thumb.

I was pulled out of my thoughts when Charlotte spoke from the passenger seat.

"So, was that Savannah's boyfriend or something?"

Just the thought of that idiot dating Savannah had me grinding my teeth. Thank God it was dark in the cab of my truck so Charlotte couldn't see my reaction. I'd be in for hours of talking about the problems in our relationship—meaning Charlotte's dislike of my ex-girlfriend. There would be no way for me to live that down.

I didn't understand why Savannah was Charlotte's least favorite person, and that just made things all the more difficult for me. She tended to get jealous of my relationship with Savannah. Charlotte also didn't like how tight-knit our group was. She'd complain that she felt like an outsider, and no matter how hard I'd tried to convince her that everyone liked her, it just never seemed to be enough.

I enjoyed spending time with Charlotte, and honestly, the sex was out of this world. But her jealousy was starting to grate on my last nerve. The only reason things had lasted this long was because I'd finally admitted that I needed to move on from Savannah.

I didn't see anything long term with Charlotte, but that didn't mean I couldn't enjoy the company while it lasted. I just wasn't planning on tying myself to the very first person I'd started dating since Savannah and I broke up. I was still young, and if I couldn't have the person I really wanted, there was nothing wrong with wanting to enjoy what I'd been missing out on all these years…was there?

I tried to make my voice as casual as possible before answering. "I don't think so. I'm sure I would have heard something if she had a boyfriend."

"Oh, that's right," she replied.

I didn't need to see her face to know she was pissed. Her words were practically dripping with sarcasm.

"I forgot that you're all BFFs and tell each other *everything.*"

I rolled my eyes in the darkness of the truck. "Charlotte, I've told you a thousand times that everyone likes you just fine. You feeling like an outsider is all in your head."

I could see her profile from the lights in the dash, and she was sporting one of her signature poses—arms crossed over her chest and an unattractive pout on her lips.

"Yeah, well, Savannah doesn't like me," she whined.

The need to defend Savannah hit me like a Mack truck. "And whose fault is that?" I asked in a condescending tone. "Maybe if you weren't so damn rude every time she was around, the two of you could actually be friends. She really is a good person, Charlotte. You'd know that if you actually made an effort to get to know her."

Charlotte let out a huff and started hopping around in the seat next to me before shoving her finger in my face. "I knew it! I knew you still had feelings for her!"

I could feel the headache building behind my eyes. I took one hand off the wheel and started to rub the bridge of my nose. "I don't have feelings for her, Charlotte. Our relationship ended a long time ago. We are *just* friends." I wasn't sure how truthful that statement was though.

A part of me would probably always have feelings for Savannah. She was the first girl I'd ever been in a relationship with and the only one I'd ever loved. She would always be special to me.

"So, you're just automatically taking her side?"

Jesus Christ! I'm talking just to hear myself talk. "Damn, woman! There are no sides. She's my friend, and you're my girlfriend. That's all there is to it."

We sat in silence for several seconds, and my headache started to recede slightly. Finally, I felt the bench seat shift as Charlotte scooted toward me, and then she started to rub her hand up and down my thigh.

"I'm sorry, baby," she cooed in my ear before licking the shell of it and slowly kissing down my neck. "I hate being jealous, but I just can't help it." Her hand went straight to the crotch of my pants, and she began massaging my dick through my jeans.

I had to hand it to her. There were times when she was almost too much for me to handle, and I thought about just throwing in the towel. But damn, did she know how to use her hands and mouth. It was almost as if she were made for sex.

I let out a deep moan as my cock started pushing painfully against the zipper of my jeans. I had to use all my willpower to keep my eyes from rolling back in my head as I tried to focus on the road in front of me.

"I just care about you so much, baby," she whispered. "Do you care about me?" She lightly bit my neck, hitting just the right spot.

I'd tell her just about anything she wanted to hear at that point. I knew it was absolutely pathetic, but my cock was doing all the thinking for me. "Yeah, baby, I care about you," I said on another moan.

I felt a tug as she undid my belt and started to unbutton my pants.

Nothing like road head to get a couple past a fight.

Savannah

"I'm so sorry about that. I don't know why Jeremy was being such a dick tonight."

I was completely humiliated by Jeremy's behavior. I'd specifically told him that Ben was an attorney at my firm, so Jeremy would know to be on his best behavior. I might not work directly for Ben, but for all intents and purposes, he was still very much one of my bosses. That meant my friends' behavior was a reflection on me if one of my bosses saw us out in public. I was going to kick Jeremy's ass the next time I saw him.

Ben gave me a dazzling smile as he patted my hand that was resting on the bar. "It's all right. I do have to ask though— did you guys have a thing or something?"

I was taken aback just a little by that question. "Why do you ask?"

"Well, that just seemed a little like jealousy to me. I just assumed you two had dated or something."

I waved my hand in an attempt to brush off his comment. "Yeah, but it was, like, seven years ago. We've been over for a *really* long time. We're just friends." Just saying those words made my heart hurt.

The look he gave me clearly showed that he didn't believe me. "You're sure you're just friends?"

I let out an uncomfortable laugh. "Yeah, I'm positive. You met his girlfriend, Ben. And tonight was the first time in months that Jeremy and I have really even talked to each other."

Luckily, Emmy and Luke picked that moment to come over and introduce themselves, giving me a reprieve from the awkward conversation I was having.

"Hey there," Emmy said, extending her hand out to Ben. "I'm Emerson Grace, Savannah's best friend." She and Ben shook hands before she threw her thumb over her shoulder. "This is my lesser half, Luke."

Ben and Luke both laughed as the two men shook hands and introduced themselves. I loved how my best friend took every opportunity to put Luke in his place. They might be nauseatingly in love with each other, but Emmy was still one hundred percent herself...unlike *Charlotte*.

"So, you're the lucky couple?"

Emmy wrapped her arm around Luke's waist, and he slung an arm over her shoulder.

"Oh, no. I mean, he's definitely lucky to have me," Emmy said as she poked Luke in the ribs, "but we aren't engaged or anything."

"Yeah, that would be those two over there," Luke said. He extended his arm and pointed out Gavin and Stacia by the jukebox. "The girl who's clearly three sheets to the wind and the guy who looks like he'd be thrilled just to clean up her puke—*that's* the lucky couple."

Emmy shoved an elbow in Luke's side as I smacked him across the back of the head.

"Play nice," I told him. "They're in love."

"Just callin' it how I see it, Killer."

I hated Luke's nickname for me, but even I had to admit that it fit pretty well. After all, I had threatened him with bodily harm—and possibly murder—several times right after he moved back to town.

I turned my attention back to Emmy and noticed she had a cheeky little grin on her face. That couldn't lead to anything good.

"So, how do you two know each other?" she asked.

Before Ben had a chance to respond, I jumped in. I didn't know why, but I had a feeling I needed to clearly define my non-relationship with Ben and fast.

"We're coworkers," I blurted out. I didn't miss the disappointed look that briefly crossed Ben's face when I said that, so I tried to ease the blow. "Ben just started at P&C a few weeks ago, and he hasn't really gotten the chance to meet new people. I thought this would be the perfect opportunity."

It's official. I am so off my game.

Ben hung around a little longer to chat with me and all my friends. He seemed to hit it off pretty well with everyone, and by the time he got up to head out, Brett had already invited him to the show their band was doing next weekend. I might not have made any progress with Jeremy, but at least I'd made a new friend and helped Ben to get to know people in town.

Score one for me.

After he took off, Emmy and Lizzy plopped down on the stools next to me while Brett, Luke, and Trevor headed off to play pool. Gavin had finally decided it was time to call it a night when Stacia declared to the entire bar that she wanted his seed and that he needed to give her a bunch of babies. They'd taken off shortly after that.

"So…" Emmy started with that smile plastered on her face. "Ben seems cute."

Ah hell.

"Don't even think about it, Emerson Grace. He's just a coworker and maybe a friend."

"Says you," Lizzy responded. "That dude looked like he wanted himself some Savannah lovin'."

I rolled my eyes and downed the last of my beer. "You bitches know I don't dip my pen in the company ink. That's just asking for trouble."

I started to stand when Emmy got serious all of a sudden.

"It's time, Savannah. You and Jeremy have been broken up for a while. He's finally moved on. Don't you think it's time you did too?"

The crushing weight I felt each time I thought of Jeremy came back, and the smile slipped from my lips. "I just don't want a relationship right now, Em. I'm good, I promise."

I hated lying to my best friend more than anything. I was so far from okay that it wasn't even funny.

"I just don't get it!" she exclaimed as she threw her hands in the air in exasperation. "It's obvious you two still love each other. Why the hell can't y'all just get back together?"

From my peripheral vision, I caught Lizzy's sympathetic look. She was the only one who knew the truth behind mine and Jeremy's breakup.

"He's with Charlotte, Emmy."

"Oh, please. You know as well as I do that he'd drop her in a minute if you'd just give him a chance!"

I'd had enough for one night. "Okay, I'm done with this conversation." I reached for Emmy and gave her a hug before releasing her and hugging Lizzy. "I'm out. I'll see you guys later."

"You are so damn stubborn!" Emmy exclaimed.

I turned back with a smile and threw over my shoulder, "Yeah, but you love me anyway."

"I can't figure out why," she called back with a laugh in her voice.

The only thing I could think of doing was getting to my house, face-planting into my huge, comfy bed, and sleeping through the next few days.

CHAPTER
four

The loud shrill of my cell phone cut through my head and ripped me out of a sound sleep. Groaning, I rolled over and willed my eyes to adjust to the sun shining into my bedroom as I reached to grab my phone from the nightstand.

"If someone isn't dead, they're about to be," I muttered to whoever was stupid enough to call me before eight o'clock on a Saturday.

"Um…" the voice on the other end replied. "I'm sorry. I must have the wrong number."

I rolled my eyes and propped myself up on my elbows. Once I was awake, there was no getting back to sleep. The asshole on the other end had just prevented me from sleeping in on the one day a week I was able to, so it was understandable that I wasn't exactly chipper.

"Who the hell are you trying to reach at such an ungodly hour?" I snapped.

"Uh…well, I was looking for Savannah Morgan?" He ended his sentence as a question, which just annoyed me further.

"Well, unfortunately for you, you got her. Who the hell is this?"

"B-Ben. Uh…this is Benjamin Bennett from P&C?" he responded, sounding almost terrified.

I was surprised he hadn't just hung up on me already.

"*Ben?*" I asked, positively horrified that I'd just acted like that to someone I worked for. "Oh my God, I am so sorry. I can't believe I just spoke to you like that. I am so, so sorry. Um…I'm not really a morning person."

He laughed across the line. "I kind of figured that out. I'm the one who's sorry. I just got my ass thoroughly chewed. Are you sure you aren't a lawyer?"

I let out an abashed groan. "I'm so embarrassed right now," I replied quietly.

"Please, don't be."

It made me feel somewhat better that I could sense he was smiling. I'd dodged a bullet. He wasn't going to fire me—or at least I hoped not.

"It's totally my fault for calling so early on a weekend. I honestly didn't even look at the clock before picking up the phone. For that, I'm sorry."

"Oh, uh...well, you're forgiven," I replied awkwardly.

"How about we start this whole thing over?"

I felt a smile spread across my face at his humor. "Sounds like a plan."

"Ring, ring," Ben said into the phone.

I cleared my throat and put on my best professional persona. "Hello?"

"Hi, I'm calling for Savannah Morgan, please."

I let out a small laugh. "You've reached Savannah. May I ask who's calling?"

"Well, good morning, Ms. Morgan. This is Benjamin Bennett. How are you this lovely *early* morning?"

A full-belly laugh escaped me when he stressed the word *early*. "I'm good, Ben. How are you?"

There was a long, awkward pause before he spoke again. "I'm well. Thank you for asking. I'd be better, however, if you'd allow me to take you out tonight. That is, if you don't have any plans already, of course."

My stomach dropped. "Like on a date?" I stupidly asked.

He let out nervous chuckle at my question. "Well, that would be ideal."

Shit!

I had no clue how to respond to that. Granted, Ben was a very attractive man, what with the piercing blue eyes and perfectly styled and cut light brown hair. Any woman would be more than willing to date him. I just didn't feel right about agreeing to a date with him. He was a really nice guy, but I had a rule against dating coworkers. Those types of relationships never ended well.

"I don't really know if that's a good idea, Ben," I said slowly. I wasn't sure about dating him, but I didn't want to hurt his feelings either. "You're a really nice guy. I just don't think it would be smart for us to date."

He was silent for several seconds before he said, "Is it because of that guy last night? Jeremy?"

"No, not at all." *Maybe just a little.*

"Oh…all right. I completely understand. I'll admit that I read a little too much into your invitation last night. I'm sorry for that, and I'm really sorry I disturbed your sleep."

He sounded so dejected that I couldn't help but feel horrible. If I were being honest with myself, he hadn't *completely* misread the situation. I *was* attracted to him. I just wasn't sure about the whole work aspect of things.

"No, Ben, you didn't read too far. I am attracted to you—"

"Oh, thank God!" He blew out a relieved breath. "I thought I was completely off the mark, and that could have been humiliating."

I had put a stop to the direction the conversation had taken before he got the wrong impression. "*But…*" I dragged it out, so he knew he needed to listen to what I had to say next. "I made this rule that I would never date coworkers. That's just a recipe for disaster. I mean, have you ever heard of that working out for anyone?"

"Well…"

He remained silent for a long time. I could only assume he was trying to come up with an example to show it could work out.

He finally let out a sigh and relented. "No. You're right. I can't think of an example where dating a coworker worked out well."

I had to laugh at his disappointment. "If it's any consolation, I'd totally go on a date with you if you didn't work at P&C."

He joined me in laughing. "If I didn't have rent and bills to pay, that might be incentive enough for me to quit."

"Damn economy."

"My thoughts exactly."

"Look…" I started, hoping to soften my earlier rejection. "I know that it's totally cliché to say this, but I mean it when I say that I want us to be friends. I had a lot of fun with you last night, and I know my friends liked you. I think you'd really fit in with all of us—that is, if you're even interested since I shot you down and all," I ended with a smile.

"Well, since you put it that way…who could possibly turn down that offer?" he said with a chuckle.

"You know what I mean. Besides, you've already been invited to the guys' show on Saturday. They'd be really disappointed if you missed it."

He finally relented and admitted that he'd had fun the night before, and he agreed to go watch the guys' band play on Saturday. We talked for a few more minutes and ended the conversation on a high note.

It felt good to have Ben as a friend. We'd dodged the awkward dating bullet, and I felt relieved with where we'd ended up.

I threw myself back on my bed and contemplated going for a jog. I despised exercise with a passion, but I'd read in a book that it was a great stress reliever. And seeing how I was normally a stress-free person who was currently living a stressful life, I was all for any method that would get rid of that shit.

My phone rang again, rescuing me from all thoughts of cardio.

"Yo," I answered after seeing Emmy's picture pop up on the display.

"What are you doing right now?"

"Lying in bed, trying to decide if I want to go for a run or not."

Emmy was silent for several seconds before finally saying, "Aren't you allergic to exercise?"

I let out a little chuckle. "I'm not allergic. I just really, *really* hate it."

"You broke out in hives just from walking around the block with me. You had to take off your shirt and lie on my kitchen floor just to cool off."

"Hey! That was *one* time. And I didn't break out in hives. I just got really hot and splotchy." I could hear the bitch chuckling on the other end of the phone. "I could work out if I wanted to," I replied defensively.

"Whatever you say, Savvy. But you're gonna have to work on your fitness some other time. We've got plans."

I ran through my mental calendar, trying to figure out what she was talking about. "What plans? I don't remember making any plans."

"Stacia called me this morning. We're going bridesmaid dress shopping today."

I let out a groan at the thought of being stuck in some stuffy dressing room covered in butt-ugly tulle and silk.

"Suck it up," Emmy responded. "She's one of our best friends, and it's our duty to go try on ugly-ass dresses."

I threw my legs over the side of my bed with a huff, and started for my bathroom. "Fine, but I reserve the right to bitch-slap her if she chooses anything close to fuchsia."

"Duly noted, honey. Now get the lead out. We have a ten-thirty appointment, so be at the diner by ten."

I hung up the phone and turned on my shower to scalding. The thought of meeting up at the diner and possibly running into *Charlotte* didn't make me any more excited about my day.

After standing in the shower longer than I should have, I only had a few minutes to finish getting ready before I had to head out the door. I threw on a pair of dark skinny jeans and matched them with a loose, off-the-shoulder, white and navy striped shirt and a pair of ballet flats. After throwing my long blonde hair into a messy bun on top of my head, I was ready and out the door.

Pushing through the door of Virgie May's ten minutes later, I had to hold in a frustrated groan at the sight in front of me. Jeremy was sitting on a bar stool at the counter while Charlotte—in her Virgie May's uniform, I might add—was wrapped around him while feeding him a bite of pancakes.

Unprofessional much?

It took an enormous amount of strength for me not to puke at the disgusting display. I sidled up to the bar and turned my full attention to Emmy and Lizzy, trying my best to ignore the lovely couple.

"All right, I'm here. Let's get this party started," I said sarcastically.

Lizzy gave me a smirk. "Don't get too excited now."

I rolled my eyes. "Where's Stacia?"

Emmy stopped from setting up her pie display and looked at me. "Princess Pukey is a little slower than normal this morning."

I laughed, remembering Stacia's drunken antics from the night before. "Okay. Well, can I at least get a cup of coffee while we're waiting?"

Emmy walked away to get my coffee, and Lizzy's phone rang, pulling her attention away from me. That left me stuck with Charlotte and Jeremy with no buffer. That was not good. I sat there and stared at the counter for several seconds, praying neither of them would pay me any mind.

I wasn't that lucky.

"Mornin', sugar," Jeremy drawled out.

It was possibly one of the worst things he could have said. *Sugar* was Jeremy's nickname for me throughout our entire relationship. The fact that it was the first time I'd heard him use that particular endearment since he and Charlotte had gotten together wasn't lost on me—or her either, for that matter. I didn't have to turn and look to catch her reaction to Jeremy's pet name for me. She made her feelings known by throwing the fork down on the counter and stomping off into the kitchen.

I turned and narrowed my eyes at him. "Are you trying to get her to poison my food, Jer? You already know she can't stand me."

He let out a frustrated breath and ran both hands through his hair. Jeremy's hair was one of my favorite features on him. His reddish-brown hair, which normally lightened up in the summer, was now a gorgeous darker bronze color. When we had been together, I could sit for hours and just run my fingers through the silky auburn strands.

"She overreacted," he responded dryly.

I didn't agree with him. I would have responded the same way if the shoe were on the other foot. But it wasn't like I could admit that. I wanted to hurl knives every time he called her *baby* in front of me.

"Whether you think she's overreacting or not, you can't call me *sugar* in front of your girlfriend, Jeremy. The last thing I need is for you to give her more ammunition to hate me. I've done that enough just by breathing."

He looked at me, and I could see the sadness in his deep brown eyes. I was always able to tell how Jeremy was feeling just by looking into those eyes.

"I don't understand why the two of you can't just get along."

I felt my defenses rising at his statement. "Why don't you ask her? I haven't done a damn thing to warrant her acting like a bitch every time I'm around."

He pinched the bridge of his nose. It was something he did whenever he was under extreme stress.

Welcome to my world, buddy.

"I know, trust me. I just hate this shit," he said with an exasperated sigh.

I couldn't help my response to that. It pissed me off to know he wasn't happy with how things were, but he wasn't man enough to do anything about it.

"Well, you made your choice, Jer, so you gotta stick with it."

His head swung back around to face me, and I could see the anger there.

"What the fuck is that supposed to mean?" he asked heatedly.

"It means that you choose to let your girlfriend lead you around by the short hairs at the expense of our friendship. If you don't have the balls to stand up to her, that's your problem, not mine. You've made it clear where I stand with you, so you might as well just suck it up and live with it."

I knew I was being slightly dramatic, but everything that had been festering inside me all these months was finally coming to a head, and I just couldn't contain it anymore. I couldn't stand feeling so miserable day in and day out. That wasn't me. I'd always been a happy person. Even growing up with the world's shittiest parents hadn't made me feel as bad as I was feeling lately.

I got up and started to head to Emmy's office in the back of the diner, but I decided to throw one last parting shot his way before I left. Turning to him again, I called out, "And don't call me *sugar* anymore!" Then, I just walked away.

CHAPTER
five

I found myself standing on a pedestal in front of a three-way mirror with my mouth hanging open in horror. I was covered from neck to knee in the most hideous excuse of a dress I'd ever seen. I looked like I'd just stepped out of a 1980s prom. The only things missing were the crimped hair and foot-high bangs. And the worst part was that the dress was *fuchsia*!

"Uh…Emmy? Remember what I said on the phone?"

"Yup," she responded, looking at herself in equal horror.

"I'm gonna do it!" I replied.

Stacia looked up from her seat at the foot of our pedestals. "Do what?" she asked innocently.

I took a step toward her and answered, "Bitch-slap you. Come here."

Stacia jumped back just as I was about to get her.

Lucky for her, Emmy was faster and held me back. "Just slow down, Savvy. I'm sure she meant for these dresses to be a joke."

Stacia looked at me, then Emmy, and then turned to Lizzy, who appeared to be frozen in horror in front of the mirror. "What? I think they're pretty."

"These aren't pretty, Stacia!" Lizzy yelled. "I look like the Kool-Aid Man blew chunks on me!"

I turned back to Stacia and planted my hands firmly on my hips. "If you make me wear this, I will ruin your wedding. I swear to God, I will get shit-faced and sing "Welcome to the Jungle" in an Axl voice while doing the running man on top of the bar during your first dance as a married couple!"

Stacia mimicked my stance and narrowed her eyes. "You wouldn't."

"I'll show the pictures," I whispered menacingly.

"What pictures?" she asked in confusion.

"*The* pictures."

Emmy gasped behind me.

"What? What is she talking about?" Lizzy asked.

Stacia's eyes widened in understanding. "You promised."

"What pictures?" Lizzy asked.

Stacia and I were in a standoff.

"Pick these dresses, and I'll do it. You know I will."

"*What pictures*?" Lizzy hollered.

After about ten more seconds of staring each other down, Stacia finally threw her hands up in defeat. "Fine!" she huffed. "Y'all can pick your own damn dresses." She threw herself down in a wingback chair, crossed her arms over her chest, and began to pout while Emmy and I fist bumped in victory.

"Will someone please tell me what friggin' pictures y'all are talking about?"

Emmy began telling the story of what had happened back in high school that led to me holding on to pictures to use as blackmail so many years later.

"Lizzy, remember that summer when your parents made you stay with your aunt and uncle in Boise because they thought we were bad influences, and they wanted to get you away from us?"

Lizzy looked up at the ceiling, trying to pull the memory back. "Yeah, I remember. That was the same year Savannah and I were suspended for two weeks because we super glued Bobby Mulroney to his desk in homeroom and drew dicks all over his face, right?"

"Little shit deserved it," I mumbled under my breath. "He told the whole school Stacia was a cock tease because she wouldn't put out after winter formal."

"Nooo," Stacia piped up. "He told everyone I gave lousy head, so he hadn't bothered with screwing me."

"That's right. I totally forgot. That peckerhead!"

"You junk-punched him a few times for good measure too," Stacia added.

"Anyway…" Emmy cut in. "The three of us decided to meet the guys over at The Ropes to go swimming."

The Ropes was a place at the creek where some kids had decided to tie a bunch of ropes to the trees along the embankment, so they could swing into the water ten feet below. Cloverleaf wasn't exactly known for being a town that had bred intelligence, so The Ropes was the best name people could come up with.

"Stacia decided to ride with me, and since my backseat was nonexistent, Savannah took her own car. We were about to turn onto Miller Road when Stacia thought it would be funny to stand out of my sunroof and flash Savannah since she was behind us."

Lizzy looked over at me. "So what? You took pictures of her boobs?"

I started to laugh hysterically as I remembered back to that day.

Ah, good times.

Emmy continued, "No, it wasn't just that she got pictures of Stacia's boobs. Stacia got stuck because of the visor on the sunroof, and she couldn't get back in. Then, her bikini top got knotted up in her hair, so she couldn't get it back on."

"Well, if you had stopped driving, there wouldn't have been a problem!" Stacia exclaimed loudly.

Tears streamed down my cheeks as I laughed harder than I had in months, and Emmy was laughing so hard that she was having trouble continuing.

"Stacia was screaming and flailing around, trying to get back inside the car, and I was laughing so damn hard that I about peed myself. We just so happened to turn onto Miller Road where a trooper had set up a speed trap. When he saw Stacia and her jiggly bits hanging out my roof, he pulled us over. She was still stuck the whole time he was writing us tickets—her for public indecency and me for reckless driving. Savannah was parked behind us, taking pictures."

I pulled my shit together long enough to add on, "My favorites are the ones when he was greasing you down with Armor All and trying to shove you back through."

Lizzy started to laugh so hard that she was snorting. "I have *got* to see these pictures...pretty please?"

I pulled out my cell and started scrolling through. "No problem. Got 'em right here. I transfer them every time I get a new phone."

"I hate you bitches," Stacia grumbled. "You're all officially out of my wedding."

Jeremy

I played Savannah's words over and over in my head all day long, and the more they ran through, the madder I got. I wasn't choosing anybody over anybody—or at least I wasn't trying to. I was just trying to move on with my life. I'd spent so long trying to get Savannah to see that we belonged together, but there was only so much rejection a man could take and still maintain his pride.

I was so busy stewing over my conversation with Savannah that I wasn't paying attention to what I was doing. My hand slipped off the wrench I was using to change the alternator on Bob Carlson's Camry, and I sliced my palm right open.

"Son of a bitch!"

"Bad day?" I heard from behind me.

I turned to see my best friend, Luke Allen, standing in the bay door of my garage with a smart-ass smirk on his face.

"That obvious?" I asked as I walked inside to clean my hand.

Luke followed behind me silently as I washed up and reached under the sink for the first-aid kit. I rubbed on some antibacterial cream and slapped a bandage over my palm.

"You wanna talk about it?" he finally asked.

"You wanna get all girlie and start talking about our feelings and shit?" I replied sarcastically.

Luke let out a lighthearted chuckle. "Well, last I checked, I hadn't grown a vagina, so I'd prefer to skip the cryin' and huggin' part of the conversation, if it's all the same to you."

"So noted."

The humor quickly died from his face, and he contemplatively stared at me. "But I do know that some serious shit is brewin' in that head of yours. You've been outta sorts for a while now, brother. I just wanted to make sure you were solid."

I made my way over to my office and threw myself down in the chair. Running my uninjured hand through my hair, I let out a deep breath. "Christ, I don't know, man. Shit is so tangled right now that I couldn't tell you up from down if my life depended on it."

Luke took a seat across from me and propped his feet up on my desk. "This got anything to do with Savannah?" he asked casually.

I threw my head back and studied the ceiling. "Yeah, man—Savannah and Charlotte. I don't know why those two can't just get along, but their animosity toward each other is really starting to become a pain in my ass. Savannah actually laid into me today, accusing me of choosing Charlotte at the sake of our friendship. Can you believe that shit?"

He sat there with a pensive look on his face, like he was thinking about how to answer me. "Well, brother, I can't say it's been lost on me—the looks Charlotte gives Savannah when they're in the same room with each other."

That comment threw me for a loop. I could sense Charlotte's attitude change when they were in the same room, but I'd had no clue that it was so bad that my other friends were picking up on it.

"What the hell am I supposed to do? I've got Charlotte on my ass all the damn time, riding me about being so close to Savvy. But it's not like I can just stop talking to Savannah, you know? Past relationship aside, she's my best friend. I can't just cut her out of my life because Charlotte is insecure. I don't *want* to cut Savvy out."

"Looks like you've got yourself a real dilemma," was all he said.

"You know, if that's all you've got to say, then you can head on out. Stating the obvious isn't doing jack to help me."

Luke threw up his hands in surrender and let out a loud laugh. "All right, man, all right. I just like givin' you a hard time."

"I'm having a hard enough time already. I don't need you to add to it."

Luke rubbed his chin, dropped his feet to the ground, and rested his elbows on his knees. "You love Charlotte?" he asked.

I didn't even bother speaking my answer. I just shook my head back and forth.

"Then, why go through all this?"

And that was the question wasn't it? Why was I subjecting myself to all this misery if I knew Charlotte and I weren't going to make the long haul? "I don't know, Luke. I've been asking myself the same questions lately."

"Look, I'm not claiming to be an expert on relationships here, but I will tell you that if you can't picture spending the rest of your life with this chick, maybe it's time to cut your losses."

"Is that why you came back for Emmy?" I asked.

"Hell yeah, man!" Luke exclaimed. "I don't have a life without that woman in it. My suggestion—find a woman you feel like that about and hold on to her for the rest of your life."

Luke knew what he was talking about in matters like that. Years ago, he'd walked away from Emmy after just one night. He'd left a ton of destruction in his wake that he wasn't aware of until he'd moved back to Cloverleaf, but after trying to live without her for eight years, he had finally sucked it up and come crawling back. It had taken more work than most men would have been willing to put in, but he'd finally gained back her trust, and eventually, he'd fixed their relationship. I'd never seen two people more crazy about each other than Luke and Emmy.

The only problem with his suggestion was that the one woman I couldn't picture living without had ended our relationship a long time ago, and she wouldn't take me back even though she knew we were perfect for each other.

"If Savannah is it for you, then you need to do everything in your power to make her see that."

CHAPTER
six

Savannah

For some insane reason, I'd decided I was going to start running that morning. The only thing I had working for me in my attempt at a three-mile jog was the fact that it was November. In Texas, that meant it was a comfortable sixty-five degrees outside with only eighty percent humidity as opposed to the standard thousand percent.

About a mile in, I decided I was a complete idiot, but I had the type of personality that wouldn't allow me to quit something once I'd started, so I finished the three miles. I'd walked a lot, but I'd finished, damn it! It was nothing short than a miracle that I was able to shower and get myself ready for work later that morning.

And for that reason, I was currently sitting in my office at work with my head on my desk, feeling like I was going to die. Maybe Emmy had been right. Maybe I *was* allergic to exercise.

"Everything okay in here?" I heard from behind me.

I didn't even have the energy to lift my head. I just turned it to the side and looked up at Ben standing in the doorway.

"You okay, Savannah?" he asked, concern evident in his voice.

"I think I'm dying," I responded in a weak voice.

At my pathetic declaration, Ben's concerned expression morphed into a smile, and he started to laugh. "What did you do?"

I slowly pushed myself off my desk and slumped back into my chair. "I went for a three-mile run slash walk, and now, God is punishing me."

He stared at me like I'd grown a second head. "All this for three miles? You're kind of a drama queen, aren't you?" he asked with a cheeky grin.

"Screw you, asshole! Get out of my office."

Ben threw his head back and let out a full belly laugh. "Oh, come on, Savannah. It was just a short little jog. I could do three miles half asleep."

I threw my staple remover at Ben's head, only missing by *thiiiis* much. "First of all," I replied defensively, "it wasn't a *short little jog.*" I shot him a death glare, hoping to melt the skin off his face. "And secondly, I'm allergic to exercise. Just ask Emmy. She'll vouch for me!"

He just stood there, still chuckling.

"You think it's funny now, but when I keel over, it's on you. Don't say I didn't warn you. I think I should at least get the rest of the day off."

"For what? Being active?"

"Mental distress due to unnecessary physical activity," I responded.

"How about I spring for lunch? You think you can live till then?" Ben asked me.

I stared up at the ceiling, giving that some serious thought. On one hand, my limbs felt like Jell-O, and I was pretty certain I'd look like a drunk Gumby if I attempted to walk, but on the other hand, I never passed up a free meal.

"You've got a deal."

Ben and I shook hands. Then, he left my office, and I went back to my paperweight routine.

"So, is this place any good?" Ben asked as we walked into Virgie May's.

I'd been working hard at avoiding Charlotte, but with Ben next to me, I was able to stand a little taller and not worry about a potential run-in with the one chick I couldn't stand. Plus, I was really in the mood for a piece of chocolate pie.

I thought making friends with Ben was one of the best decisions I'd ever made. There was just something about him that made me instantly comfortable. After our little misunderstanding, we'd comfortably fallen into the friend-zone with no issues. I felt a sense of calm around Ben that I hadn't felt in a long time. I loved all of my friends equally, but maybe the fact that Ben was just mine and I didn't have to share his friendship with Jeremy was what made it so easy.

"It's only the best food in all of Cloverleaf. See…" I declared, pointing to the hand-painted sign in the front window of the diner. "It says so right there."

"Well then, it has to be true."

We took our seats at a table off in the corner, and Ben started looking over his menu while I scanned the diner for Charlotte. I breathed a sigh of relief when I noticed she wasn't working.

"So, what should I get?" Ben asked me, still scanning the menu.

"You can't go wrong with the meatloaf, but the smothered pork chops are really good too."

"All right, I think I'll take your word and get the pork chops."

"You won't be disappointed, I promise."

A few minutes later, Emmy came walking over to take our order. I could tell by the grin on her face that she'd instantly misinterpreted my lunch with Ben. I was probably going to be grilled about my relationship with him later, and that was the last thing I wanted.

"Well, hey there, you two. Don't you look all cozy?"

I'm gonna punch her in the throat.

"Hey, Emmy," Ben replied with a bright smile. "How are you today?"

"I'm fantastic," she responded.

She turned to face me, and I could see her evil mind working.

"So…is this a date?"

Then, I'm gonna stab her with my fork.

"Wow. You're as subtle as Liberace," I deadpanned.

"When have you ever known me to be subtle? That would be like you claiming not to be a drama queen."

Ben attempted to stifle a laugh behind his hand, but he failed miserably. Choosing to ignore him, I kept my glare on Emmy.

"Ben and I are just friends, *Emerson*." I used her full name, hoping to get my point across that she was walking on thin ice.

No such luck.

"If you say so. But if it matters for anything, I think he's fine as hell, girl." With that, she sauntered off.

"You didn't even take our order!" I hollered after her.

"You're getting the meatloaf because that's what you always get, and Ben is getting the pork chops because they're awesome!" she yelled back as she made her way to the kitchen.

"She's like a food ninja," Ben said, totally in awe of Emmy's gift at guessing people's orders.

"Yep, being annoying clearly isn't her only skill."

"I didn't find her all that annoying," Ben said with a smile.

"That's because she called you fine."

He glanced over at me with a little grin. "Well, she's obviously a very smart woman."

Ben and I sat for a while longer, enjoying each other's company and our delicious lunch. Of course, Ben loved the pork chops, and Emmy couldn't help but come by to gloat a little.

Shortly after we finished eating, Ben excused himself and headed to the restroom. I'd just finished putting the rest of our lunches in a to-go container when the chair across from me squeaked loudly against the tile floor. Looking up, I was surprised to see Jeremy sitting in Ben's unoccupied seat.

"So, you two dating now?" were the first words out of his mouth.

No hello or how's your day going? Nothing like that.

It didn't take a genius to realize this conversation was going to go downhill fast.

I rolled my eyes and leaned in to prevent the other diners from eavesdropping. "No, we aren't dating, not that it's any of your business. We're just two friends who had lunch together."

I could see the muscle twitching in his jaw as his brows furrowed.

"That guy wants in your pants, Savannah."

My anger was starting to slowly boil beneath the surface. If Jeremy pushed me any further, I was going to go off. "Again, Jeremy, that's none of your business," I snapped.

I started to stand, but he reached across the table and grabbed my wrist, keeping me in my seat.

"So, you *are* screwing him then." It wasn't a question.

I jerked my wrist out of his hold and leaned in close enough for only him to hear. "Despite what you might think of me, I don't fuck every guy I'm seen in public with."

"I didn't—"

I raised my hand to cut off his protest. "When I said it was none of your business, I meant that you have no right demanding to know who I am or am not sleeping with because you have a *girlfriend,* Jeremy. The day you got into that relationship, you lost all right to worry about my sex life."

"We're still friends, Savannah. Or have you forgotten that?" he said between clenched teeth. It was obvious he was having a hard time keeping his anger in check.

Unfortunately for him, I didn't have that kind of strength. "No, I'm not the one who's forgotten we *were* friends. *You're* the one who's been AWOL for months. *You're* the one who runs away the minute your girlfriend snaps her fingers. And *you're* the one who hasn't said more than a handful of words to me since you and Charlotte got together. I knew that things would be different when you started dating, but I didn't expect you to act like we hardly know each other."

"That's not how I've been acting," he insisted.

"Isn't it? We might not have been a couple, but you still picked up the phone and called me every night just to see how my day was. When was the last time you called me?" I didn't even give him a chance to answer. I just continued to pour out everything I'd been keeping locked inside me for so long. "Tell you what—you go about your business, and I'll go about mine. I'm officially releasing you of any obligation you might feel you have toward me. I don't need people in my life who are only there out of a sense of responsibility. I grew up with that, and I won't tolerate it from anyone—least of all, you."

I stood up just as Ben was walking back to the table.

"Everything okay here?" he asked as he eyed Jeremy speculatively.

"Everything's fine," I replied, grabbing Ben's arm and pulling him away from the table. "We need to get back to work."

"You sure?" He still hadn't taken his eyes off Jeremy. They were in some sort of stupid macho-guy standoff.

"Positive. Let's go."

We started walking and were just about to the door when Jeremy spoke again. "We aren't finished talking, Savannah. You said your piece, and you're damn well gonna listen to mine."

I glared at him over my shoulder and replied, "The hell I am! I don't need to hear anything you've got to say, Jer. This conversation is *over*."

I watched as the anger slowly crept out of his beautiful brown eyes, and a slow smile spread across his lips, showing his gorgeous dimpled smile.

God, I hate that stupid smile!

"That's where you're wrong…*sugar*."

I let out an exasperated huff, and I could hear him laughing behind me as I finished pulling Ben out the door.

"You know, one of these days you're going to have to tell me what the story is with you two."

"Hmph, there's no story to tell."

48

I could hear Ben chuckling beside me, but I refused to look at him.

"For some reason, I highly doubt that," he muttered under his breath.

CHAPTER
seven

Jeremy

I didn't know how it was possible to want to ring Savannah's neck *and* bury my dick deep inside her at the same time, but that was the effect that woman had on me. How pathetic was it that her little rant gave me a semi in the middle of a crowded diner?

I hadn't been able to help myself. I'd known I was just trying to get a rise out of her when I called her *sugar* as she walked out the door. I'd needed to see her eyes flash with something other than sadness. Every time she looked at me, I could see the sorrow in those gorgeous honey colored eyes and I felt like I was dying a slow, agonizing death.

If she was angry at me, at least that meant she still had that fire inside her. That fire made her the strong, stubborn, pain-in-the-ass girl I'd fallen for when I was fourteen years old.

I had been a little confused after my conversation with Luke, but after getting into it with Savannah at the diner, something had just clicked in my head, and I knew what I had to do. That was why I was sitting at my kitchen table, sweating bullets.

When I heard a knock on my front door, I sucked in a fortifying breath and prepared myself for the scene I was about to walk into.

I opened the front door, and I was immediately assaulted by Charlotte's perfume. She'd said it was some expensive name brand—Coco something-or-other—but to me it just smelled like an old lady's closet, and it gave me a killer headache. I couldn't stand the smell of it. The bad thing was that Charlotte insisted on drowning herself in the shit every time we were together. Whoever Coco was, I wanted to kick his ass.

"Hey, sweetie," she squealed in that nasally baby voice she thought was cute. Just the sound of it made my teeth hurt. "I missed you so much. Did you miss me?" She peppered my face with kisses, smearing her sticky lip gloss all over me.

I knew I wasn't being fair, picking out every little thing she did that annoyed me, but I couldn't stop myself. I'd started comparing everything about her to Savannah, and there was no way Charlotte could ever measure up.

"Hey, Charlotte. Why don't you come in and have a seat?" *Here goes nothing.*

Charlotte pranced into the living room like she belonged there and plopped down on my sofa. "What's up, baby?" she asked. "You sounded kind of weird when you called earlier. Is everything okay?"

I roughly ran my hands through my hair before bringing my eyes to hers. Everything about her was the polar opposite of Savannah. Charlotte's hair was a light brown, and Savannah's was a golden blonde. Charlotte had pale blue eyes, and Savannah's were light brown, the color of whiskey. Charlotte wore way too much makeup, but Savannah didn't need all that shit caked on her face to make her look good. She rocked the natural look, and to this day, I still thought that she was the most beautiful woman I'd ever seen.

"Shit," I muttered under my breath, knowing the best way to go about saying what I had to say was just to spit it out.

Charlotte's back went straight, and the smile slipped from her face. "What's going on, Jeremy?" she asked seriously. The baby voice had disappeared, and she finally sounded relatively normal.

Say it quick. Just like ripping off a Band-Aid. "I'm really sorry, Charlotte, but this just isn't working for me anymore." *There— you did it. That wasn't so hard.*

She silently sat there for several seconds. "What's not working for you?"

Well hell, she's not going to make it easy after all. "This relationship," I replied carefully. Just because I didn't want to be with her didn't mean I wanted to hurt her any more than what was already inevitable.

She stared into space for what felt like an eternity before turning back to me. She hauled her hand back and slapped me on the face as hard as she could. It was like she'd morphed into a whole other person all of a sudden. Gone was the sweet, loving Charlotte, and in her place was a red-faced, shrieking banshee. I was almost scared she was going to pop a vein or something.

"*Are you fucking kidding me*?" she screamed. "This relationship isn't *working* for you? Is this a fucking joke?"

She was on her feet, stomping back and forth through my living room, while I sat on the couch and out of the line of fire.

"I'm sorry, Charlotte. I really am. I'm just being honest."

"I thought you loved me!"

The hell? That threw me for a loop. "Now, hold on, I never once told you I loved you. I said that I *cared* about you. There's a huge friggin' difference," I insisted.

"Oh bullshit!" she spit out. "Don't give me that. I know you love me."

Was she delusional? I'd never said or done anything to make her think I loved her. "No, Charlotte, I don't love you. If you were under the impression that I did, I apologize. I never meant for you to get the wrong idea. I have been totally upfront with you from the very beginning. I think you're a great person, but I never saw this turning into something serious. I thought I'd made that perfectly clear." I hated sounding cruel, but she needed to step back into reality—fast.

"This is because of Savannah, isn't it?" Her lips curled up into a sneer when she said Savannah's name. "That bitch has been trying to break us up this whole time!"

That was it. I wasn't going to sit there and let her talk about Savannah that way. She hadn't done anything to deserve being called names behind her back without the chance to defend herself.

"Stop. You aren't going to stand here and blame Savannah for something that had nothing to do with her. She hasn't said or done a single thing against you, and I am *not* going to let you talk shit when you clearly don't know what you're talking about."

"I never stood a chance with you! It's always been about Savannah. She's not that fucking perfect, Jeremy. *God*, she's not even pretty!"

"ENOUGH!" I shouted, finally getting her attention. "You're being ridiculous. I've already told you that Savannah has nothing to do with this. It is *my* decision. You've had something against her since we got together, so any problems you and her have are your own damn fault!"

"You asshole!"

She lunged at me, trying to scratch at my face with her perfectly manicured nails. I had to grab both her wrists and pin her against my chest until she finally stopped fighting and broke down in tears. She was sobbing so uncontrollably that her whole body was shaking.

All I could do was stand there, feeling incredibly uncomfortable, while I held most of her weight. Her arms wrapped around my waist so tightly that I felt like she was squeezing the life out of me. Finally, she pulled herself together enough to stop the tears, but then she grabbed a hold of my neck with both hands and tried to force my lips to hers.

"Charlotte," I said softly as I pulled on her death grip, trying to release myself, "I think you should go."

It was the only thing I could think to say. I'd told her the truth, and I just needed our conversation to be over. I felt guilty about it, but the only thought running through my head was that I needed to get my ass over to Savannah's as quickly as I could. I didn't want to waste any more time trying to get her back.

"I can't believe this." Charlotte sobbed into my chest. "I l-love you s-so much."

"I'm sorry," was the only pathetic response I could come up with.

After a while longer, Charlotte finally left, and I was able to take my first real breath in what seemed like hours. Hurting someone was never something I wanted to do, but I felt like a weight had been lifted off my chest.

I was finally kicking my ass into gear and going for what I wanted. And this time I wasn't going to let Savannah make excuses for why we shouldn't be together. Everything in my gut told me that Savvy was my world, and I wasn't going to live without her for another day. I didn't care how long it took me to convince her that we belonged together. I'd drill it into her head for the rest of my damn life if I had to. I was going to get Savannah back if it killed me. Knowing her fiery personality, it just might.

Savannah

When I was a child, my mother always made me take tap dancing classes, ballet classes, piano lessons, and basically anything else that I could use as a talent in the countless beauty pageants she had forced me into while growing up. The only thing I'd remotely enjoyed was the singing lessons even though I was completely awful. People around me had constantly informed me that I was tone deaf, but I hadn't thought I was *that* bad. It didn't matter though, good or bad, absolutely loved to sing.

That was why I was currently shaking my ass all around my living room in my Hello Kitty sleep shorts and tank top that Emmy had gotten me for Christmas last year while belting out the lyrics to Heart's "All I Want to Do Is Make Love to You." My taste in music normally leaned toward alternative, but I was in a self-pitying mood and Heart seemed the way to go.

I was in the middle of the first chorus, giving it everything I had, with my eyes closed and hands in the air when I heard a noise from behind me. I spun around and screamed at the top of my lungs while simultaneously tripping over my coffee table as I attempted to run from whatever I'd heard. I finally face-planted onto the carpet with a *hard thud*.

I'd like to think I would have been smart enough to continue my escape had I not knocked all the wind out of my lungs, which forced me to curl up in the fetal position while gasping for air. But who the hell knows? Knowing me, I'd probably be the dumb bitch who attempted to lock herself in the bathroom instead of going for the back door.

"Christ, sugar, are you okay?"

It took a couple of seconds for my brain to clear so I could figure out what the hell was going on.

"What the hell, Jeremy? You scared the shit outta me!" I screamed. I was breathing too fast, and my heart felt like it was about to pound through my chest.

"I kinda figured that when you attempted to do a Superman over your coffee table." That asshole actually had the nerve to laugh.

I narrowed my eyes and replied, "If I wasn't pretty sure I just broke a rib, I'd kick your ass right this second. How the hell did you get in my house anyway?"

"You left the door unlocked. Not smart, by the way."

"Just because it was unlocked doesn't mean you have the right to just walk on in, Jeremy."

He tried to help me off the ground, but I batted his hand away and pushed myself up. I tried really hard not to flinch in pain when I put pressure on my right ankle.

"I heard the radio and figured you were singing. I didn't want to interrupt. I was really enjoying the show."

Okay, maybe I forgave him just a little for that comment. It was kind of sweet after all. But I was stubborn and didn't want to let go of all my anger right away. "Yeah, well, knock next time," I replied grumpily. I was totally embarrassed that he had caught me in all my glory.

"Will you stop being so damn stubborn?" he harrumphed when I brushed off another attempt from him to help me up. "You're clearly in pain. Just let me help you up already."

"Fine."

He reached for my elbow and gently pulled me all the way onto my feet. Then he carefully led me back to the couch. Once I was seated comfortably, he lifted my right foot, placed it on his lap, and started inspecting my ankle. For what, I had no clue.

All I knew was that his fingers on my bare flesh made my entire body break out in goose bumps. The skin-on-skin contact felt so familiar, yet so painful at the same time. I wanted nothing more than to grab hold of his copper colored hair and kiss the breath out of both of us, but I knew that wasn't going to happen. He wasn't mine anymore, and that thought caused me physical pain.

"What are you even doing here? I told you that we were done talking." I was trying to sound mad, but I knew I was coming off sounding more mournful than anything else.

"Charlotte and I are done."

CHAPTER
eight

Charlotte and I are done.

I couldn't have possibly heard that right. "Say what now?"

"I broke up with Charlotte."

I had so many questions running through my head, but the one that was at the forefront was, "When?"

"Just before I came over here."

Everything skidded to a halt. I went from wanting to throw myself at him to wanting to pummel him into the ground.

"So you dumped your girlfriend and thought…what? That you could just drive by my house for a late-night booty call or something?"

Jeremy's head shot back like I'd just slapped him and he looked at me with confusion. "What? No!"

"Well then, why else are you here, Jeremy? You think you can just end your current relationship and then jump into bed with me a minute later? There's no reason for you to be here at ten o'clock at night unless it's for sex!"

"I never said that! You're putting words in my mouth."

He tried to say more, but I was on a roll. "Well, let's see, you accused me of banging my coworker earlier today, and then you turn up at my place in the middle of the night, informing me that you broke up with Charlotte. That's all pretty convenient, don't you think? What conclusion would you like me to come to? It's obvious you think I'm a slut or else you wouldn't be here!"

"I don't think you're a slut, Savannah. Stop saying that."

His face was getting red with anger, but I was heated, and once that happened, there was no stopping me. "Well, let me tell you something, Jeremy Matthews. If you think you're getting in my panties, you got another thing comin'."

"Woman, would you just shut the hell up for a second?" he hollered.

Oh no, he didn't!

Commence the dramatic female neck rolling and hand waving in three, two, one…

"You did *not* just tell me to shut the hell up! And just who the fuck do you think you are, calling me *woman*? Talk to me like that one more time, and I'll beat the ever-loving shit outta—"

I didn't get the chance to finish my statement before he shot up to stand. He bent at the waist, leaning in so that we were practically eye to eye. He was so close that he forced me farther back into the couch. I could smell the intoxicating scent that I'd grown to associate fully with Jeremy. It was a combination of fresh air and clean laundry with just the slightest hint of motor oil from his work at the garage. It was all man and a smell that had haunted me for as long as I could remember. I loved that smell.

"I ENDED IT FOR YOU!" he shouted.

"WELL, DON'T DO ME ANY FAVORS!" I spit back.

"Have you always been this damn stubborn? Or do you just get a rush out of pissing me off?"

I let out a snort of laughter and dramatically rolled my eyes. "Where the hell have you been? Of course I've always been this stubborn. You might have noticed if your head hadn't been shoved up Charlotte's ass for the past few months."

A slow grin spread across Jeremy's lips, causing my stomach to drop. I didn't know what was running through his head at that moment, but whatever it was—judging from that evil grin on his face—it wasn't good.

"Sounds like you're a little jealous there…*sugar*."

That set my blood boiling. "*Pfft*, please. I'm so not jealous." *Bullshit, who was I kidding? I was totally jealous.*

But there was no way I was going to let myself admit that to him. It wasn't something I was necessarily proud of, but my pride stung a little at his accusation. I wasn't saying it was the smartest decision, but when I felt backed into a corner, my claws had a tendency to come out.

"What do I have to be jealous about? I was simply pointing out the fact that she's been carrying your balls around in her little designer purses ever since you two started dating. That wasn't jealousy, Jeremy. That was pity."

I wasn't sure what reaction to expect from him, but the booming laughter filling up my living room certainly wasn't it.

"You're a piece of work, Savvy. You know that? Why can't you just admit that you still want me?"

I stood up on the balls of my feet in an attempt to come off as more intimidating. "Because I don't!"

"Bullshit," he responded calmly.

"It's *not* bullshit!"

"You want me."

"Do not!"

"Do too."

A torrent of different emotions was coursing through me. I didn't know if I wanted to slap that smug smile off his face or kiss it off. By how my body was heating up at our exchange, I was leaning toward the latter.

"Nu-uh!" *When all else fails, resort to childishness.*

"That's it."

My stomach dropped to my feet, and all the air rushed from my body. I was so certain that he meant he was leaving, so when he grabbed my arms and jerked me up, all I could do was let out a startled yelp before he plastered his lips to mine.

It took a second for my brain to respond to what was happening, but once it did, I instantly melted into him. It felt like Jeremy was pouring every ounce of himself into that kiss, and I greedily took everything he had to give me. I'd wanted him for so long that I was completely desperate for him. I couldn't stop myself. I needed him more than I needed air. Running my fingers through his hair, I grabbed it and held on for dear life. I was terrified of what would happen when the kiss ended.

All too soon, he pulled away and stared into my eyes. Our breathing was erratic, and I could feel the quick rise and fall of his chest pressed against mine.

We stared at each other for what felt like an eternity before I could finally summon the courage to speak. "What was that, Jeremy?" I asked so quietly that I thought he might not have heard me.

He placed his forehead against mine, still not breaking eye contact. "That was what we've both needed to happen for a really long time, sugar."

He sounded so sure of himself that I could feel a piece of myself breaking inside.

Several months ago, I'd stupidly let my emotions and hormones take control, and Jeremy and I ended up having sex for the first time since we had broken up all those years ago. It'd been absolutely perfect, but when I woke up the next morning, reality had come crashing back down, and the bad decisions I had made at nineteen had still been there. I knew there was no way we could be together, so even though it killed me to do it, I'd walked away from him for a second time.

I didn't have the strength to do it a third time. "Jeremy, I can't do this," I whispered as tears welled up in my eyes.

I tried to shove him away, but it was like trying to move a brick wall. When he grabbed my hands and held them to his chest, even more of my resolve crumbled. I could feel his strong muscles through the thin cotton of his T-shirt, and all I wanted to do was slide my palms across those hard ridges.

I shook my head in an attempt to clear it. When I glanced back up, Jeremy was smiling down at me. I couldn't understand how he could be smiling when I felt like my world was crumbling around me...again.

"You're not getting away this time, sugar," he replied.

His mouth came back down on mine, and he kissed me like he owned me—and damn, if I didn't want him to in that moment.

Just as quickly as the kiss had started, it ended. Jeremy pulled away and began heading for the front door, leaving me in a quivering pile of limbs.

"Where are you going?" I hated the shakiness in my voice, but there was no controlling it.

Jeremy had just ripped my walls down, and pretending to be unaffected was impossible.

"I'm going home," he replied with a nonchalance that had me wanting to smack him and climb him like a tree all at the same time.

"*What?*" I squeaked. "Why?"

He turned to face me and crossed those strong arms across that even stronger chest. I felt my face heating up as images of what we could have been doing right then—had he not walked away—played on fast-forward through my head.

Yeah, I was *totally* affected. And it was driving me crazy that he seemed so casual. I wanted him to be panting and as hot for me as I was for him.

He squeezed his eyes closed and gave his head an irritated shake, and I was finally able to see that he wanted me too. I breathed a sigh of relief that the feeling was mutual.

"You made it clear that you thought all I was looking for was sex, so I'm leaving to prove you wrong. I'm gonna head home, take a cold-ass shower, and maybe jerk off once or twice."

My jaw dropped. He was just as affected as I was. Then why was he leaving?

"But…you said…"

"I know what I said, and I meant every word of it."

Oh, thank God.

"But," he continued, and my hopes for him staying deflated a little, "that being said, for the past seven years, I let you control how things went between us whether I agreed with them or not."

I opened my mouth to interrupt him, but he held up his hand and cut me off.

63

"I wasn't lying when I said I wasn't letting you go this time. But from here on out, we're doing this my way."

I felt my hackles rising again. "Excuse me?"

He shot a smile at me that had my knees quaking. "Now, don't start the attitude again. It won't change a damn thing."

I let out a huff and narrowed my eyes at him.

"There's no doubt in my mind that you want me just as badly as I want you, and sugar, you gotta know I love that. But I'm done letting you dictate how things are going to be between us. It's my turn now."

I felt the effect of his words deep in my gut. This unexpected dominant side of Jeremy was new to me. And it was Totally. Freaking. Hot!

I was contemplating tackling him to the ground and ripping off his clothes when he turned and started for the door again.

Once he got it open, he looked back and gave me a wink over his shoulder. "Don't worry, sugar. I won't make you beg me to get in your panties *too* much."

Oh hell, I'm so screwed!

CHAPTER
nine

Sleep did not come easy that night. I spent hours tossing and turning, replaying every kiss and every word out of Jeremy's mouth. I was a bundle of nervous energy, bouncing between wanting him and knowing it wasn't a good idea.

I lay there, staring at the ceiling while my heart and my brain battled it out over what I should do. After hours of constant back and forth, I finally managed to doze off around four in the morning.

The lingering smell of bacon woke me up way too early for my liking the next morning. Groggy and still half asleep, I kicked the covers off my bed and padded my way down the hall. If I'd been awake all the way, I might have been bothered by the fact that it appeared someone had broken into my house in order to make breakfast.

When I turned the corner, the first thing my eyes feasted on was Jeremy's back as he stood at my stove in a tight gray T-shirt and worn jeans that fit his ass to perfection. The second thing was the delicious meal of bacon, eggs, and pancakes that was set up on my kitchen island. Everything looked as wonderful as it smelled. He must have been here for a while.

"Uh…what's going on here?"

He turned and hit me with that hot-as-sin smile, throwing my sleep-muddled brain off even more. "Well, good morning to you too, sleepyhead."

"Good morning. What's going on here?" I repeated, still unable to wrap my brain around it.

He grinned and then turned back to flip another pancake. "What does it look like? I'm making you breakfast."

I pulled out a bar stool and planted myself at the island. Then, I started to pour syrup on a couple of pancakes before digging in with gusto. "How did you even get in here?" I asked around a mouthful of food." Classy was my middle name.

Jeremy turned off the gas burner and slid the pan into the sink to rinse. Then, he turned to face me and pulled a key out of his pocket. "Got a key, remember?"

I rolled my eyes at that. "I have *got* to stop giving out keys."

I'd made the mistake of giving a key to my house to all of my friends. They had a tendency to act like my house was open for them whenever the hell they wanted to come over, no matter how inconvenient it was for me. Between Luke, Trevor, Jeremy, Brett, and Gavin, I had to restock my pantry and fridge *way* too often.

Jeremy leaned back against the counter and crossed his arms. "You know, for someone acting all pissy, you sure are shoveling that food in pretty damn fast."

I glanced up and glowered at him, not even bothering to inhale between bites. The food tasted divine. I hadn't even realized how hungry I was. "Whatever," I grumbled between bites while he stood there all cocky and full of himself.

We stayed in companionable silence while I ate until I had absolutely no room left in my stomach. When I finally finished, I dropped my fork, leaned back on the stool, and let out a content sigh.

"Good?" Jeremy asked with a laugh.

"Oh, yeah," I said happily as I rubbed my full belly. "So good."

He leaned his elbows on the island across from me and studied my expression. "When was the last time you had a decent home-cooked meal?"

I shot my eyes to the ceiling and scrunched my face in thought. "What's today?" I asked.

"Tuesday."

"Three years ago?" I guesstimated.

He shook his head. "That's just sad."

I crossed my arms and leaned against the counter, mimicking his stance. "No more avoidance, Jer. What's all of this about?" I asked, waving my hand around the kitchen to indicate his cooking.

He stared right in my eyes while responding, "This is me showing you what you're getting by being with me."

My heart started to speed up at the same time my stomach dropped while I looked down at my lap. The whirlwind emotions I was experiencing were driving me insane. The majority of me wanted nothing more than to be with Jeremy. But that little voice in my head was still reminding me that I didn't deserve him, that I'd screwed up, and if he ever found out, he would hate me forever.

I took a fortifying breath and looked back up at his beautiful face. "Jeremy, we aren't together."

"Keep telling yourself that, sugar." He rounded the island and came to stand right beside me, ignoring my personal space. "Did you forget what I said last night? We're doing this my way. If you insist on being your typical stubborn-ass self, that'll just make proving you wrong even sweeter."

I tried to scoot back to put a little bit of room between us. Having him so close was shattering my resolve. "You aren't going to prove me wrong," I said with as much determination as I could muster. My words still sounded weak, even to my ears, so I knew he didn't believe me.

"If you say so."

With that, he leaned into me and kissed me so fiercely that it stole the breath from my lungs. My lips parted on a gasp, and Jeremy took that as an opportunity to slide his tongue between them. The flavor of maple syrup and coffee overwhelmed my senses, and before my brain had a chance to click on, my arms were wrapping around his neck, and I was pulling him to me in an attempt to deepen the kiss. My body heated, and it felt like a swarm of butterflies had been let loose in my stomach.

Before I was ready for the kiss to end, Jeremy pulled my bottom lip between his teeth and gave it a playful nip before disentangling himself and stepping away. "Have a good day, sugar."

My mind couldn't play catch-up. "What? Where the hell are you going?" I demanded as he headed for the front door.

"Work. Gotta busy day today, and I'm sure you do too."

Before I could formulate a response, he was gone, leaving me aching for him *again*. I was going to kick his ass the next time I saw him.

Jeremy

It was inevitable that walking out on Savannah for the second time in only a matter of hours meant that I was going to be stuck with a raging hard on for the rest of the day. But I could tell I was wearing her down, and that was worth every second of discomfort I would have to deal with. I'd watched as the struggle played across her eyes this morning, and after I kissed her, I could see the indecision had vanished and been replaced with hunger.

It wasn't going to be an easy fight, but I refused to give up. That girl took pride to a whole new level, but there was no doubt that I was going to win out in the long run, and I was going to savor her telling me I was right.

I was leaned over the engine compartment of my 1967 Pontiac GTO, working on restoring the engine, when Luke walked in.

"What are you so happy about?"

I looked up to see him decked out in his full deputy uniform. "Do you ever work, man?"

Luke rolled a chair over and plopped down, making himself comfortable. "What the hell does it look like I'm doing right now?"

I pulled out the rag that was tucked into my back pocket and wiped at the grease on my hands. "I don't know. Wasting taxpayer dollars?"

He kicked his feet up on the bumper of the GTO and leaned back. "What can I say? Since I got back, crime has been down. I must scare people straight. I'm a badass."

I leaned back against the car and let out a laugh. "I don't suppose it has anything to do with the fact that Cloverleaf is small and never really had a high crime rate to begin with?"

"Nope, it's because I'm a badass."

"Whatever."

"You still working on this thing? Damn, Jer. If I didn't know any better, I'd say you must be a shitty mechanic."

I kicked his feet off the bumper and laughed as he tried— and failed—to keep himself from falling. "It's a slow process, asshole. I'm just about finished with her."

Luke propped himself back in the chair and dusted off his pants. "Whatever. I still say you suck."

"Don't you have a speed trap to set up or underage kids to catch smoking?"

"Nah, I'll let the little punks get a few more packs in their lungs first. That way, I won't have to chase 'em very far."

"You're a disgrace to the badge."

He waved off my comment without even a blink and switched topics. "So, you never answered my question. What are you so happy about this morning?"

There was no way in hell I was going to tell Luke about Savannah. Breaking her walls down was a work in progress, and Luke had a bigger mouth than every damn woman in Cloverleaf combined. If Savvy found out that people knew about us, she would shut herself off tighter than she'd ever been. Nope, no way I was risking it.

"What are you talkin' about? I'm always in a good mood."

He eyed me skeptically. "Yeah, but not like this," he said, waving his hand at me. "You were whistling when I walked up. You're downright chipper this morning. What's going on?"

I turned back to the car and began working again. I needed him to get of here before I found myself spouting shit about Savvy that would undo all the work I'd already put in. "I don't know what you're talking about, man. Nothing's going on. Just a good day, I guess."

Like an answer to my prayers, the radio on his shoulder screeched and pulled his concentration away from harassing me. He mumbled a few words into the radio and stood. "Gotta go. Got a drunk and disorderly."

I looked at my watch and glanced back up at him. "At nine thirty in the morning?"

Luke chuckled as he called out over his shoulder, "Yeah. Apparently, Forrest Hendrix had a hard night of partyin'. Barb got pissed and locked him out of the house...naked."

The image of a naked Forrest Hendrix sent a chill down my spine. "Wear gloves," I hollered after him.

Savannah

I was sitting at work later that morning, trying to concentrate on my job and not that smokin' hot kiss Jeremy gave me before walking off again, when my cell phone rang on my desk. I looked down to see Emmy's gray eyes smiling back at me, and slid my finger across the screen to answer. "Hello?"

"OMG!" she exclaimed before I ever got the full word out.

"Emmy, we've discussed this. I will hang up on you if you insist on text-talking. You're better than that."

Her tinkling laughter rang through the speaker. "IDK what you're talking about BFF, Savvy."

"Hanging up now," I said with a chuckle. "I'm kind of busy right now, Em." *Trying not to spontaneously combust from thinking about Jeremy.*

"So, you're telling me that you don't want to hear the latest in the Cloverleaf grapevine?"

That instantly piqued my curiosity. "You're telling me you got gossip?" I asked, sitting up straighter in my chair.

"Jeez, you're such a gossip whore," Emmy replied with a laugh.

"Guilty as charged. Now, spill it, sister."

As Emmy spoke through the phone, my thoughts trailed back to Jeremy—how the muscles on his back had flexed while he'd been making breakfast this morning, how his chest and stomach felt when I ran my hands down them, how the kisses he'd given me were enough to crack the foundation I'd built over seven years of regret and self-denial. I was so wrapped up in everything Jeremy that I hadn't listened to a single word Emmy had been saying.

"Are you listening?"

Emmy's annoyed tone broke through my lusty haze and pulled my attention back. "Sorry…what?" I asked.

"Ugh! You didn't listen to a damn word I just said."

I rolled my eyes before responding, "Oh, untwist your panties, you big baby. You enjoy telling gossip as much as I like hearing it, so just start again from the beginning."

"Okay, well"—she took a breath for dramatic emphasis—"this is coming straight from the source, so you're the first to find out."

The anticipation was killing me. I really was a gossip whore.

"So," Emmy continued, "I'd just opened up Virgie May's, and I was setting up the pastry case when Charlotte came bursting through like her ass was on fire. And she just up and quit. Can you believe it?"

My back went stiff at the mention of her name. "What? Did she tell you why she quit?" I asked, completely shocked.

With everything that had happened between me and Jeremy since last night, I never stopped to think about how Charlotte might have handled the breakup. Clearly, she hadn't handled it well.

"She was totally hysterical," Emmy said dramatically. "I'm talking tears and snot—the whole ugly-crying thing. I could barely make out a word she was saying."

Oh God.

"What was wrong with her?" I asked in a small voice. I knew damn good and well what had been wrong with her.

"Well, my lovely Savvy, that's the good part. Charlotte and Jeremy broke up!" Emmy screeched into the phone.

I had to pull it away from my ear to prevent any permanent hearing loss.

"Um…did Charlotte say why they'd broken up?"

"No," Emmy replied. "She didn't say why. She just said that he'd dumped her, so she couldn't work here anymore because she knew we were all friends, and she didn't want to risk running into him."

I sat there, trying to figure out how I should feel. While part of me was glad they had broken up because she was a horrible person, the other part couldn't help but feel a little bad for her.

"Well, it sucks that you're out a waitress," was the only lame-ass reply I could come up with.

"You don't sound surprised. Why don't you sound surprised?" she demanded.

"What? No! I'm totally surprised!"

I was so full of shit. I knew Emmy saw right through me, but there was no way I was going to be the one to tell her about Jeremy's little epiphany from the night before. She would sink her teeth into that one and never let go. Besides Jeremy himself, the only person more determined to get us back together was Emmy. I needed to keep this one close to the vest while I figured out what in the world I was going to do.

Faking a work deadline, I quickly hung up the phone and dropped my head down on my desk. When had my life turned into such a roller coaster?

CHAPTER
ten

I was losing my freaking mind. There was no doubt about it. It had been two weeks since Jeremy had started operation Prove Savannah Wrong, and it was official, I was losing—*big time*!

The Thursday after he'd made me breakfast, he'd shown up at my job with Chinese takeout, and he'd eaten with me in my office. Friday, I'd pulled up to my house after work, and he had been there, cleaning out the gutters that I had neglected for as long as I'd lived in the house. The following Monday, he'd fixed my leaky bathroom faucet.

Everything that had needed fixing around my house managed to be fixed over the last two weeks. He'd shown up with takeout or cooked for me at least four times each week. And every time he'd left, he would make sure to leave me with a skin-tingling, brain-muddling kiss that was hot enough to make my panties combust.

Lizzy was the only friend who knew the full reason behind the end of my relationship with Jeremy. Therefore, she was the only one I could call to vent my sexual frustrations.

"So, what's he doing now?" she asked from the other end of the phone.

I stood at the bay window in the small kitchenette area off of my kitchen with a cup of coffee in my hand. "Mowing my lawn."

"Well, that doesn't sound so bad," she replied.

I pulled the phone from my ear, snapped a quick picture and texted it to her. A few seconds later, she put me on hold to check out what I'd just sent.

"Hot damn! Has he always been built like that?"

I looked back out my window at Jeremy, taking in the broad chest, ripped abs, and muscular arms pushing the mower around my front lawn. Sweat was running down his sexy-as-sin torso, pulling my eyes to the worn out jeans that were resting low on his hips. The white T-shirt he'd shown up in earlier had been discarded and was hanging out the waistband of the back of his pants. He was a walking advertisement for sex, and even my neighbors couldn't help but come outside to appreciate him.

I let out a sexually repressed sigh and went back to my conversation with Lizzy. "He's bulked up a bit over the years, but yeah, for the most part, he's always been pretty cut."

She was silent for several seconds. "No offense, babe, but how in the ever-living hell did you give up having sex with *that* for the past seven years?"

I leaned my head against the glass and squeezed my eyes shut. "With an iron will."

She started laughing on the other end of the phone. "How's that working out for ya right now?"

"Well, considering I'm two seconds from knocking his ass out just so I can take advantage of him, I'd say not so good."

"So, he's still leaving you hot and bothered every night?" she asked, still chuckling.

I wanted to reach through the phone and choke her out.

"Yes, he is. And it's really starting to piss me the hell off."

"Oh, someone's edgy when she isn't getting laid."

I let out a low growl. "It's not just that. It's the fact that he insists on turning me on almost every friggin' day, and then he leaves me high and dry. If I had balls, they'd be blue as a fucking Smurf right now."

That set Lizzy off into a fit of hysterics. I couldn't appreciate the humor in my situation at the moment.

"I'm serious, Lizzy! Maybe I should roofie him. Can guys still get it up when they take that shit?"

"Why don't we try to stay away from the felonies? Have you tried something simple like, I don't know, maybe seducing him?" She said it like I was an idiot for not coming up with that plan already.

A light bulb went off, and I knew exactly what I had to do. "Lizzy, I gotta go."

"It's about damn time you pulled your head outta your ass!" she shouted right before I disconnected the call.

Armed with a plan, I ran to my bedroom and started stripping out of my ratty sweats, and then I went on the hunt for the perfect outfit. Five minutes later, I headed out to my front yard just as Jeremy was finishing up. If we lived anywhere other than Texas, my plan wouldn't have worked. It was one of the only times I was thankful for Texas weather.

I spread my beach towel out on the freshly cut grass, and began rubbing sunscreen onto my bikini-clad body. Thank God I'd never been all that modest about my body, or I might not have been able to pull this off. After I was properly SPFed, I slid my sunglasses on, stuck my earbuds in my ears, scrolled through my playlist for The Neighbourhood, and lay back, propping one knee up in an attempt to look sexy yet casual at the same time.

After about five minutes, I started to doubt my plan when Jeremy hadn't made his way over to jump my bones, but then a large shadow spread over me, blocking out the sun. I lifted my sunglasses and saw Jeremy standing above me, wearing a knowing grin. Without a word, he reached down for the glass of iced tea I'd sat next to me and guzzled it.

"Thirsty?" I asked with a sassy smile.

He gave me a crooked smile and laughed. "Yeah, just a little."

I propped myself up on my elbows and crossed my feet at my ankles. "Kinda hot for November, isn't it?"

"Seeing as you're lying there in a bikini, I'd say, yeah, it is."

Why isn't he all over me yet?

"You know"—he took a seat beside me on the grass and lay back with his hands behind his head—"I know what you're doing, and it's not gonna work."

Shit.

I could feel a blush creeping up my neck to my cheeks. "I don't know what you're talking about," I lied. "I'm just trying to get a little sun."

"Sugar, all you have to do to get me to sleep with you is say four little words. We. Are. A. Couple. It's not that hard."

I let out a huff and lay back down, completely defeated that my plan hadn't worked. The asshole was even more stubborn than I was! I didn't know that was possible. "Is it a crime for a girl to work on her tan?" I replied testily.

Jeremy stood, and to my displeasure, pulled his shirt from his waistband and put it on. "Jesus, you're stubborn, woman!"

I shot to my feet, full of not-so-righteous indignation. "Look who's talking, asshole! You kiss me like you want to fuck me every damn time you see me, but you absolutely *refuse* to make a move. What do I have to do? Put it out there on a silver damn platter for you?"

Jeremy crossed his arms over his chest and stood his ground. "You know exactly what you have to do."

"Damn it, Jeremy! Have sex with me!" I yelled at the top of my lungs, not caring that my neighbors were still on their porches, enjoying the view of Jeremy.

"Say we're a couple."

"Oh!" I turned and stomped off toward my house. "Kiss my ass!" I shouted over my shoulder.

"I'd do that too—if you'd just admit we're together!" he called after me.

I flipped him the bird and slammed the door before he could say anything else.

Jeremy

Two weeks.

Two. Fucking. Weeks.

That was how long I'd been making Savannah suffer, but I was starting to think I was the only one suffering.

If my dick hadn't hated me before, it was a sure thing now after two weeks of self-induced agony. I was crazy!

That damn woman was going to drive me completely batshit crazy. There was no way in hell I would ever admit it to her, but I'd come so close to just caving many times. If I had to jack off one more time, I was scared I might actually go blind. Every time I was around her, my cock turned into a friggin' heat-seeking missile pointed right in her direction.

I had been determined before, but she'd turned this into a fucking war. I was going to break her like a wild horse if it was the last thing I did.

I headed to my truck, muttering curses about Savannah the entire way. When I climbed in, I had to adjust the ever-present hard on in my pants to get comfortable enough to drive. If any of the guys knew the torture I was putting myself through, they'd never let me hear the end of it.

If the blood loss to my brain—because it was all stored in my dick—didn't kill me, I knew Savannah was going to be the death of me. But *damn* was it going to be sweet when I finally had her.

Even after all these years, I remembered almost everything of our time together. For how hard we fought each other, we loved twice that. She was playing hard to get, but no one on Earth could convince me that Savvy didn't still want me.

And all the pain and suffering I was going through was going to be so worth it once I had her. I just had to stick to my guns. I already had a very creative, very detailed list of how she could make up all my current *physical* pain up to me.

Savannah

I was starting to wonder if I could get away with killing Jeremy and using temporary insanity as my defense. I felt that all the sexual frustration he was intentionally causing was sending me over the deep end. The women in that jury would *have* to understand my dilemma when they saw a picture of Jeremy without his shirt on.

"Savannah? Are you listening?"

For the past few weeks, my brain had been on one channel, and all that channel played was Jeremy Matthews, twenty-four/seven. I was even dreaming of the bastard every night.

I looked up to see Ben standing in the doorway of my office. "I'm sorry. What did you say?"

Ben gave a little chuckle before tucking his hands in the pockets of his designer slacks as he leaned against the doorframe. "Where's your mind been the past few days?"

Nowhere I want to admit to you. "I don't know. I guess I've just had a lot on my mind lately. But don't worry, I won't let it affect my work."

Embarrassment washed over me at the idea that I'd been so transparent to someone who didn't even know me that well. Just because I didn't *need* my job financially didn't mean I didn't *want* it. I liked what I did and who I worked with, so I always tried my hardest not to let me personal life bleed into my professional life.

Ben pushed off the wall and made himself comfortable in the only other chair in my office. "I'm not worried about your work. I'm more concerned about you. You've been…on edge for several days now."

I could tell by the twitch at the corner of his mouth that he'd wanted to phrase that statement very differently. "You mean, I've been acting like a raving bitch?" I asked with a smile of my own.

"Hey, you said it, not me."

I threw my head back and laughed for the first time in days. If I couldn't appreciate the humor in my situation, it was going to drive me batshit crazy. "Yeah, sorry. It's been a trying few weeks, I guess you could say."

"Anything you want to talk about?"

The last thing I was going to talk to Ben about was my sex life—or in this case, the lack thereof. "Nah, I'm pretty sure everything will work itself out soon." Either Jeremy and me were going to go at it like rabbits soon, or one of us was going to end up in jail.

Ben stood from the chair and headed for the door. "Okay. Well, I'm here if you need me."

His sincerity made me happy that we'd been able to stay friends after his failed attempt at a date. "Thanks, Ben."

"I'm heading to the deli around the corner to grab some lunch. Want to go with me?"

My stomach let out a sound, selling me out to the fact that I hadn't eaten anything for breakfast. "Yeah, that sounds good." I grabbed my purse from the bottom drawer of my desk and shut down my computer. "Let's go."

CHAPTER
eleven

Jeremy

I'd managed to get away from the garage long enough to grab a bite to eat. The last thing I'd expected to see when I turned the corner on Briar Street was Savvy walking into Briar Deli with that dickhead, Ben. That was all it took for the fine thread my control was hanging by to snap. Before my brain could register my actions, I was storming through the door and straight up to the table where they were sitting, looking all fucking cozy.

"Well, don't y'all look too cute?" I spit out before I could think about what I was saying. The only things I could concentrate on were Savannah looking like a walking pinup model in a tight ivory skirt that should be illegal with her legs and the twat who was sitting way too close to her.

She looked up at me with surprise and confusion in her eyes. "Jeremy? What are you doing here?"

The innocence in her voice just made me want to wring her neck. I'd been busting my ass at the sake of my poor neglected dick for weeks, and she was sitting there with another guy, looking like they were on a damn date?

I don't think so.

"Well, sugar, I thought I'd stop in for a bite to eat. Didn't know I'd be interrupting something here."

"Oh, for Christ's sake," she muttered under her breath. "Jeremy, stop being an ass. You aren't interrupting anything. We're just having lunch."

Bull-fuckin'-shit. I decided I needed to cut this off at the source. Turning to Ben, I responded, "You're sittin' a little too close to my girl, buddy."

That caught his attention. "Your girl?"

I pulled a chair over and forced it between the two of them. "Yeah, my girl. You didn't know we got back together?"

His eyes bounced back and forth between me and Savannah. It was obvious his discomfort with our little trio had just grown. "Uh…no, I didn't know. We're really just having lunch, man. Nothing's going on here."

I put my elbows on the table and leaned in, so he had no doubt how serious I was. "Damn straight, nothing's goin' on here because you'd have two broken arms if there was."

The sound of a chair scooting back broke the lock I had on Ben. I turned to see Savannah standing up and grabbing her purse.

"This is fucking ridiculous," she said between clenched teeth as she grabbed my arm and tried to jerk me up. "I'm so sorry for this, Ben."

"Why the hell are you apologizing to this asshat?" I cut in.

Her gaze shot to mine, and her eyes narrowed. I was instantly afraid for the safety of my balls.

"Shut the hell up, Jeremy, before I break both of *your* arms." She turned back to look at the douche she'd been having lunch with. "I'll see you at work tomorrow. I've got to take care of this little problem."

Ben stood, still obviously uncomfortable. A quick glance around the deli showed that we'd garnered quite a bit of attention.

"Yeah, I'll see you later. You two have a good day."

"Oh, we will, *Benjamin*," I replied even though I knew nothing good was about to come from the conversation Savannah and I were about to have.

She jerked me toward the door, no doubt to my imminent castration. She walked at a fast clip to the door, her shoes clicking on the tile floor the whole way. I might have been in fear of what was to come, but I was still a guy. That meant I was walking a few paces behind and admiring just how perfect her ass looked in that tight skirt and fuck-me heels. The burn-in-hell look she shot at me over her shoulder had me going from semi to fully hard instantly.

She finally made it to the sidewalk outside the deli and turned to face me. "Be at my house in fifteen minutes, or I swear to God, I will hunt you down and beat the ever living shit outta you."

Oh, I'd be there. This shit between us was going to end today. Seeing her with another man was the straw that broke the camel's back. She was going to admit what was going on between us *today*, or I was going to tie her ass to the bed—preferably naked—until she did.

Savannah

He was dead—so freaking dead that it wasn't even funny!

I'd already wanted to kill him for the past two weeks, but that little show back in the deli was just the icing on the cake. I pulled my little Lexus into my driveway and shut it off just as Jeremy pulled in behind me. I slammed the door and headed into the house without even looking back. I'd just thrown my purse onto the loveseat in the living room when I heard the front door bang shut behind me. Completely prepared for a fight, I spun around to see he was just as geared up as I was.

"I can't believe you just did that. Ben is an attorney at my firm. Do you not get that? You could have just cost me my job!"

I could actually see him losing some of his steam at that statement. He'd been so consumed by jealousy that he hadn't even taken into account that Ben was technically one of my bosses.

"What the fuck was that about, Jer?"

He roughly ran his hands through his hair and collapsed on my couch. "Why do you insist on making this so damn difficult, Savannah?"

The desperation in his voice and the fact that he'd called me Savannah instead of *sugar* didn't sit well with me. It hurt me to see him in distress. And I hated that I'd caused him to feel that way.

I took a seat on the other end of the couch and let out a heavy sigh. "Why are you pushing this so hard? It's been seven years, Jeremy."

He turned to me with a look of anger. "That's bullshit. Yeah, we might have broken up seven years ago, but we fucked a couple months ago. Stop acting like there hasn't been something between us this whole time!"

I felt a lump forming in my throat. "Jeremy, please…"

He stood and pulled me to him, wrapping his fingers in the long strands of my hair to force my face to his. "You belong with me and you know it. There's no one else out there for you. Just like there's no one else for me. I'm not letting you go."

I cocked my head back, shocked at how sure he sounded. "Excuse me?"

Jeremy ran his fingers through my hair and rested them on the nape of my neck, all the while looking unflinchingly into my eyes. "Seven years ago, I was stupid enough to let you walk away from me, and I've been letting you do it every day since. I'm tired of trying to convince myself that the little bit I have of you is enough. It's not. I want all of you. I *need* all of you. And I know you need me too."

I swallowed audibly past the tears clogging my throat. Everything he said was one hundred percent true. I did need him. But I couldn't have him.

"Jeremy, you know this won't work. Our past—"

He cut me off with a gentle kiss before pulling back again. "Our past doesn't matter. I don't care what happened seven years ago. I'm talking about right now, sugar. I don't want to look back. I want to move forward, and I can't do that if I'm not with you. I tried to move on, and I failed miserably. I'll say it again—there's no one else for me."

Every wall I'd worked so hard to build over the past seven years started to crumble, and I was having a hell of a difficult time holding the pieces together. "You know it's not that easy," I pressed.

"Do you love me?"

If only it were that simple…

Standing so close to him—the only man who could ever piss me off and turn me on all at the same time—was torture. I loved everything about him—his milk chocolate eyes, his burnished hair, those rippling muscles, each one earned from the years of back-breaking work he'd put in at his garage. Everything about him was rugged and sexy as hell.

"It's not that easy, Jer. You know that."

He dipped his head and ran his lips from my collarbone up to my ear before whispering, "But it *is* that easy, sugar."

His breath on my skin sent a shiver through my entire body, and I knew he could feel it. He was too close not to.

"Do you love me? Because I've loved you since I was fourteen. I've loved you every single day that's passed since the day I met you."

I couldn't hold myself back any longer. When he told me he'd never stopped loving me, all my instincts to fight him flew out the window. I lunged, wrapping my arms and legs around him as tightly as I could, effectively ripping my pencil skirt in the process.

"I love you too," I said between the kisses I was planting all over his face. "God, Jeremy, I love you so much."

Holding on to Jeremy was the only thing I could think about. Tears ran down my cheeks unchecked as I put my heart and soul into showing how much I had missed him.

He wrapped both arms under my bottom, tearing the fabric even more, and held on to me as tightly as I was holding him. "I've missed you so much, Savvy," he said against my lips as he walked us away from the couch and over to the wall that separated my living room from the kitchen. "You mean everything to me."

A low moan escaped my throat when he pressed his denim-clad hips into me, hitting just the right spot. I could feel how hard he was through the layers of clothes between us, and I desperately wanted to tear everything away. I needed to feel him, skin against skin. My nipples tightened to almost painful points under my shirt. I was sure that Jeremy could feel them.

Using his body to pin my weight to the wall, Jeremy released one hand to trail it down my side, brushing against my breast with a whisper-light touch, and traveling down to where my now ruined skirt was bunched around my waist.

"Sugar, I need you so bad," he said as he dragged wet kisses down my neck to the swell of my breasts.

I couldn't contain the whimper of need that bubbled up. "I need you too, Jer. God, I need you."

"Say it," he demanded.

I couldn't think clearly when he was touching me. "Say what?"

His breath felt hot on my skin.

"You know what I need to hear, sugar."

I couldn't deny it anymore. He'd won, hands down.

"We're a couple," I whispered against his lips.

"Thank God!" he exclaimed with as much desperation as I was feeling.

I let out a sound of distress when he pulled his hips away, but he quickly slid his hand between my legs, pushing my lace panties to the side and plunged a finger deep inside me.

"Christ, baby, you're so perfect."

He brought his lips back to mine as he kept up a quick pace, turning me inside out with just his hand.

"Jeremy, I'm so close." I craved the release that was building up quicker than I could have anticipated. I needed Jeremy to take me there so badly.

He inserted a second finger, pushing as deep as he could, and curled them in a come-hither motion while pressing his palm harder against my clit. "Give it to me, Savvy. I want to hear you."

"Oh God!" I cried, throwing my head back against the wall and squeezing my eyes closed. I was so close to falling over the edge.

"Eyes on me, sugar. I want you to see who's in control of your pleasure."

I lowered my head and looked at Jeremy through hooded eyes. He was still so beautiful. Everything about him was perfect to me.

"Tell me you're mine," he demanded.

"I'm yours, Jeremy."

"Only mine," he said, his voice a growl.

"Only yours. Only ever yours."

"*Fuck*," he ground out. "I love you so much, Savannah."

And with that, I flew right over the edge, crying out Jeremy's name, as he continued to thrust those talented fingers in and out, over and over, coaxing every drop of climax from my body until I wasn't capable of holding my own head up.

It took me several seconds to catch my breath, but once I did, I was finally able to respond. "I love you too, Jeremy. Only ever you."

When he flashed me that brilliant dimpled smile that made me fall in love with him all those years ago, he captured my heart completely, all over again.

CHAPTER
twelve

Somehow, as the night had progressed, we'd finally made our way into the bedroom. After having some of the best sex of my life, Jeremy and I had both passed out.

Unfortunately, I woke up a few hours later, giving myself plenty of time to think about why us getting back together was such an epic mistake. I replayed the reason over and over again until I was filled with so much anxiety that I felt like I couldn't breathe.

The only light in the room was drifting in from the hallway, illuminating Jeremy's naked back. He had the best back. I hadn't even known it was possible for a man to have a sexy back until Jeremy.

I lay there, watching the toned golden skin rise and fall with each breath he took. He seemed so peaceful while sleeping, and the thought of not being able to keep what we'd started just hours before caused my eyes to sting with tears. I rolled to my back and stared at the ceiling, trying to figure out what I was going to do next.

"I can hear those wheels turnin' in that head of yours from here," Jeremy mumbled in a sleep-filled voice. Even if I hadn't been able to see his gorgeous body, the gravelly tenor of his voice was enough to turn me on.

"Hey," I responded softly, "I didn't know you were awake."

He rolled to his side and propped his head in his hand, making the muscles in his bicep and chest stand out even more. I was pretty sure I was starting to drool.

Keep your head in the game, Morgan!

"I know you didn't," he responded with a sly smile. "If you had, you'd probably be tryin' to kick me out the door right about now."

I shot up into a sitting position, holding the sheet to my naked chest. "No, I wouldn't!" I replied incredulously.

He might have been totally correct, but that didn't mean I liked him assuming the worst of me.

He threw his head back in laughter, enhancing his abs. It took everything I had not to jump him.

"Sugar, you've never been any good at bullshitting me. I know you better than you think."

I threw myself back onto the pillows in a huff of defeat. He knew me better than anyone, sometimes better than I knew myself. But that didn't mean I liked it. It made keeping secrets from him damn near impossible.

"Come here, sugar," he whispered softly, opening his arms for me to scoot into him.

I buried my face in his chest and breathed deep, inhaling the scent that was inherently Jeremy.

He held me tight and started rubbing a hand over my hair. "I told you that you weren't getting away again and I meant it. You can try all you want, but it's me and you from here on out."

I bit his pec playfully before looking up into those chocolate eyes of his. "What if that's not what I want?"

He grabbed a handful of my hair and pulled it back, just hard enough to make me gasp, before his head shot down and he sealed his lips to mine in a forceful kiss. It was as if he was taking ownership of me with that kiss.

"You want it, baby. You're just scared, but that's okay. I'm not going anywhere, and you'll eventually get over your fears."

God, I loved him something fierce.

He nipped my bottom lip with his teeth, causing a pleasurable sting to form, before soothing it with his tongue. He pulled back slightly, and I instinctively followed after him, not ready to stop kissing him yet. The desire I felt for him was consuming me. I couldn't touch or taste him enough.

Jeremy gently rolled me to my back and pushed himself between my legs. I could feel him growing harder against my lower stomach, and desire pooled deep in my core.

"Mmm, I love how you taste," he murmured as he ran his tongue along my collarbone. "You smell fuckin' good too, sugar."

I'd forgotten Jeremy's gift of turning me on with just a few words. He could always light me up just by talking.

"Jeremy, I need you," I pleaded breathlessly.

"I'll never get enough of hearing you say that, Savvy."

Jeremy rolled, taking me with him, so that I was straddling his trim waist. I ran my tongue across his lips before kissing my way past his chin and down his neck. I could spend hours licking and kissing every inch of his amazing body.

As I wandered farther and farther down, I couldn't help but feel invincible when I looked up through my lashes and saw an expression of complete satisfaction and adoration on his face. It was a heady feeling, knowing I could make a man as strong as Jeremy crazy with want.

By the time I made it all the way down, positioned with my chest between his legs, his breath was coming out in rapid pants. I took him in my hand and squeezed slightly, loving the silky yet hard feel of him. When I licked my lips in anticipation, a low growl rumbled from deep within his chest. I ran my tongue from the base, all the way up the underside of his cock, and to the tip where I licked a drop of pre-cum before sealing my lips around the head completely.

"*Fuuuuck*, baby," he ground out between clenched teeth.

His reaction spurred me on, and I started moving up and down his rigid length, over and over, taking him as deep as I could. I hollowed out my cheeks and sucked harder on my way back up then flicked the tip of my tongue over the sensitive underside.

"Savvy, I'm gonna come if you don't stop," he breathed.

The thought of him losing control like that made me moan around his dick, which sent a shiver through him. Grabbing his sac in one hand, I began to massage as I used the other hand at the base, working him faster and faster. I knew Jeremy's control was slipping when he grabbed a hold of my hair tightly and started thrusting his hips, making me take him even deeper. I wanted him to let go. I thrived on the idea of taking him over the edge, like he had done for me.

I glanced up at his face and saw his eyes squeezed shut and the muscle in his jaw twitching. After releasing him with a pop, I mumbled, "Eyes on me, baby," repeating his words from earlier. "I want you to see who's in control of your pleasure."

"You're all I've ever seen, sugar, even when my eyes are closed."

The intensity reflected in his look as he spoke caused the breath to rush from my lungs. I didn't know if I'd ever loved him more than I did right at that moment.

Before I had the opportunity to get back to my task, Jeremy bent at the waist, reached under my arms, and hauled me back up his body, shifting so that I was lying underneath him once again.

"Do you have any clue what you do to me?" he asked.

The sincerity in his voice made me tear up. It took me a few seconds to be able to speak past the lump in my throat. "Yes," I whispered. "Because you do the same to me."

Jeremy leaned back down and kissed me with so much passion that the tears I'd been fighting back had no choice but to escape. I was so consumed by it that my brain almost didn't register when he shifted his hips and started to slide into me.

"Baby…condom," I said against his lips.

He pushed up on his forearms and looked down at me. "You on the pill, sugar?"

"Yes, but…"

"I'm clean, honey. You're the only one I've ever been with without protection."

I took a deep breath, and my eyes drifted to the side of his face. I couldn't look directly at him and ask the question that needed asking. "What about Charlotte?"

Grabbing my chin, he tilted my face, so I had no choice but to look directly at him. "You're the only one, Savannah, I swear. No one else was worth that risk—ever."

My mouth dropped open, and all I could do was nod.

"You trust me?" he asked.

Again, all I did was nod. His words, *No one else was worth the risk*, were on repeat in my head, making it impossible for me to form a coherent sentence.

"I need words, sugar. You trust me?"

My mind finally started working. I looked into those deep brown eyes and smiled. "Yeah, Jer, I trust you."

At my response, Jeremy pushed all the way in with a fast, hard thrust, burying himself completely. I gasped at the initial intrusion, but my body quickly adjusted to his length, and the gasp turned into a deep moan.

"Oh shit, baby. You feel so damn good."

Jeremy kept up the same brutal pace the entire time and I could feel my orgasm building with each deep, brutal thrust. His amazing stamina might have turned my brain to mush, but my body knew exactly how to respond, and my hips began to rise quickly in an attempt to meet his.

"Oh God, Jer. It's so good. I'm close," I said between gasps.

He buried his face in my neck and let out a low moan. My core tightened as I got closer and closer to the edge and I threw my head back against the pillows.

"Don't stop, Jeremy," I panted desperately.

Before I could even register his movement, Jeremy sat up on his haunches, pulling me with him so we were both sitting face to face with me straddling his lap. At the new angle, I took Jeremy even deeper inside me. I let out a whimper at the new sensation as I ground down on him. Our movements were becoming erratic, and I was so close that I started losing rhythm with Jeremy. I arched my back, pushing my breasts against his chest and threw my head back as my climax started to take over.

"Look at me, Savannah," Jeremy said as he wrapped a large chunk of my hair around his hand and pulled my face back to his. "I want your eyes on me the whole time."

The combination of his words and the sting in my scalp from where he held my hair caused my orgasm to rock through me, and I came with a sharp, loud cry.

"Christ, Savvy. So. Damn. Beautiful." His words were punctuated with each thrust just before he found his own release seconds later.

I could feel him, hot and hard inside me as he came and the sensation set me off again.

"*Jeremy*," I cried out in a horse voice as the intense pleasure became almost too much.

Jeremy continued pumping his hips until there was nothing left for either of us. Once we were both completely sated, we collapsed on the bed in a heap of twisted, sweaty limbs, neither of us having the strength to lift a finger.

"I think you just killed me, sugar," Jeremy said with a chuckle once our breathing had finally calmed.

I laughed in response. "Perfect way to die."

Jeremy grabbed the back of my neck and jerked me to him, sealing his lips against mine. "Hell yeah, it is."

I could feel his smile against my lips, and I couldn't help but smile back. I didn't remember a time in my life when I'd felt more at peace than I did right then. I knew, no matter what, that in Jeremy's arms was exactly where I was supposed to be.

CHAPTER
thirteen

My cell phone went off at the ungodly hour of six in the morning, waking me from a perfect deep sleep. Still not quite awake all the way, I rolled toward the device from hell with a groan, only to have a strong arm pull me back into an equally strong chest.

"Let it ring." Jeremy's voice was husky from sleep.

My body became instantly aroused by the rumbling tone. *Good Lord, is there anything about him I don't find attractive?*

"Mmkay," I replied sleepily, turning back over into the warmth of his body and nestling in comfortably.

I'd just about dozed back off when the phone started ringing again. I was seriously contemplating throwing the bastard against the friggin' wall.

"Sonofabitch! You've got to be kidding me." I pulled away from a laughing Jeremy to give the person calling a ration of shit for waking me up—*twice*. I didn't bother looking at the display when I answered, "Swear to God, when I wake up all the way, I'm gonna hunt you down and make you suffer."

"WHAT THE HELL IS GOING ON?" Emmy shrieked into the phone, nearly blowing my eardrum out.

"Emmy, it's six in the morning. I'm not properly caffeinated, and I'm half-deaf now. You better have a damn good reason for calling this early."

"And you better have a damn good reason for not telling me that you and Jeremy are back together!"

Oh shit.

She kept going before I could utter a word. "Half the town is talking about the little scene between you two at Briar's yesterday—and don't even get me started on the fact that you were eating at Briar's instead of Virgie May's. That's a whole other conversation you and I need to have. I can't *believe* you didn't tell me!"

I was trying to pay attention to Emmy's rant, but Jeremy sat up and started placing kisses across my shoulders, wrecking my concentration as my skin broke out in goose bumps.

Stop it, I mouthed, trying to scoot away from him so I could hear Emmy.

He didn't care.

I tried to focus on Emmy, but it was so damn hard with a naked Jeremy pushed up against my back.

"I'm sorry I didn't tell you, Em, but it just kind of happened yesterday. It's not like I've had the opportunity to talk to you about it."

Jeremy's tongue darted out and ran over the shell of my ear, sending shivers down my spine.

"Something like this doesn't just happen overnight, Savvy. You expect me to believe this hasn't been going on for a while?"

At that very moment, I really didn't give a damn what she believed. All I could think about was straddling Jeremy.

"Oh my God!" she exclaimed. "This is why Charlotte quit two weeks ago, isn't it? This has been going on for *two weeks!*"

Charlotte was the last person I wanted to think about when I was curled up on a warm bed with the only man I'd ever loved.

"Look, Em, I know how this appears, but we really did just *officially* get back together last night."

"Not saying I'm not ecstatic that you two finally got your shit together, but you owe me a waitress."

In exasperation, I rolled my eyes and dropped my head back to stare at the ceiling. All that did was give Jeremy better access to my throat and that sensitive spot between my ear and collarbone, which he took complete advantage of. I had to work hard to choke down the moan that wanted to escape.

"How does you needing a waitress fall on me? That shit is not my fault!"

I could feel Jeremy's body shaking with laughter from behind me. He was used to the childish arguments between Emmy and me.

"Yes, it is! If you and Jeremy hadn't fallen all in love and shit, I wouldn't be a waitress short."

"Well, then you shouldn't have let dating the help. You were always rooting for us to get back together, so it's technically you're fault that you're a waitress short," I demanded.

She stayed silent for several seconds. "Hmm, you might have a point there."

I let out a very unladylike snort. "What do you mean, *might* have a point? I'm right, and you know it. And why am I even fighting with you about this at the butt crack of dawn? It's too early for this shit."

That was the moment Jeremy chose to push me onto my back and plant his hips between my legs.

"Stop it," I hissed under my breath, trying to wriggle my way out from under him.

"What's going on over there?" Emmy demanded from the other end of the phone. "Who are you talking to?"

His fingers started a seductive path down my ribs, and just when I started to think he was going to turn the heat up on his seduction, he did the complete opposite and began tickling me. I let out a loud burst of laughter and fought even harder to get out from beneath him.

"Ah! Jeremy, stop!" I shouted between laughs.

"Hang up the phone," Jeremy said in a deep baritone voice that sent an electric spark through me.

"HOLY SHIT!" Emmy screeched. "Jeremy's there! You're with Jeremy! HOLY SHIT!"

"I'll call you back!" I hollered, dropping the phone on the bed near my head as I tried to escape Jeremy's tickling fingers.

"AHHHHHHHHHH!" Emmy screamed so loud that I was afraid my ears would start bleeding.

Jeremy let out a loud belly laugh at Emmy's scream, and I couldn't help but laugh along with him.

"Pickupthephone. Pickupthephone. Pickupthephone," I heard coming from the bed next to me.

Before I could get a hold of the phone, Jeremy had already grabbed it.

"Good morning, darlin'," he drawled into the phone.

I couldn't make out exactly what she was saying to him, but from the high pitch, I knew she was still screaming with excitement.

"Can Savannah call you back, Emmy girl?" he asked as he shot me that killer dimpled smile.

"OHMYGOD! Jeremy!" she started but didn't get to finish before he disconnected the call.

I was pinned beneath his body, still laughing, when I told him, "Great. You know she's gonna lay into your ass later for hanging up on her."

"She'll deal with it," he said with a chuckle.

I shoved at his shoulder playfully. "No...*I'll* deal with it. I'm the one who's gonna have to hear it."

He swiveled his hips, causing me to throw my head back and let out a needy groan.

"I'm pretty sure I can make it up to you, sugar."

Oh, I had no doubt about that.

He leaned in and planted a kiss on my lips. "I guess we should deal with it sooner rather than later." He pushed up, flexing those sexy arms, and hopped out of bed.

"What? Where are you going? I thought we were about to have sex!" I pushed my bottom lip out in a pout. I wasn't nearly done with him yet. I didn't know if I would ever be done with him.

He grabbed his jeans, doing the exact opposite of what I wanted him to do, and began to get dressed. "We're goin' to breakfast, sugar. Might as well kill two birds with one stone and deal with Emmy while gettin' some grub."

I crossed my arms over my chest and shot him an ugly look.

"Ah, don't be that way, Savvy." He pulled his jeans up and zipped them, but left the button undone before crawling across the bed to give me a lingering kiss. "Besides, I gotta feed my woman," he said before biting down on my bottom lip lightly. "We need to keep our strength up with everything I've got planned for you."

I licked across his lips and wrapped my arms around his neck. "Mmm, I forgot how insatiable you are."

"I'm gonna have one hell of a time reminding you, baby."

I slung one leg over his waist and ground my pelvis against his. "Why don't you remind me right now? I think I might have forgotten," I said playfully.

"Oh, is that right?"

I nodded and seductively bit down on my bottom lip.

He reminded me twice before we finally made our way out of bed.

CHAPTER
fourteen

"Looks like she called in the cavalry," I muttered to Jeremy as we pushed through the door to Virgie May's.

Luke, Emmy, Lizzy, Stacia, Gavin, Brett, and Trevor were all huddled around the counter. As soon as the bell over the door dinged and they saw us, all of them started yelling and jumping around like a bunch of idiots.

"I changed my mind. I'm not hungry."

I tried to turn and walk back out, but Jeremy had a death grip on my hand and he wouldn't let go.

"Uh-uh, sugar. I'm not walking into the lion's den alone. This is a team effort."

I turned to him and placed my hands on my hips. "Screw team effort! This was your idea. I should just throw your ass in there and make a run for it."

He let out a chuckle and gave me a kiss on the forehead. "I love you too, honey."

I mumbled a few choice words under my breath as we made our way over to all our friends.

"Which one of you assholes hung up on me this morning?" were the first words from Emmy's mouth, which was totally what I'd expected.

"That would be this asshole right here," I said as I pointed to Jeremy. I was *not* above throwing him under the bus when it came to dealing with the wrath of Emerson Grace. Nuh-uh. No way.

Emmy directed her heated glare right at him. "Oh, we're gonna have words, my friend."

Jeremy turned on the charm full force. "Ah, Emmy girl, don't be mad. I just wanted to spend as much time alone with Savvy as possible. I just got her back. I didn't want to share her just yet."

"Aww," came from Emmy, Lizzy, and Stacia.

He was good. He'd just played Emmy like a fiddle. All I could do was roll my eyes.

"So, it's official then?" Lizzy asked. "You guys are back together?"

I saw underlying concern beneath her happiness, and I could understand, but I just chose to ignore it. Lizzy was the only one who knew the whole truth.

"What can I say? She just can't stay away from me," Jeremy responded, giving me a swift slap on the ass.

I turned and punched him in the arm. "I think I just changed my mind," I said as I raised a brow.

Jeremy grabbed hold of my waist and pulled me flush against his body. "That's not what you were saying last night. If I remember correctly you were actually screaming—"

I slapped my hand over his mouth. "You finish that sentence and what happened last night will *never* happen again."

"Oh God," Brett chimed in. "I don't need to hear this shit. She's like a sister to me."

Jeremy nipped one of the fingers covering his mouth. Then, he grabbed me by the nape of my neck and pulled me to him, kissing me fiercely. When he finally pulled back, I breathlessly glanced around. Lizzy, Emmy, and Stacia were looking at us like they were so happy they wanted to cry or break out into song. I prayed they didn't do either of those things. Luke, Trevor, Gavin, and Brett looked like they wanted to hurl.

"Damn, Killer," Luke began. "I didn't think you'd go all girlie when you started gettin' some. I'm a little disappointed in you."

I reared back and punched him in the stomach as hard as I could.

"Ouch. Damn it!" Luke started rubbing the spot I'd just hit as Emmy came over to baby him.

"Still disappointed?" I asked.

"No." Luke pouted from his hunched over position.

"Good. Remember that. I'll still kick your ass."

We sat and joked for a while before I had to leave to go to work.

"We staying at my place or yours?" Jeremy asked as I picked up my purse and grabbed two cups of coffee to go.

I smiled and leaned in to give him a quick kiss. "Look at you, just assuming you're gettin' some two nights in a row."

He gave me another peck before saying, "Whether we have sex or not doesn't matter. I'm not sleeping without you next to me. I spent seven years worth of nights like that, and I refuse to do it anymore."

I looked at him for several seconds, just soaking in everything about him, before sitting my stuff back down. I wrapped my arms around his waist, buried my face in his chest, and inhaled deeply. "I love you so much," I said into the soft cotton of his T-shirt.

Jeremy grabbed my face in both hands and tilted it up toward his. "I love you too, sugar. Only ever you."

"Only ever you," I repeated in a whisper.

Finally tearing myself away from him, I turned and gave everyone a wave before heading off to work. I wouldn't have been able to wipe the smile off my face if I'd tried.

"Good morning," I said in a singsong voice as I walked into Ben's office.

I pushed some stuff around on his desk to make space for the coffee I'd brought him. It was an attempt at a peace offering after the stunt Jeremy had pulled at Briar Deli the day before.

"Oh God, you're a lifesaver," he said dramatically. He picked up the cup and took a generous gulp.

"Long night?" I asked as I planted myself in a chair across from his desk.

"You have no idea."

I was a little concerned by the tone of his voice. He seemed fine when I last saw him.

"Is everything okay?"

Ben ran his hand over his jaw, and I noticed that he had apparently skipped shaving this morning. The scruff looked nice on him.

"Yeah," he said on a sigh. "Just some family stuff. But I don't want to drag you down with it. It's a little hard to understand."

A clip from my childhood played on fast-forward in my head. "You might be surprised," I replied with a sarcastic laugh.

"Your family can't possibly be as dysfunctional as mine."

I waved a finger in the air at him. "I wouldn't place money on that bet if I were you. But this isn't the time or the place to get into the drama of our families."

He lifted his cup and saluted me. "Agreed. So, since we're changing the topic of conversation, I'm guessing it's safe to say that everything worked out with you and Jeremy last night? You're rather pleasant this morning."

That ridiculously corny smile spread across my face again at Ben's statement. "I don't know what you're talking about."

He said with a laugh, "Your poker face is horrible."

"Well, there's a reason I'm a paralegal and not a lawyer."

I shot him a cheeky grin, and he just rolled his eyes.

"I'm just hoping now that you two seem to have patched things up, he'll quit looking at me like he wants to beat the shit outta me. I have to admit, that's getting a little old."

Humor was evident on his face, but I still cringed slightly at the mention of Jeremy's behavior toward Ben.

"Yeah. I'm really sorry about that. I'm gonna have a talk with him."

Ben gave me a good-natured smile. "Nah, you don't have to do that. I understand where he's coming from."

"Ha! Well, how about you fill me in? Because, apparently I don't, and alpha isn't a language I'm fluent in."

Ben leaned back in his chair and steepled his fingers. The look on his face said he was about to school me on all things male. "Well, you see, young grasshopper—"

I immediately interrupted him. "Oh, gag! Spare me the *Karate Kid* bullshit."

"Okay, fine. In a nutshell, Jeremy has/currently is/or wants to sleep with you. Any man who thinks that way about a woman will automatically get possessive when he feels like another guy is encroaching on what he assumes is his."

"But you aren't encroaching on anything. We're just friends."

"Doesn't matter. That's just how we function. If a member of the opposite sex is talking to our woman, it's in our DNA to view that man as a threat. I'm pretty sure there are medical journals and scientific studies out there that back up my theory."

I remained silent for several seconds, thinking about what he'd said. I could only come up with one response. "Penises make y'all stupid."

"That's why we're the weaker sex," he replied with a grin.

I threw my head back and laughed. "At least you're willing to admit it."

"Well, if he's the reason for your good mood today, I'm happy for you."

I stood, smiling brightly at Ben, as I started toward the door. "He is, and thank you."

"You're welcome, Savannah. I'm just glad to see you happy."

And I really was. For the first time in years, I was one hundred percent genuinely happy.

CHAPTER
fifteen

"Get a move on, sugar. We're already late," Jeremy hollered from the living room.

I was running around my bedroom in nothing but my bra and a pair of jeans, freaking out. I would have been perfectly content to spend all evening in bed with Jeremy. But was I ever that lucky? Of course not.

"Not that I don't love what you already have on, but you show up to my folks' house like that, and Pops is liable to go into cardiac arrest."

I turned to see Jeremy casually leaning against the doorway of my bedroom, like he didn't have a care in the world, and threw him an evil look. Dinner with Jeremy's family—I'd done it a million times when we dated in the past, but that had been years ago. After we'd broken up, I'd only seen members of his family here and there around town. They were always pleasant, but I knew they hated how things had ended between us.

"I don't have anything to wear." I pouted. "I can't go."

Rolling his eyes, Jeremy pushed off the doorframe and made his way over to my closet. "I find that hard to believe, considering it looks like the entire Cloverleaf mall is in your closet."

He wasn't kidding. I had a serious retail-therapy issue, but that didn't mean I had anything appropriate to wear to a family dinner at my boyfriend's parents' house.

"What about this right here?"

He held up a top that said *Classy Girls Say Fuck* that I'd gotten as a gift from Brett on my last birthday.

"Yes, because nothing says, 'I'm a suitable girlfriend for your son,' like a shirt with the word *fuck* in eight inch hot-pink letters." I threw myself down on my bed with an exaggerated sigh.

I felt the bed dip with Jeremy's weight, and then his fingers began to lightly trail across my stomach.

"It's not like this is the first time you're meeting my folks, Savvy. Hell, you were practically part of the family when we were dating."

"Yeah, but that was a lifetime ago, honey. I wouldn't be surprised if they hated me for dumping you and breaking your heart."

I could feel Jeremy's body shaking in silent laughter. "They don't hate you, baby. They hated that we broke up because they loved you like a daughter, but they never hated you. Besides, none of that matters anymore. We're together now, and it's gonna stay that way." With that, he hopped off the bed and pulled me up after him. "Now, put on a damn shirt before I rip off what little you're wearing and make us even later."

Ten minutes later, we were in Jeremy's pickup, heading toward his parents' house. I was pretty happy with my decision of an ivory silk camisole that flowed slightly and a coral-colored jacket with cuffed sleeves. Paired with jeans and tan heels, it was the perfect combination of dressy and casual.

"So, who all is coming to dinner?" I asked, wondering exactly how many of Jeremy's siblings were going to be in attendance.

I prayed it wasn't all of them. The Matthews were amazing people, but Jeremy had three brothers and a sister. How his parents managed with five kids was beyond me, but having four boys? No, thank you. They were loud and boisterous by themselves. Getting them all together in one room had a tendency to become overwhelming.

"Well, Olivia's school hasn't let out for winter break yet, so she's still in Louisiana, and Daniel had to go out of town for some conference, so they won't be there."

Olivia was Jeremy's little sister. At nineteen, she was the youngest. Add the fact that she was the only girl stuck with four overbearing older brothers, and it didn't take a genius to guess how difficult life had been for her growing up. To say they were protective was an understatement. Poor Olivia had to go to college in Louisiana just to get a date.

Daniel was thirty-five and the oldest of all the kids. He'd gone on to medical school, and was currently working at a hospital in Houston's Medical Center.

That meant Chris and Michael were coming. Three out of five wouldn't seem that bad, but between just those two, Jeremy had five nieces and nephews. *Five!* That didn't even count the other four kids that Daniel had.

It wasn't hard to see why Jeremy was all about a big family. At that thought, I was hit with a twinge of sadness.

Jeremy must have sensed the change in my mood and interpreted it to be nerves because he reached for my hand and shot me a reassuring smile. "It'll be okay, baby. You'll see. Everyone's excited to see you again."

I knew the smile I gave him didn't quite meet my eyes, but I just couldn't muster up anything more genuine at that point.

A few minutes later, we pulled up in the driveway of Jeremy's childhood home. The red brick house was just as I remembered it. With a porch that extended the length of it and the same white shutters, I was instantly hit with memories from my past. I'd spent so much time at this house, soaking in all the love that was missing in my own home. I almost forgot how much Jeremy's family meant to me growing up, especially his mom. Everything I'd never received from my own mother, Mrs. Matthews had given me in spades.

God, I missed her.

Before my nerves had a chance to take over, the front door was thrown open, and she came flying out, straight toward Jeremy's truck. For a woman who had given birth to five kids, she was such a tiny little thing. She was all of five feet tall with a sleek bob that was the same reddish-brown color as Jeremy's. The only sign of her age was the smattering of gray hair lightly spread throughout it.

I didn't even have time to blink before the passenger door was flung open, and I was wrapped up in her familiar arms. "Savvy, honey, I've missed you so much!"

I let out a laugh and returned her hug, squeezing her back just as tight. The scent of lavender wafted up, and any anxiety I'd felt earlier was washed away by the familiarity. My arms constricted, hugging her even tighter, before I finally let her go and stepped out of the truck.

"I missed you too, Mrs. Matthews."

"*Pffft*, what's this Mrs. Matthews business? You're family, sweetheart. It's Kathy."

My breath hitched, and I had to fight to hold back the tears. To still consider me as part of her family after so long was even more proof of what a phenomenal woman she truly was.

I'm not gonna cry. I'm not gonna cry.

She grabbed hold of my forearms and stepped back to look me up and down. "Look at you—just as beautiful as ever. You look absolutely stunning."

She smiled up at me, her brown eyes glimmering, and I was reminded where Jeremy got his eyes from.

"You look beautiful too, Kathy. Thank you for inviting me."

She linked her arm through mine and started leading me to the house. "Of course you're invited. I'm just so thrilled you and Jer got your heads outta your asses long enough to see what was good for y'all."

"Jeez, Mom, how about we at least get in the house before you start in on us?"

I turned and gave Jeremy a wink from over my shoulder.

Just as we crossed the threshold, I heard a booming voice coming from the kitchen.

"Is that my sunflower?"

I squealed in excitement and started jumping up and down as Jeremy's dad rounded the corner.

"Burt!" I hollered, launching myself at the giant teddy bear of a man.

"Sunflower!" he replied as he scooped me up and started spinning me around.

Jeremy's hair and eyes might have come from his mom, but he'd gotten everything else from his dad. Burt Matthews was definitely a handsome man. Standing well over six feet, he was all broad shoulders and muscular arms. His midsection might have gained a little paunch over the years, but it didn't detract from the fact that he'd most definitely been a lady-killer back in the day. Jeremy was built just like him—well, with the exception of his dad's extra weight around the middle.

I'd totally forgotten about Burt's nickname for me. He'd started calling me *sunflower* when Jeremy and I were just kids, and for the longest time, I'd thought it was because of my blonde hair. That was before he told me that I shined like the sun and lit up all their lives when I was around. I loved him calling me *sunflower* almost as much as I loved when Jeremy called me *sugar*.

"How you doin', darlin'?" he drawled as he put my feet back on the ground. "We've missed you something fierce around here."

"I'm so sorry I waited seven years to see y'all again." I could feel the tears welling up. To my horror, my voice cracked, and everyone standing by me knew I was about to lose it.

"Hey now, sunflower, it's okay." Burt pulled me back into his barrel chest and squeezed gently. "We understood, darlin'. We're just glad you and Jeremy came to your senses. It's nice to have you back."

I pulled away and ran my fingers under my eyes to fix any smudged mascara. "It's so good to be back," I whispered.

Sensing I needed a change of subject, Jeremy wrapped his arms around my waist from behind and pulled me to him. "Don't be tryin' to steal my woman, Pop," he said with a smile in his voice.

I could see the pride shining in both of their eyes as they looked at me and Jeremy together.

How did I ever walk away from all these wonderful people?

Then, just like anytime I started to feel happy, I was hit with an ugly reminder. I'd walked away because I couldn't risk seeing the disappointment on their faces if they found out what I'd done. Walking away had been easier than letting them down. I couldn't stand the idea of that.

I was pulled from my ruminations by the sound of Burt's deep belly laugh.

"Wouldn't dream of it, son," Burt replied as he wrapped an arm around Kathy's shoulders. "Got everything I need right here."

The love that they had for each other was written all over them. Not many people were lucky enough to have that, and all I could do was hope I hadn't ruined my chance at having the same thing with Jeremy.

A loud thundering sound caught my attention, and I turned just in time to see four kids come flying into the living room like a destructive hurricane.

"Eww, Poppy's kissin' on Granny!" one of them yelled.

"Uncle Jeremy smells like butt crack!" another shouted.

That was quickly followed by, "Get back here, you little monsters!"

All four kids let out delighted shrieks loud enough to break every window in the house, and ran from the living room just as Chris and Michael came after them.

Chris was the second youngest at only twenty-three, but he'd married his high school sweetheart, Michelle, right after graduation. From what Jeremy had said, they were insanely happy. They had a three-year-old boy and a newborn baby girl, the only girl out of the whole bunch. I'd been an only child growing up, and I didn't have any close family, so I'd never really gotten the chance to be around babies. I was kind of excited about meeting her.

Michael was thirty-two, and had been married to Sandra for the past ten years, so I'd gotten to know her pretty well before Jeremy and I broke up. She was one tough woman, mainly because she had to be. Michael and Sandra were the parents of the remaining three children—all boys ranging from ages seven to two. Sandra was my kind of people, all attitude on the outside but with a soft, caring center. I really liked her.

"Savannah!" Chris and Michael both yelled and immediately stopped chasing after the kiddos to engulf me in a group hug.

And just like that, it was like I hadn't been gone for the past seven years.

"What's your name?" Cameron, Michael's four-year-old son, asked.

I smiled at the adorable towheaded boy. "I'm Savannah, but all my friends call me Savvy."

His face scrunched up like he'd just smelled something disgusting. "Why they call you that?" he asked. "That's a stupid name."

"*You're* a stupid name!" Johnny yelled at Cameron.

Johnny was Chris and Michelle's three-year-old son—the one who had informed everybody that Jeremy smelled like butt crack.

"Am not!" Cameron hollered back. "Mama, Cam said I'm a stupid name. Make him take it back!"

"Are too, poop face!"

I sat there with Jeremy, both of us trying to suppress our laughter, as the kids went back and forth, and the adults tried to holler over them with threats of time-outs, no TV, and no Christmas. Michael even went as far as pulling out his cell phone and threatening to call Santa. All that did was send the kids into a fit of hysterical tears while Sandra threatened to murder him for making the situation worse.

Dinner was eventful to say the least.

As the evening passed and we moved the party into the living room, I soaked in as much of the family dynamic as I could. I hadn't grown up in a home with so much love, and I wanted to experience as much as possible.

I sat in a rocker, snuggled up with baby Caitlyn, while chatting with Burt and the women as Jeremy and his brothers wrestled on the floor with the boys, trying to expel as much of their energy as possible.

Staring down at that beautiful little girl, I felt an ache inside my chest that I'd worked years to ignore. Guilt pushed its way to the surface as I tilted my head down to inhale that wonderful baby powder scent that all babies seemed to have. She began to stir in my arms, so I ran my fingers over her downy hair to try and comfort her.

My eyes lifted to catch Jeremy staring at me with a huge smile on his face, and I couldn't help but question if I deserved the happiness I'd been feeling since we had gotten back together.

Shoving those painful feelings deep down, I summoned up a half-hearted smile, hoping he couldn't notice the sorrow I was feeling shining in my eyes.

When Jeremy finally called it a night, Caitlyn had fallen asleep in my arms. I was so exhausted from the emotional turn I'd experienced that I was ready to leave. We said good-bye to everyone, and I spent the whole ride to my house trying to pull myself out of the self-induced funk I was in.

If I knew anything, it was that there was one sure-fire way to get my mind off of all the bad things swirling around. He might not have known it right then, but Jeremy was definitely about to get lucky.

CHAPTER
sixteen

Jeremy

"Oh God, Jeremy, I'm close."

Thank Christ! "That's it, baby," I replied, trying to coax her orgasm out of her.

If she didn't come soon, I was liable to explode. The girl was riding me like it was an Olympic event, and she was going for gold. And considering I was seconds away from blowing harder than I'd ever had before, she deserved it!

I sat up, wrapped my lips around a gorgeous pink nipple, and began to suck, knowing how sensitive it was. I could feel her clenching tighter around me. I knew she was close, so I reached up and wrapped her hair around my hand and pulled just hard enough to make her scream.

"Oh FUCK! Baby!"

The sexy noises coming from her pushed me over right after her, causing me to moan her name like a friggin' prayer until there was nothing left. My girl fucked like a dream, that was for sure. She milked every last drop until I collapsed back onto her bed and pulled her down with me.

"Holy shit," she whispered into my neck once she caught her breath. "It gets better every damn time. I think you just about killed me."

If she hadn't just wrung me dry, I probably would have jumped out of bed and run naked through the streets, letting everyone know I'd fucked Savannah Morgan to near death. "The feeling's mutual, sugar. I feel like I should write you a thank-you card or something."

She bit my chest playfully and let out a quiet laugh. "In lieu of thank-you cards, I'll accept monetary donations."

I leaned up and nipped at her shoulder. "Ah…like a hooker."

She smacked me on the arm and sat up, still straddling my hips and giving me an amazing view of her perfect body. "High priced call girl—get it right."

I sat up and gave her a smacking kiss before falling back down. I still hadn't fully recuperated.

"I had a nice time tonight," she said as she ran her fingertips in random patterns over my chest. "I didn't realize how much I missed your parents."

I looked at my beautiful girl and smiled. "You think we could refrain from any talk of parents while I'm still inside you?"

She huffed out a sigh and rolled her eyes before sliding off of me and out of bed, leaving me with a killer view of her ass as she walked into the bathroom to clean up.

"I'm glad you had fun, Savvy," I said as she crawled back into bed with me minutes later. I pulled her to me and wrapped my arms around her, never wanting to let her go. "I know everyone was thrilled to see you."

She laid her head on my chest and hugged me back. "I know. I could feel it. I forgot how nice it was to be around a family who are so open and loving with each other."

She said it nonchalantly, but I knew how much it bothered her to have parents who were so disinterested in her life that she only saw them on holidays for the required family time. My heart broke for her. If there was anyone in the world who deserved all the love a family could give, it was Savannah. There wasn't a person on the planet who went out of her way more than Savannah. The woman would bend over backwards for the people she cared about. She spent her entire life putting everyone else before herself, and I admired the hell out of her for it.

We lay silent for several minutes, just enjoying being with each other, and I caught myself thinking about how much I loved watching her with Caitlyn. Growing up with my family, I'd known from an early age that I wanted to have children of my own. When I'd seen Savvy holding my perfect little niece, in that moment, there was no doubt in my mind that I wanted to make that family with her. She was my world, and I was never going to let her go.

"So, what did you think of Caitlyn?" I asked casually, not wanting to jump right in at the risk of causing an infamous Savannah Morgan Freak-Out.

I could feel her smile against my chest, and I couldn't help but grin in return.

"She's so beautiful. I could've just held her all night. I love the way all little babies smell. I seriously wanted to steal her from Michelle and Chris."

"How do you feel about having a baby?"

She lifted her head and looked at me. "Like right now?"

I knew the nervousness was setting in when she started biting her bottom lip. I needed to ease the tension.

"No, not right now. I might be a stud, but I don't think I could pull it off right this second. Gimme a few minutes."

She punched me in the gut and laughed when I let out an *oomph*. Once I got my breath back, I looked at her expectantly. She took a deep breath, and I held mine in anticipation.

"Yeah…" she finally answered although I could see something lingering in her eyes. I just wasn't able to tell what it was. I had told myself over and over that her hesitancy wasn't a big deal, that she'd eventually let her guard down, but I wasn't completely confident that it was true.

I didn't like the way she would start to shut down whenever we got on the topic of our future. I knew she loved me, but it seemed like she was always waiting for something bad to happen, for the other shoe to drop. I just couldn't figure out what she was waiting for.

"I'd like to have a baby one day." A playful grin slowly spread across her face. "Maybe after I'm done slumming it with you and settle down with the right guy, you know? Have the white picket fence, a golden retriever named Scout, and two point five kids."

There's my sarcastic girl.

I slid my hands to her waist and started tickling. There wasn't a woman in the world more ticklish than Savannah.

"Take that back," I demanded. I refused to stop even as she flopped all over the bed, laughing and trying to get away.

"All right, all right!" she squealed. "I take it back, I swear!"

I stopped tickling and quickly flipped her over to pin her beneath me. "Who are you having kids with?" I tried my hardest to sound casual, but a large part of me needed her to acknowledge what we were to each other. I couldn't give a shit if I was acting like a vagina. I needed her to say it.

She stared up at me, and I thought I saw something flicker across those beautiful eyes, only for it to disappear before I could tell what it was.

"Who are you having kids with, Savannah?" I asked again with a little more conviction. I knew I should try not to freak her out, but I needed an answer.

Finally, after a few heart-stopping seconds, she whispered, "You."

With just that one little word, I was able to breathe again. "That's right, sugar, no one else. It's just me and you from here on out." I leaned down and kissed her like my life depended on it—because in some ways, it did. After just a few short moments, I started getting hard, and I needed her again.

I trailed my lips down her neck and nipped at her collarbone as I moved my hand between her legs. She was already dripping wet, ready for me. I loved how her body instantly responded to my touch.

I gently brushed over her clit, intentionally trying to make her beg. I had to hear how desperate she was for me. I ran a finger through the wetness and slowly pushed it in before pulling it out at the same pace. Her hips jerked in an attempt to get my finger back, but I wasn't done playing.

"Tell me what you need, baby," I whispered before teasingly flicking my tongue over her nipple.

"Please…Jeremy," she moaned.

A light sheen of sweat covered her flawless skin, and I knew she was getting desperate.

"Please what, sugar? Tell me what you want."

She grabbed my wrist and held it tightly. "Quit playing around and fuck me already," she demanded.

There's my Savannah.

I loved it when she got fiery in bed. Never one to play the timid little thing, she knew what she wanted and accepted nothing less.

"Yes, ma'am," I replied with a smile as I drove myself balls-deep into that perfect, tight warmth of hers.

Christ, I wanted to stay there for the rest of my life, but when she started writhing and moaning underneath me, I couldn't help but move with her.

Savannah's hips lifted, meeting me thrust for thrust. "You feel so good."

"Tell me you love me," I demanded.

She opened her eyes and locked in on mine, so I could see how serious she was.

"I love you so much, Jeremy," she whispered.

And I could hear the conviction in her words.

"Only ever you, sugar."

Savannah

I tried to roll out of bed for the third time, but was yanked back into Jeremy's rock-hard chest…for the third time.

"Jer, I gotta go. You've already made me late."

"Mmm," he mumbled into my neck as he brushed my hair aside.

I loved it when he did that. It was like he was trying to commit my scent to memory.

"Blow 'em off, Savvy. I'm not ready to let you go yet."

I started laughing hysterically. "I'm so telling the girls you just said that."

That got him to let me go. He flopped onto his back and looked at me, wide-eyed. "You wouldn't dare."

I looked at the clock and gave him a cheeky grin. "Well, I don't know. I'm already ten minutes late, and I'm gonna have to deal with the wrath of Stacia. You'd have to come up with something pretty amazing to keep me from ratting you out."

He rolled back over me and started kissing down my neck. "Anything you want, baby. Just name it."

I planted a kiss on his lips and pushed him off of me. "I'll take you up on that...later. Now, I really have to go."

I laughed as Jeremy smacked my ass before I headed to the bathroom.

I rushed in to the diner twenty minutes late and fully prepared to have Stacia lay into me. For such a soft-spoken, sweet, sometimes ditzy woman, she took Bridezilla to a whole new level. I knew I could be a bitch, but she had even me scared to death.

"I'm so sorry I'm late," I tried explaining quickly. "It's just that Jeremy—"

"It's okay," Stacia interrupted, immediately making me question her cheerful demeanor when she should have been tearing my head off. "Jeremy already called and explained."

Ah, he's so damn sweet.

"He told us you couldn't keep your hands off of him this morning and that you were running late because you said you couldn't function without a quickie."

That son of a bitch!

"That son of a bitch!"

Stacia looked at me with a less than genuine smile. "It's okay, really. I'm just so happy you guys are back together that I can't even be mad you were late on such an important day."

And cue the guilt trip.

Emmy's head dropped down on the counter and Lizzy started cursing under her breath. It had been weeks of Stacia's bipolar attitude. One minute, she would be sweet as pie, and the next, I wanted to strangle her with the ribbon she'd picked for the bouquets. Enough was enough already.

I placed my hands on Stacia's shoulders and looked her directly in the eye. "Sweetie, you know I love you, but if you don't knock off this crazy, bitch-ass, bride-to-be routine, I'm gonna take those dyed-to-match heels you forced me to buy and shove them into something that God created strictly to be an out hole."

Emmy and Lizzy busted up laughing while Stacia crossed her arms and began to pout.

"I haven't been that bad," she whined.

"Uh…yeah, you have, honey. You told the cake lady that you'd burn her store to the ground if she put so much as one fondant flower on your cake."

"And Gavin told Luke you threatened to neuter him," Emmy piped up. "I believe he said, and I quote, 'If you order that white tux, I swear to Christ, I will cut your balls off and shove them down your throat.' Does that sound about right?"

Stacia jumped off her stool and stomped her foot. She actually stomped her damn foot. "It wasn't that it was *just* white. It had fucking tails, for Christ's sake! And one of those ugly ass ruffled shirts. He said it made him look like Prince! Who the hell wants to look like Prince? All three of you would have done the exact same thing!"

She had a valid point on that one. None of us could argue with her logic when it came to Gavin's tuxedo choice. It sounded almost as bad as the disastrous ring he'd originally picked out for her. That reminded me—he still owed us a *massive* thank you for that save.

We gave her a few more seconds to simmer down before I asked, "Feeling better now?"

She took a deep breath and exhaled slowly. Then smiled like she hadn't just gone postal in the middle of Virgie May's. "Yeah, I feel much better." She grabbed her purse off the bar and headed for the door.

The only thing the rest of us could do was follow in stunned silence.

CHAPTER
seventeen

"What's up, bitches?"

As soon as we walked through the door of the bridal shop, Mickey was standing there with a bottle of champagne in one hand and a glass filled to the top in the other. We all let out a collective squeal of excitement. She got more and more beautiful every time I saw her with all her glossy, dark long hair and bright hazel eyes. Dressed in low-rise jeans, black Chucks that had seen better days, and a Rolling Stones T-shirt that was cut off at the midriff, her gorgeous tattoos and curves were on display for the world to see. I always envied that she could make so much ink look good. The piercings in her nose and lip added even more flair.

Mickey was Stacia's cousin and her maid of honor. Emmy, Lizzy, and I had gotten to know Mickey when her parents had shipped her off to Cloverleaf to stay with Stacia's family during the summers when we were younger. She'd been living in Austin with her boyfriend for a couple of years, so we didn't get to see her as often as we wanted, but it was always a blast when she came to visit. She was one of the most outspoken and loud people we'd ever met, and we all adored her for it.

"Drinking already?" I asked.

She wrapped me in a hug and replied, "It's happy hour somewhere. Don't be jealous. There are glasses over there for all of you."

I headed straight for the table she was pointing at. "Oh, score!"

Lizzy and Emmy booked it over right behind me, each grabbed a glass and promptly filled up. Since the three of us had already been subjected to the torture that was bridesmaid dress shopping, we got to relax. We were mainly there to be supportive of Stacia as she tried to pick out her wedding dress, and since Mickey hadn't been able to come into town when we all got fitted, it was the perfect chance.

A few minutes later, Mickey came out wearing the dress we'd all finally agreed on after the fuchsia nightmare. The dress was a pale yellow chiffon that worked perfectly with Stacia's springtime wedding. It fell about knee length and the halter neckline was my absolute favorite aspect of the dress. It cut down to about mid-cleavage, but considering none of us could be classified as stacked, it looked totally awesome as opposed to trashy. Don't ask me how a dress that low cut worked for a wedding. It just did.

"Okay," Mickey stated in a whisper as she looked back over her shoulder. "Before Stacia comes out, can I just say thank you from the bottom of my heart? She showed me a picture of the dress she originally wanted us to wear." She made a face that looked like she'd just finished sucking on a lemon. "I was two seconds away from disowning her, so I wouldn't have to be in the wedding and wear that dress."

"You're welcome," we all said at once.

A few seconds later, Stacia came walking out of the dressing room and stepped onto the platform in front of us. The smile plastered across her face was only slightly more beautiful than the amazing dress she was wearing. "So, what do you guys think? Is this the one?"

"Don't you dare try on another dress," was Emmy's response.

The rest of us couldn't even form a reply. We were too busy taking in how stunning she looked. The ivory dress was a mermaid cut that hugged her curves like it had been made for her. The elegant lace overlay had delicate pearls sewn in throughout the entire dress. It had a sweetheart neckline and tiny lace cap sleeves that pulled across the back to form a gorgeous diamond cutout across her shoulder blades. Stacia had opted out of any type of tiara or anything like that, and instead, she had gone with a beautiful mantilla veil edged with the same lace on her dress. I couldn't even form words for how much I loved it.

I did something I wasn't normally known for doing. I went totally girlie. "You look so pretty," I whisper-sobbed before covering my mouth with both of my hands.

"Holy shit. You made her cry!" Mickey exclaimed. "I thought Savannah Morgan crying was an urban legend. I think we found a winner, cuz."

I punched Mickey on the arm and looked over to see Emmy and Lizzy were both crying like little bitches as well.

"I'm getting married!" Stacia screamed before doing her goofy-ass happy dance.

Right there in the middle of a crowded bridal salon, the four of us jumped up onto the platform in front of a million mirrors and joined her.

After telling Stacia ten more times that it was, in fact, the perfect dress and she shouldn't even bother trying on anything else, we all made our way to our favorite Tex-Mex restaurant, Mama Maria's, for lunch and celebratory margaritas.

"So, Mickey, how long are you going to be in town?" I asked.

She took a sip of her margarita. "I'm not really sure. It's looking indefinite."

That got all of our attention.

"What happened with you and Dale?" Lizzy asked.

Dale and Mickey had been together on and off for the past four years. None of us really liked him. He was a loser who enjoyed smoking pot, playing Xbox, and mooching off of Mickey. Working wasn't something that was high on his list of priorities, and there was no doubt that she could do so much better. But he was who she'd chosen, so as long as she was happy, we were happy for her.

Stacia answered for Mickey, "She finally wised up and saw him for the leech he is. She's gonna be staying with me and Gavin until she finds her own place."

"What about work?" Emmy asked. "If you're looking, I need a waitress down at the diner."

The look Mickey gave Emmy was of sheer disgust. "I love ya, babe, but I'd rather rip my fingernails out with tweezers than serve people food."

I couldn't help but laugh, mainly because I totally agreed. I always helped Emmy out when she needed it, but I absolutely despised waiting tables.

"You know, our friend Trevor just opened up a shop in town. I bet he'd hire you on with all your years of tattooing experience," Lizzy replied.

"Who's Trevor?" Mickey asked.

"He's Luke's friend from the Corps," Emmy replied. "He moved to Cloverleaf not too long ago."

I chimed in, "That's actually a pretty damn good idea. I know he's looking for good people, and you're freaking brilliant. He'd hire you in a heartbeat."

The waitress stopped off with our food, and we all dug in.

"That's actually perfect," Mickey responded between bites. "So, what's this Trevor guy like? Is he hot?"

My eyes instantly cut to Lizzy to see how she would react to Mickey's question. We were all convinced that something was going on between Lizzy and Trevor, but both had denied it incessantly, insisting they were strictly friends. But every time they were around each other, Trevor tracked every move Lizzy made, like he couldn't stand not having her in his sight. And she would cater to him like she'd been in a relationship with him for years. She'd do little things like grab him a beer when he needed one, and he wouldn't even have to ask. Because he was allergic to nuts, she always made sure to bring something he could eat whenever there was a party. The two of them would even finish each other's sentences. It would have been adorable—if they weren't so damn ignorant about what was going on.

I thought I might have seen a brief flutter of something flash across Lizzy's face, but before I could be sure, it was gone and she was her composed, normal self.

"Yeah," she responded. "He's actually really good-looking. You definitely need to meet him. You're totally his type."

What the hell?

I glanced around the table to see Emmy and Stacia both wearing the same confused as hell expression as I was.

Before any of us could cut in to point out what was obvious to everyone but Lizzy, Mickey spoke up, "Huh…well then, I'm looking forward to meeting him."

I just picked up my margarita and drank deeply. If Lizzy refused to see what was right in front of her face, that was her prerogative. Who was I to try to dictate other people's love lives? I barely had my own under control. All I could do was sit back and be her friend. Sometimes you had to let people fall on their own and be there to help them up when the time came.

All I could do was hope that Lizzy didn't fall as far or as hard as I had.

CHAPTER
eighteen

Days had gone by, and true to his word, Jeremy had been in my bed every night since getting back together. I knew it was only fair that I stay over at his place sometimes, but I wasn't quite comfortable with that yet. His breakup with Charlotte was still a little too fresh. I didn't want to rub our relationship in her face, so I thought it would be best not to run the risk of her seeing my car in his driveway. At least my house was a few minutes outside of town. The risk of her driving by and seeing Jeremy's truck there was pretty slim.

Saturday night Jeremy drove us to Colt's to watch the guys' band play, and I was stoked to be wearing my *I'm Banging a Rock Star...Don't Be Jealous* T-shirt.

I was sitting at the bar with the girls, Luke, and Trevor when Ben walked in and joined us. He hadn't even gotten a chance to order a drink before Jeremy honed in like he had some sort of freaky sixth sense.

I was just standing to give Ben a friendly hug when an arm wrapped around my waist and pulled me back. Jeremy had me glued to his side, and when I glanced up at his face, he was giving Ben a look that could have peeled the skin off his face.

I'd officially had enough. I wasn't a possession, and there was no way I was going to sit by while my boyfriend and my friend needled each other for no good reason.

Pulling out of Jeremy's hold, I stepped between the two men. "Outside. Now," I demanded to the both of them.

I didn't give either of them a chance to speak before stomping off. If they knew what was good for them, they'd make sure to follow.

Luckily, they could both be smart at times. When I spun around, they were standing there, neither one looking too happy to be next to the other.

"We're going to start over," I began, talking to them like they were children. "Jeremy, this is my *friend* from work, Ben. Ben, this is my *boyfriend*, Jeremy." I crossed my arms over my chest, cocked a hip and narrowed my eyes at them. "Now, was there anything lost on either of you just then?"

"No," they both mumbled, each one looking down at his shoes.

"Do I need to be more specific on where each of you stands?"

Jeremy said, "No," again and Ben just shook his head.

"Good. I'm tired of you two acting like jackasses." I turned to Jeremy. "Whether you want to believe it or not, Ben *really* is just a friend, so can you please try to be nice?"

Before Jeremy could answer, Ben cut in, "It's true, man. There really isn't anything going on with Savannah and me. You've got my word."

I could see Jeremy's shoulders relax marginally at Ben's statement and I was sure Ben saw it too.

"Sorry about that," Jeremy replied as he held out his hand for Ben to shake. "I've just waited a long time to get her back, so I get a little jealous, I guess."

"Understandable."

"Yay! Now, you two keep playing nice, or I swear to God, I'll make you both miserable, and you know I can do it."

I turned and started back in when I heard Ben tell Jeremy, "Your girlfriend's kinda scary, man."

"You've got no idea," Jeremy replied.

When I got back to the bar and grabbed my beer, Trevor and Luke were both smiling at me.

"What?" I asked.

"They still alive out there?" Luke asked with a chuckle.

"For the time being."

Ben and Jeremy finally made their way back in, and from the looks of it, everything was good between them. Jeremy had to go up on stage to finish setting up, and the rest of us were hanging out when we heard a loud voice cut through the buzz in the bar.

"What's up, losers? I'm here, so the party can finally start."

"Hey, babe. Stacia said you found a place. How's moving going?" I asked as I wrapped Mickey in a tight hug.

"It's good. I'm just getting myself settled and trying to get everything in order. I figured I'd give myself a little break for a while. You know, so I can see what kind of trouble I can get you ladies into."

I finally released her from my death grip and turned to introduce her to Trevor and Ben since she already knew everyone else.

"Guys, this is Stacia's cousin, Mickey. Mickey, this is Trevor. He's Luke's friend we were telling you about. He just opened Ink Addictz." I turned to Trevor. "Mickey's an amazing tattoo artist. She's looking for work."

He gave a slight nod. "Oh yeah?"

Mickey gave him a little grin. "Yeah, I'm pretty decent."

"Well, stop on in and we'll see what we can work out."

"Sounds like a plan."

I figured Trevor would be all over her since she seemed right up his alley. And the lustful look in Mickey's eyes wasn't lost on me, but he just politely shook her hand, never once leaving Lizzy's side. Why the two of them wouldn't just hook up was beyond me. The sexual tension was almost thick enough to cut with a damn knife.

Ben, on the other hand, was staring at Mickey like she was a drink of water and he'd been stuck in the desert for a year.

Oooh…interesting.

"Mickey, this is my friend Ben. He works as an attorney at P&C with me."

Mickey must have noticed his expression as well because I saw a sexy smile spread across her lips. Trevor was obviously completely forgotten in just a matter of seconds. Ben wasn't going to know what hit him by the time the night was over.

"You gonna sing with the guys tonight?" Emmy asked.

I hated Mickey for her God given musical talent. She had such a low, smoky voice that when she sang, people would be instantly captivated.

131

"I don't know. I might," she said with a shrug.

Ben, in the meantime, looked like he was about to swallow his tongue. For a guy who was always so composed and professional in the courtroom, it was hysterical to see him so flustered around a woman.

"You might want to pick your jaw up off the floor, Ben. It's kind of dirty in here," I whispered when Mickey stepped up to the bar to order a drink.

He didn't even bother to take his eyes off her. "Yeah, sure thing," he replied.

He obviously hadn't heard a word I said. I let out a laugh and turned to Emmy and Luke, leaving Ben to his drooling.

A few minutes later, we all stood to head to the stage when I heard Stacia suck in a gasp.

"Heads up. Three o'clock, Savvy."

I turned to my right to see what she was talking about.

"No, the other way," she said in a loud whisper.

God love her. "The other way is nine o'clock, Stacia."

"Whatever," she hissed. "Just turn to your left."

We all made an obvious show of looking over to see what she was talking about just as Charlotte and her group of Barbie dolls came walking through the door.

"Ah shit," I said on a sigh.

Things had been going so well that I hadn't even realized that Mickey hadn't been around to know the latest goings-on in our circle.

"What? What's happening?"

Emmy leaned towards us to fill Mickey in. "That's Jeremy's ex."

"Which one?" Mickey asked, eyeing the group in disgust.

Where Mickey looked like a rocker, Charlotte and her friends were the complete opposite, wearing pastel sundresses, pearls, and too much makeup. They stuck out like sore thumbs.

"The brunette who looks like she belongs at a country club instead of a bar," Emmy replied.

"Okay…no accounting for taste or anything, but what's the problem? And what does it have to do with Savannah?"

"Savvy and Jeremy got back together," Stacia squealed a little too loudly.

I cringed and shot up a prayer that her voice hadn't carried all the way across the bar.

"No shit?" Mickey yelled. "Why the hell am I just now finding this out?"

It was obvious those two were family. If Charlotte's posse hadn't heard Stacia, they'd definitely heard Mickey.

Charlotte's eyes cut in my direction before she leaned in to her friends and whispered something. All of them turned their attention my way, each scrunching up their fake noses like they smelled something gross. I was sure they would have had wrinkled brows too, but the Botox was obviously preventing that.

I turned my eyes back to Mickey, trying to ignore the looks coming from the other side of the bar. I would typically let something like that roll right off me, but for some reason, knowing that Charlotte and her minions were staring me down was really getting to me. But I'd be damned if I let Charlotte see that.

Jeremy must have seen her walk in and sensed my discomfort because he was behind me before I could even turn around. "You okay, honey?"

The concern on his face was moving, and when he ran his fingers down my cheek and tucked a loose strand of hair behind my ear, I couldn't stop from leaning in to his touch.

"Yeah, I'm fine. It's just a little awkward, you know."

"I know." He leaned in and gave me a slow, thorough kiss.

I probably would have stayed there all night if the sound of breaking glass hadn't pulled me out of my lust filled daze.

We all turned to see her friends leading a tear-soaked Charlotte out the door. I didn't like the woman, but that didn't mean I wasn't sympathetic.

I turned back to Jeremy with a frown. "You shouldn't have done that in front of her."

He ran his fingers through my hair and crouched down to my level to look directly in my eyes. "I can't worry about her, Savannah. The only person I care about is you, and it was obvious you weren't happy. It's my job to make sure you're always happy."

He is so getting lucky as soon as we get home! I stood up on my toes to kiss him and whispered, "I am happy, Jeremy. I love you."

"Only ever you," he whispered to me before heading back toward the stage.

We all made our way to the front of the crowd as the band started up. I always enjoyed watching them play, but now that I was actually with Jeremy, his sex appeal on stage skyrocketed. The only thoughts I had running through my head as we danced and sang along were all the naughty things I was going to do with him when we got home.

After several songs, the guys called Mickey up to the stage with them. Anytime she came to a show when she was in town, they made sure she sang a couple of songs with them. She always sounded beautiful and the crowd ate it up.

The music started, and after a few seconds, Mickey's hypnotic voice began drifting through the microphone. I was so busy listening to her voice that I almost missed the song she was singing—*almost.*

As she poured her heart into Coheed and Cambria's "Dark Side of Me," I couldn't help but relate to the lyrics. When she got to the chorus and started singing about giving her everything for all the wrong things, my mind wandered back to the decisions I'd made all those years ago, and the tears began welling up in my eyes.

As the song played on, the guilt started weighing heavily on me, and it took everything I had not to let the tears fall. I knew Jeremy would notice if I started to cry, and I couldn't risk him asking questions.

Lizzy saw my face and came over to wrap an arm around my waist. "You okay?" she asked discreetly, her voice full of concern.

I sniffed and pasted on a fake smile. "Yeah…yeah, I'm good. Mickey just sounds so beautiful that I got a little emotional."

It was obvious she saw right through me. "You have to tell him, Savvy," she whispered in my ear so that no one else could hear her over the music.

I looked into her eyes and nodded. "I know," I whispered, fighting back a sob. I refused to make a scene in the middle of a crowded dance floor.

Seeing that I was desperately trying to pull myself together, Lizzy turned us back toward the stage and we swayed along with the music as it continued.

For the rest of the night, I did my best to act as if nothing was wrong, but in the back of my mind, I couldn't stop worrying that I was at risk of losing the one thing that made me the happiest.

CHAPTER
nineteen

Jeremy

The sad look that clouded Savannah's face earlier when Mickey was up on stage singing with us hadn't been lost on me. I asked her about it after the show and she brushed it off, saying she'd just loved the song and Mickey's voice, so she had gotten a little emotional. I wanted to push the topic more, but when Savannah didn't want to talk about something she would completely shut down if it was forced.

Things had been going so good between us that I wasn't willing to risk her closing any part of herself off from me—at least not this early on.

We went back to her place after leaving Colt's and she practically jumped me the minute we got through the door. I had no clue that she'd be so turned on from watching me play the guitar, but now that I knew, I was going to carry that damn thing around with me everywhere.

Hours later, after I'd successfully worn her out, I was lying in her bed with her naked body partially draped across my chest as I ran my fingers up and down her back.

"Mmm, that feels so good," she mumbled in a sleepy voice.

Something had been on my mind ever since we'd gotten back together, but I was never sure of a good time to bring it up. With her worn out from great sex and half asleep in my arms, I figured she'd be much more agreeable than usual, so I went ahead and blurted it out. "I think we should move in together."

My hand stopped moving when I felt her whole body tense up.

After a couple of seconds, she lifted her head and looked at me with shock written all over her face. "Are you serious? Jeremy, we've been together for, like, a minute. Don't you think it's a little soon to discuss moving in together?"

I knew that would be her argument so I'd made sure to prepare a kick-ass rebuttal. "Savannah, it's not like we just met and started going out. We were together for five years, and we were friends long before that. We've been a huge part of each other's lives since we were kids."

She sat up, and to my disappointment, wrapped the sheet around her, covering that delectable body of hers. "Jer, we were just kids when we dated. Things have changed. We aren't the same people we were back then."

I pushed myself up and rested my back against the headboard. "We're not that different, sugar. You still chew on your bottom lip when you're uncomfortable." I pointed to her mouth where her lip was currently pulled between her teeth to make my point. "You still have a tendency to be volatile when things don't go your way, and you're still a god awful singer."

She reached over to slap my arm and I used the opportunity to pull her onto my lap so that she was straddling my thighs.

"You and I both know that this is it for us. What's the point in wasting any more time than we already have?"

I could see it in her eyes. She was starting to come around to the idea of us living together so I went in for the kill.

"And besides, you're gonna be twenty-seven in, like, a month. Don't you want to get the ball rolling before you get too old?"

She pinched my nipples as hard as she could and I let out a yell as I tried to grab her wrists.

"I'm not old, you asshole!" she said with a laugh. "You're the one who's finding gray hairs."

"Baby, you're practically ancient," I responded as we started wrestling around on the bed. "You wait any longer and you're gonna dry up."

"None of this is making me want to move in with you."

I rolled her underneath me and settled between her thighs. I knew I had her where I wanted her when she looked at me with those hooded whiskey-colored eyes. Her lustful expression told me everything I needed to know.

"No more wasting time, sugar. I've waited seven years to begin my life with you. I don't want to keep waiting."

She started to chew her bottom lip and I wanted to ask her what she was worried about, but I couldn't risk her shutting down during such an important conversation.

"Can I think about it?" she asked.

I knew it was a lot for her to take in over such a short amount of time, so I was willing to give her a chance to think it through. I knew what I wanted, and I knew I wasn't going anywhere.

"Yeah, baby. You can think about it."

The smile she gave me lit up her entire face and I was lost in her.

"I love you so much, Savannah."

"Only ever you," she replied.

Savannah

Jeremy had to work the next morning, so when he left, after giving me a brain-scrambling kiss and reminding me to think about moving in with him, I immediately grabbed my phone and texted Lizzy.

911. My house in 30.

"What's up, chica?" Lizzy asked as she breezed through my front door exactly thirty minutes later. "I had a feeling this conversation would require booze, but since it's only nine thirty in the morning and neither of us is Irish, I brought Virgie May's coffee and doughnuts."

"But you are Irish," I replied, grabbing the coffee and taking a big gulp.

There was no denying Lizzy's heritage. The red hair, green eyes, and fair skin gave her away.

"Only half," Lizzy chimed. "Besides, I'm also Catholic, and this being Sunday and all, I have to wait until after noon to start floating my liver."

"Ah, fair enough."

Lizzy sat on the chaise lounge in front of the bay window in my living room and tucked her feet underneath her as I took a seat on the couch.

"So what's going on?" she asked.

"Jeremy wants to move in together," I spit out quickly. I figured I might as well dive right in. There was no use in dragging it out.

"Huh," was all she said.

For a while, I sat there, nervously waiting for her to say something else. When I couldn't wait any longer, I jumped in. "Huh? That's all you've got?"

"Look, you know I'm thrilled that you and Jeremy got back together. I'd love nothing more than for the two of you to move in together and get married and all that stuff, but you've got to tell him, Savannah. He deserves to know."

I reached up to rub my temples. I was already starting to get a killer migraine. "You're right, you're right. I know that. I just...he's going to hate me, Lizzy." I felt the tears coming and I couldn't do anything to hold them off.

Lizzy got up and came over to me, wrapping her arms around me and running a comforting hand in circles on my back. "I'm not going to lie to you. He's going to be mad, but he won't hate you, honey. He loves you too much. You just have to trust that."

I sniffed and lifted my head off her shoulder. "Oh yeah, I can just see that conversation going well," I replied sarcastically. " 'Hey, Jeremy. I know you're from a large, tight-knit family, and you've always wanted kids of your own, but I got pregnant when we were nineteen and decided not to keep it without ever giving you a say in the matter. Oh, then I dumped you and broke your heart because I couldn't deal with it and felt guilty every time I looked at you.' Lizzy, I took something away from him that he's always wanted, and I never even told him."

"Stop it, Savannah," Lizzy demanded. "You were both kids. Neither of you were prepared for something like that. We'd all been there when Emmy lost her baby, and you thought you were doing the right thing. It was the wrong choice, but you didn't make it easily or out of spite. It came from a good place."

"Good place or not, Lizzy, I was wrong."

She grabbed my face in her hands and forced me to look at her. "I know that, but I also know you've been carrying that guilt with you for seven years. You're still not over it, are you?"

Tears streamed down my cheeks as I shook my head in response.

"It's time, Savvy. You and Jeremy won't have a real shot at making it if you keep carrying this all by yourself."

I let out a deep breath and tried to convince myself that everything was going to be okay even though I knew deep in my gut that it probably wouldn't be.

CHAPTER
twenty

A week and a half had passed since my conversation with Lizzy, and I still wasn't any closer to coming clean about the abortion to Jeremy. I knew it was selfish of me, but I couldn't stand the idea of losing him all over again.

Every time we were alone, I found myself opening my mouth to tell him the truth, but then I'd freak out and make up some lame ass story to cover up what I was about to say. I knew he was starting to notice, and I was terrified by the knowledge that I could potentially break his heart—again.

"So, have you given any more thought to moving in together?" Jeremy asked that night as we were lounging on the couch, watching *Sons of Anarchy*.

Jeremy didn't particularly care for the show, but he had no problem letting me indulge in my Charlie Hunnam obsession one night a week.

Thank God for understanding boyfriends.

We'd already had the conversation about how I was totally allowed to bang the British hottie if our paths ever crossed. All Jeremy had said was that if I got Charlie, he got Jennifer Love Hewitt, no questions asked.

I froze up at his question, not even able to fully appreciate a shirtless Jax Teller walking across the TV screen. Jeremy, sensing my instant anxiety, let out a deep sigh and sat up, lifting me from my place on his chest and depositing me next to him.

He reached for the remote and turned off the television. "You think you can clue me in on how long it's gonna take for you to stop freaking the fuck out every time I bring up our future? Because I gotta tell you, Savvy, this shit is getting more than just a little old."

Anxiety bubbled up in my throat as he spoke. The feeling of dread was sinking deep down in the pit of my stomach. I had officially run out of time. Tears began to sting my eyes and my vision blurred as I looked into his eyes. I was minutes away from losing the love of my life and there was nothing I could do to stop it. I'd made my bed and I was going to have to lay in it. I had absolutely no one to blame but myself.

"Hey, hey," Jeremy said, concern laced through his words. He grabbed me by my shoulders and pulled me into his chest. "It's okay, baby. We don't have to talk about this right now. We can wait until you're ready."

I pressed my face into his chest and inhaled his scent, knowing it would probably be the last time. I wanted to commit everything about him to memory before it was all gone.

"I have to tell you something," I whispered, my voice cracking as I spoke.

"Savvy, baby, honestly, it's okay. I'm sorry I pushed you. We don't have to—"

I put my finger to his lips to silence the rest of his words. "I have to say this, Jer, because I haven't been fair to you. I've been selfish as hell because I knew the minute I told you the truth, I'd lose you."

Jeremy reached up and grabbed my face with both of his hands. "There's nothing you could ever do that would make me walk away." He spoke with so much certainty that I almost believed him.

Reaching up and wrapping my hands around his wrists, I pulled them away from my face. "I made a mistake, baby, and I *wish* I could go back and undo it, but I can't." I tried to swallow the sob that was building up in my throat, but it was pointless. I was dying inside and there was nothing I could do to stop it.

"You're starting to freak me out here, babe."

I looked up to see worry in Jeremy's expression.

"Did you...did you cheat on me?" he asked in a quiet voice as if he was almost too scared to say the words out loud.

"What? God, no! Jeremy, honey, I never cheated, I swear to God."

His shoulders visibly slumped and he exhaled the breath he'd obviously been holding. "Oh, thank Christ," he said with a relieved laugh. "I don't know what I would've done—"

"I had an abortion," I spit out, eyes squeezed shut. My heart was pounding so hard that I was sure it was about to leap from my chest. I couldn't bring myself to look at him. I was a fucking coward, and I hated myself for it.

Silence descended on the living room while I held my breath and waited for his reaction. After what felt like an eternity, I couldn't take the quiet any longer. I finally peeked through damp lashes to look over at Jeremy. He was sitting there, completely still, just staring at me with disbelief on his face.

"Please say something," I begged in a pathetic voice.

Jeremy shook his head, like he was trying to clear it out. "You had an abortion? When?"

"When I was nineteen."

"When you were nine—"

I could see the realization dawning on his features as my admission fully sank in. Before I could register his movements, Jeremy was off the couch and pacing the living room, grabbing his hair and pulling roughly.

"Jesus *fucking* Christ, Savannah!"

He continued pacing as the tears streamed down my face.

"I'm so sorry, Jeremy," I pleaded. "I didn't know what to do." I jumped off the couch and placed myself in front of him, desperate for him to understand. "I made a mistake. If I could take it back—"

He cut me off with a wave of his hand as he took a step away from me. "Before or after, Savannah?"

"I don't understand," I said in confusion, wringing my hands in front of me.

Jeremy took a step toward me. He was so close that I had to strain my neck to look into his anger-filled eyes.

"Did you get rid of my child before or after you fucking ended it?" he asked through clenched teeth.

I cringed at his harsh tone. I knew I deserved so much worse than just his anger, but I also hated having it directed at me. "Before," I cried.

"FUCK!"

I grabbed hold of his arms and tried desperately to get him to look me in the eyes. I *had* to get him to see how sorry I was, to understand why I'd felt like I had no other choice. "*Please*, Jeremy! God, I'm so sorry. I didn't know what else to do!"

"You didn't know what else to do? How about not getting rid of *my* baby without fucking talking to me first? How could you, Savannah?"

"Jeremy, please try to understand," I begged. "We were just kids. I didn't have the first clue how to be a mother. All I could think was that I was going to fuck my child up the way my mom had with me."

He stayed unbearably quiet so I pushed forward, trying to explain every factor that had played in my decision to end the pregnancy.

"Emmy had just lost her baby. Everything was turning upside down!"

"Don't!" he yelled. "Don't use what happened to Emmy as an excuse. You did that seven years ago, and you're doing it now. It's BULLSHIT!"

"I swear, baby, I didn't think there was any other way!"

Jeremy brushed off my hands in disgust and stepped away from me again. "You knew. Goddamn it, Savannah! You knew how much I wanted a family with you. You didn't even give me a fuckin' choice. We could've talked about it and tried to make it work."

I placed my hands on top of my head and tried to breathe past the fear clogging my throat. "I made a mistake—"

"A mistake? A MISTAKE! Are you fucking shittin' me right now? You got rid of my kid, then you crushed my goddamn heart! And you call that a mistake?"

I tried reaching for him again. "Jeremy, honey, I love you. I'm so sorry."

"Don't...touch me. And stop saying that! Sorry doesn't matter for shit. I loved you, Savannah. You're the only damn woman I've ever loved."

"You're the only man I've ever loved, Jer. You *have* to believe me!"

"You want me to believe you? Are you kidding? You never gave a shit about me, Savannah. It's clear I registered a *very* distant third to Emmy and your own selfishness."

"No! That's not true!"

I ran after him as he charged toward my front door. I couldn't let him leave without making him understand. I had to make him understand.

"Don't go. *Please!*"

Jeremy spun around with his hands up, palms facing out. "Just stop. I can't even look at you right now."

With that, he turned on his heels and walked right out the door. He never once looked back before peeling out of the driveway and away from me.

Jeremy

I felt like I'd been punched in the gut so damn hard that all the air was knocked out of me. My mind was spinning, trying to process what Savannah had just told me. I felt like I was living in some sort of twilight zone. There was no way the girl I loved could have done something like this to me, something so selfish and deceitful.

I couldn't wrap my brain around it. Earlier, when I'd been standing in her living room, I didn't even recognize the person in front of me. All I knew was that I had to get out of there. If

I stayed, I knew myself well enough to know that I'd say something I could never take back.

Going home wasn't an option. There was no doubt that sitting in my dark apartment with the walls closing in on me was just going to make matters worse.

Before I even registered what direction I was driving in, I saw the bright lights of Colt 45's lighting up the parking lot. I found myself swerving in and pulling my truck into an empty spot. Drowning my sorrows had never sounded more appealing. My feet dragged me through the motions of walking across the gravel parking lot and past the doors into the dimly lit smoky bar until I reached a vacant bar stool.

"Shot of Jack," I told the bartender. "And might as well leave the bottle."

The guy didn't even blink twice before sitting a shot glass and a bottle of Jack that was three-quarters of the way full in front of me.

I was five shots in, and the knot in my stomach was finally starting to unravel slightly when I felt a hand slap my shoulder.

A voice called out from behind me, "Hey, brother. How's it goin'?"

I looked over my shoulder to see Trevor standing there with a casual grin on his face. The smile slowly slipped off when he caught my expression. "Jesus, Jeremy. You look like shit, man."

I turned back to my shot glass and downed number six. "Thanks. And here I was, feeling fine and fuckin' dandy," I deadpanned.

Trevor planted himself on the empty stool next to me, and then with his empty beer bottle, he signaled for another to the bartender. "You want to tell me what's going on?" he asked after taking a pull from his full Budweiser.

I set up another shot and twirled the amber liquid around in the glass before downing it. "Not really, man. No offense, but I'm really not in the mood for company right now."

"How many shots have you had so far?" he asked.

My brain was thankfully beginning to get fuzzy, so I was having a little trouble remembering how many I'd had. "Don't know. Six or seven, I guess."

"Shit," he muttered. "You typically only drink like that if you're celebrating or trying to forget something. And seein' as you're here alone, I'm thinking it's the latter."

I let out a deep exhale and turned to look at the two Trevors sitting next to me. *Shit. When the fuck did he get a twin?* "You aren't going away until I talk, are you?"

The Trevor twins gave me a shit-eating grin. "Nah, probably not."

I ran my palms over my face and tried to clear my vision. "Fine. Fuck it. I found out some stuff tonight that I'm having trouble processing. I figured getting shit faced was the best option."

"This stuff have anything to do with you and Savvy?"

"Yeah," I grumbled into my shot glass before emptying it again.

What the hell happened to all my Jack? Somehow, the bottle was only a quarter full. *When did that happen?*

Trevor took another drink before clearing his throat. "Look, I'm not gonna sit here and make you pour your guts out or anything. But can you at least tell me that you set up a ride home before you got here and buried yourself in the bottom of a bottle?"

I let out a humorless laugh and turned to see concern in his features. "I didn't really get that far, man. I just bailed out of there and found myself here."

"I think you should let me take you home now before you do something you'll regret."

"Want to know the funny thing, Trevor?" I asked, not really caring if he wanted to hear it or not. "For the past seven years, I've been living with regret, thinkin' that if I'd just done something different, I wouldn't have lost her. Turns out I'm not the one who should have been regretting anything. It's all on her."

Trevor blew out a breath and ran a hand through his hair. "I'm not even sure what you're saying right now, but I'm guessin' that whatever went down between you and Savvy was some pretty heavy shit."

"You've got no clue," I replied before finishing off the last of the Jack.

After hopping off the bar stool, Trevor dropped some bills on the counter and waved to the bartender to take my shot glass. "Well, brother, whatever it was that happened isn't worth the hangover you're definitely gonna have in the morning. I think it's time I get you home."

A large part of me wanted to tell him to go fuck himself, but seeing as I was three sheets to the wind and the bottle of Jack had miraculously disappeared, I decided it was for the best, so I let Trevor lead my wobbling frame out the door and into his car.

The rest of the night was a blank.

CHAPTER
twenty-one

Savannah

My eyes felt gritty and my lids were puffy and heavy. Crying all night and lack of sleep were making me feel delirious. I'd been in tears from the moment Jeremy walked out my front door the night before, and I hadn't been able to stop. I'd worn a path on the carpet in my living room from pacing. My cell phone was still clutched in my hand. I'd gone back and forth between texting and calling him every few minutes. He'd never once picked up or responded, not that I'd really expected him to, but I couldn't bring myself to stop trying.

"You've reached Jeremy. You know what to do."

I released a defeated sigh and left *another* message. "Jer, please call me back. I know you're beyond mad at me right now, but I know we can get through this. I just need you to talk to me," I pleaded before finally disconnecting.

Anxiety was clawing at me from deep inside, and I felt as if the only thing holding me together was my skin. I was frantic, panicked, sad, and fearful. Basically, every horrible emotion people try never to feel was bundled up inside of me, trying to make its way to the surface. I was losing it. I needed to talk to Jeremy more than I needed to breathe.

I finally resigned myself to the fact that I'd tried to reach him by phone, and he'd chosen not to answer. Knowing I had no other choice, I grabbed my keys and purse off the small table next to my front door, and ran out to my car. I hadn't even bothered looking in the mirror before leaving. There was no doubt my hair was a matted, tangled mess, and any makeup

I'd had on from the prior day had already been cried off. I knew I looked like a mess, but I just didn't care. Since Jeremy refused to pick up his damn phone, I was giving him no other choice. I'd stand at his door and yell his house down if that was what it was going to take to get him to speak to me.

Jeremy

Oh God. I couldn't remember the last time I'd been so hungover.

I managed to peel my eyes open enough to notice that I'd somehow gotten myself to bed even though I wasn't sure how. Still in my clothes from the night before, I was splayed across the middle of the bed, lying on top of the comforter, with my booted feet hanging off the side.

The relentless pounding in my head refused to let up, and I was seconds away from losing the contents of whatever was in my stomach from the night before. Just as I rolled over to drag myself into the bathroom, I noticed that the pounding wasn't just coming from inside my skull.

"The fuck?" I muttered as I made my way to the front door.

Whoever was standing on the other side refused to let up, continuing to beat the shit out of my front door like their life depended on it. I didn't care if the damn apartment complex was burning to the ground around me. Whoever was standing at my door was about to pay for my bad mood.

"Knock it the fuck off!" I shouted as I jerked the door open to see a red faced, puffy-eyed Savannah standing before me. Just the sight of her brought back all the pain I'd tried to drink away the night before.

"Jeremy," she whispered in a broken voice.

Her teeth were biting into her bottom lip, and I noticed her white-knuckled grip on the handles of her purse in front of her.

"What are you doing here?" was all I could manage to say.

Reaching up, she brushed away a tear from her right cheek. "I needed to talk to you. You wouldn't answer any of my calls. I didn't know what else to do."

"Typically, when a person doesn't pick up the phone, that means they don't want to talk to the person calling. Obviously, you didn't get the hint."

I hated myself for being so callous, but the pain was still there, and it was too fresh in my mind to spare her feelings. I just couldn't control what came out of my mouth.

The sight of her shoulders shaking as she fought to hold back tears managed to break what little of my heart had been left intact after last night. I almost reached out to comfort her, but the memories from the night before caused my hand to pause in midair before it dropped back down to my side.

"Sorry," I grumbled, not being able to fully help myself when it came to consoling Savannah. I didn't know if it was possible to love and hate someone at the same time.

"Can we please just talk? Just for a minute, please."

Letting out a loud sigh, I ran a hand through my already sleep-rumpled hair and stepped out of the way so she could come inside.

I couldn't help but question how we'd gotten here. This girl, the love of my life, was standing in my living room, and her nervousness was practically palpable. And I could hardly bring myself to look at her.

I collapsed onto the couch and placed my head in my hands, waiting for her to talk, as she stood in front of me, fidgeting with her hands.

"What do you want to say?" I finally asked after she remained silent for too long.

She sucked in a deep breath and let it out slowly. "Jeremy," she finally began after several more seconds. "I know that what I did was horrible, and I've regretted my decision every day for the past seven years." Her voice cracked as she spoke. "But you have to know that I didn't do it to hurt you. I love you more than anything, baby, I swear. I thought I was doing the right thing."

I couldn't listen to her anymore. Every word she spoke was like a knife to the heart. "That's bullshit and you know it."

Her head jerked back in surprise at the venom in my words.

"You don't love me more than anything. You never have. I've always been second fucking place to your relationship with Emmy—"

She started shaking her head frantically as she interrupted, "That's not true!"

"Yes it is!" I shouted. "Who did you think you were doing the right thing for, Savannah? Huh? Was it me or Emmy?" I didn't give her a chance to respond before continuing to talk, "You knew having an abortion would mean the end of us, but you did it anyway. All you cared about was Emmy and how she would feel if she found out you were pregnant. Or how you didn't want to be like your own fucked up mother. You didn't give a shit about me or whether or not I wanted that baby. What I wanted didn't even register in your decision. If it had, you'd have realized that I would have been with you every step of the way. I could have helped you. I never would have let you turn into your mother."

Savannah hit her knees right in front of me just before grabbing at both of my hands. "I'm sorry, Jeremy. God, I'm so sorry," she sobbed. "Emmy was the only real family I had."

Those eight words hurt worse than anything. Snatching my hands from hers, I shot up from the couch and began pacing in an attempt to control my temper. It didn't work.

"*I* WAS YOUR FAMILY!" The words forced themselves out, almost of their own will. "Why couldn't you see that? I knew your relationship with your parents was all kinds of fucked up, and I busted my ass every damn day to try to be enough for you. But I never was, was I? No matter what I did or how much I loved you, you never looked at me like I was your family, did you?"

She couldn't even answer me past the tears streaming down her face.

"I wanted so badly for you to see me, Savannah, really see me. You were a part of my family from the very beginning. I tried my hardest to make sure that you felt like you belonged there, but you refused to let me in. You always kept me at arm's length."

She just kept repeating, "I'm sorry. I'm sorry," over and over as she rocked back and forth on the floor with her hands covering her face as tears leaked through.

"Why couldn't I be enough for you?" I whispered, finally letting my own tears break free.

"You were," she whispered back. "I just didn't realize it until it was too late."

With that sentence, I knew there was no fixing what had been broken between us. I wanted to be what Savannah needed, but she was always going to doubt me.

I couldn't live with that.

It took several minutes, but eventually we both managed to get our tears under control.

"We can't come back from this, can we?" she asked.

"No," was all I could manage to say past the crippling weight that was sitting on my chest.

I watched through tear-blurred vision as she stood from the floor and reached for her purse before walking toward me. I hated seeing her so broken. I wanted to fix her, to heal her pain, but I couldn't. Since I was being honest with myself, I had to finally admit that I'd never been able to. She had never let me close enough to be what she needed. I squeezed my eyes closed, trying to bury the pain.

Standing on her tiptoes, she placed a hand on one cheek as she pressed a kiss to the other. "I hate myself for hurting you, Jeremy," she said quietly. "I really do love you. I'm sorry I was too foolish to see what I had right in front of me all along. I'll regret that for the rest of my life."

I opened my eyes to the sound of the door closing and Savannah walking away from me again.

Savannah

I wanted to punch whoever started that saying, *Time heals all wounds*. I knew it was true. I knew that eventually, it wouldn't hurt so damn much, but that stupid ass saying did jack shit to ease a person's pain when living in the moment. I couldn't look beyond what I was feeling in the here and now. I couldn't imagine not wallowing in the grief of losing the one person who meant the most to me, the one person I'd always taken for granted without even realizing it.

Hindsight was twenty-twenty. Yeah, that was just another saying that I hated at that moment. I was such an idiot. I deserved every ounce of pain that was coursing through my body.

I'd done this—no one else, only me.

But the one thing that hurt me the most was knowing that I'd caused Jeremy pain. I didn't care about how much I was hurting, only that he was hurting too.

It had been three days since the end of Jeremy and me, and every day, the feeling that I'd lost the most crucial piece of myself grew worse and worse.

I hadn't dragged myself out of bed since leaving his apartment. I'd called in sick to work and ignored my cell phone every time it rang. With my friends, solitude wasn't usually something I got much of, so I was determined to bury myself in my own misery for as long as I could.

As if fate was listening to my thoughts at that very moment, someone began pounding on my front door. Fate was a stupid bitch, and I hated her.

I pulled the down comforter over my head and tried to ignore the knocking, hoping that whoever it was would get the hint and go away. Of course, I wasn't that lucky.

I heard the sounds of a key sliding into the lock and the turning of the deadbolt just seconds before Lizzy's voice echoed through my house.

"Savannah Morgan, where the hell are you?" she shouted.

I have got to quit giving people keys to my fucking house.

I ignored her and burrowed deeper into my bed, willing a hole to open up and suck me in.

"I know you're in here," she called out.

I knew by her voice that she was getting closer and closer to the bedroom. My suffering in silence was about to come to an end.

"Dear God," she said from the doorway to my bedroom. "How many pizzas have you eaten in the past few days?"

So I'd stuffed my face with mushrooms, black olives, and extra cheese from Joe's Pizza every day. So what?

"Jesus, Savvy, what's that smell?"

I pulled the comforter down just enough that my forehead and eyes were peeking out.

"Oh God, that smell is you!" Lizzy exclaimed as she made her way to the bed. "Your funk is burning my eyes from here."

"Eat shit and die," I mumbled as I pulled the covers back over my head.

She promptly grabbed hold of the bedding and ripped it off of me. "It smells like you've already done both of those. Get up. You're getting in the shower—*now*. And I'm burning these sheets while you're in there."

I rolled to my side, giving Lizzy my back. "Go away. I'm not ready to join the land of the living just yet."

I felt the mattress dip with her weight as she settled next to me.

"Savvy, honey, you need to get out of this bed. Everyone's freaking out. You won't answer your phone, and Jeremy's been walking around, looking like shit. People know something is

157

going on. Trevor had to drag Jer out of Colt's the other night. Said he was wasted beyond belief."

"I just can't talk to anyone right now," I whispered as fresh tears ran down.

"I know, honey, but you don't have a choice. Emmy has had it with waiting for you to call. She's heading over as soon as she gets off work."

Damn it. That was the last thing I wanted to deal with. Admitting to her that Jeremy and I had broken up was going to be hard enough. Confessing why was going to kill me.

"Go and get in the shower before she gets here. Please."

I looked at Lizzy and saw the concern in her eyes. Seeing that made the pain even worse.

"I ruined everything, Liz."

"Oh, Savvy."

She wrapped her arms around my neck and pulled me to her. I didn't know how long the two of us sat there, hugging each other, but by the time we pulled apart, both of our eyes were red-rimmed from crying.

"Can you just call her and tell her to stop by another day?" I pleaded. "Please, Lizzy. I just can't do this right now."

She gave me a sad smile. "Okay, I'll call her, but only if you swear to get out of this bed and take a shower. This isn't healthy, Savannah."

"I know." I nodded. "I'm going." I rolled off the bed and padded toward the bathroom.

"I'm gonna clean up a bit and throw your bedding in the washer. We'll talk when you get out, okay?"

I looked over my shoulder and gave a small chin lift in acknowledgment. I planned on dragging the shower out as long as I possibly could. I had no desire to talk.

CHAPTER
twenty-two

As time passed, I'd somehow managed to get myself to work every day, but I was a zombie the entire time I was there. Ben had tried to talk to me, to see if there was any way he could help, but I just couldn't bring myself to open up to him about everything that had happened. I'd told him as politely as I could manage that I'd be fine, but for the time being, I just wanted to come to work and do my job. I could only fake so much, and acting like everything was fine and dandy wasn't something I could pull off. So I would stay in my office and bury myself in my job, praying it would be enough to clear my head, if even just for a little while.

It didn't work.

Lizzy's call to Emmy had managed to buy me a few days of reprieve, but that was it. When I pulled into my driveway after work on Thursday, her car was sitting there, and my stomach plummeted. My time was up. I got out and made my way to the front door as slowly as possible, dread churning in my gut the entire time. Before I made it to the front porch, the door flew open and Emmy stood there with her arms crossed over her chest.

"Get the damn lead out, Morgan. We need to talk."

I had no clue what to say, how to even start the conversation that we needed to have, so I just shuffled into my house like I was walking to my own execution. Something told me she wasn't going to handle my confession any better than Jeremy had.

I headed straight into my kitchen and proceeded to uncork a bottle of red wine. I was going to need it. Emmy sat on a bar stool at the island, watching me intently the whole time. I lifted the bottle to her, silently asking if she wanted a glass for herself. She simply cocked an eyebrow at me and shook her head. I finished pouring myself a very large glass before finally looking up at her. The worried expression blanketing her face caused the tears to threaten to spill again.

"What's going on?" Emmy finally asked when it became obvious I wasn't going to start the conversation.

I cleared my throat uncomfortably and looked down into my wine glass. "Jeremy and I broke up," I said in a quiet voice.

"Yeah, I gathered that. He's been walking around looking like death warmed up and then run over, and you've basically disappeared. What the hell happened, Savvy?"

I tried to put it as delicately as possible. "I kept a secret from him for a really long time. I finally told him, and it was something he just couldn't forgive."

I glanced up quickly to see her brows wrinkle in confusion.

"What secret did you keep from him? I know everything about you, Savannah. There's no way possible you could have done something so bad that he'd break up with you."

I would have given anything for that to be the case.

"That's not true," I informed her.

"What's not true?"

I squeezed my eyes closed against the burn of tears. "That you know everything about me."

The sarcastic sound she made let me know she didn't believe that for a second.

"Yeah, okay, Savvy. What deep, dark secret do you have that I don't already know? We've been best friends practically our whole lives. We know everything about each other."

"Emmy," I said, trying to keep my voice from cracking too badly, "I had an abortion when I was nineteen. It was Jeremy's, and I didn't tell him before doing it. I kept it from him this whole time."

Her eyes grew wide as she absorbed what I'd just said. "You...what? No, you didn't. You didn't," she said, like she thought she could change the outcome if she kept insisting it wasn't true. "You wouldn't do something like that," she said matter-of-factly.

"I did," I choked out on a sob.

Emmy placed a hand over her mouth as her eyes welled up with tears, confirming my fear that she wouldn't handle it well. Emmy was the least judgmental person I knew, but she was extremely sensitive to certain things after losing Ella. I couldn't fault her for that. I'd been there, and I'd seen how it had nearly destroyed her. That was a large part of the reason why I'd convinced myself that I'd done the right thing. I'd been so sure that Emmy wouldn't have been able to handle seeing me pregnant that I'd given no thought to future consequences.

"Why would you do that, Savannah?" she asked, her voice almost pleading that I take it back.

I dropped my chin to my chest and tried to breathe past the pain that had taken up residence in my chest. "We had no business having a baby! We were only nineteen, for Christ's sake. And it's not like I had the best role model growing up," I replied sarcastically.

"You had just lost Ella," I explained. "I didn't want to hurt you. You were having a hard enough time trying to deal with it. I didn't want to make things worse."

When I finally found the courage to look up at her, she was shaking her head in disbelief.

"You can't be serious, Savannah. I'm your best friend," she said, emphasizing the last two words. "How could you possibly think I would be anything but happy for you? Jesus!" She stood and began pacing the kitchen. "I can't believe you never told me…after all these years. I can't believe you did that to Jeremy!"

"I thought I was doing what was right," I insisted, finally starting to let my anger at her judgment outweigh my guilt.

"How could you think that was right? You saw what that miscarriage did to me. How could you ever think that having an *abortion* would be something I'd be okay with?"

"I was hoping you'd never find out," I stupidly admitted.

That caused her to let out a cruel, sarcastic laugh. "Oh, wow. Well, that came back to *really* bite you in the ass, didn't it?"

"Emmy—"

"I can't approve of what you did, Savannah. I *don't* approve of it. I've always told you *everything*. I was supposed to be your best friend. How could you keep something like this from me? And for seven years. I don't know what else to say. I thought you trusted me."

"I do trust you, Emmy!"

"Obviously, you don't." With that, she turned and did something she'd never done before. She walked away from me.

The harshness in her words was completely foreign to me and cut down to the bone. She was the one person in my life who I always thought would stand beside me no matter what, whether the decisions I made were wrong or not. I never expected to see disapproval or disappointment on her face when she looked at me, but that was exactly what had been in her eyes as she stared me down.

Something in me shut down at that look. The smallest piece of happiness that I'd managed to hold on to when Jeremy walked away had shattered with that look. I hadn't grown up with a loving family. Truthfully, they had barely tolerated me.

My friends were the closest I had to any type of real family, and Jeremy and Emmy were the two most important people in all of that. With both of them turning their backs on me, I had nothing left.

The phrase *beating a dead horse* was the perfect description for how my life had become. Only, it felt like someone had beaten the horse to death and then ran over it with a Mack truck for good measure.

Apparently, losing Jeremy and Emmy avoiding me like the plague wasn't enough. I'd just finished boxing up the last of Jeremy's things when my cell phone started ringing. I was so consumed by what I was doing that I didn't even bother looking at the caller ID. That was my first mistake.

"Hello?"

"Savannah, darling, how have you been?"

Talking to mommy dearest was the last thing I wanted to do. I wasn't fooled by the polite greeting. I knew she wasn't calling to check up on me. She never did. She was calling because she needed something.

"Mother," I replied dryly. "I've been fine. How are you?"

With that question, I knew the small talk would come to an end and she'd get to her point.

"Fine, fine," she rushed out. "Listen, darling, I need a favor."

Here we go.

"As you know, your father is running for senator."

This was news to me. I had no idea my father had political aspirations. I guess I shouldn't have been really surprised. I couldn't help but think that I would definitely have to move if the people in our district were stupid enough to actually vote for him.

"Your father and I are hosting a dinner at the country club tonight for some potential contributors. We need you to join us."

In other words, they needed me to come to the dinner to put on a show that we were some loving, happy family unit. My father needed me there so he could snow those people into thinking he was a decent family man and father. That way, they'd feel comfortable shelling out their money. I would rather give myself an at-home Brazilian wax than be caught dead at that country club with my sorry excuses for parents.

"Sorry, Mother. I've just got a lot going on right now. I'm not going to be able to make it."

"Savannah Morgan! Your father and I ask so little of you, and you can't even be bothered to attend one little dinner to help him. When did you turn into such a self-centered brat? I know I raised you better than to be so selfish."

If I had it in me, I would have laughed. She hadn't raised me to be anything. She'd left that job to nannies and maids. Robert and Victoria Morgan hadn't lifted a hand in raising me.

The only thing either of them had ever done was knock me down every chance they'd gotten.

There were many instances to recall, but at that moment, my mind flashed back to one time in particular.

I was sixteen years old, and my parents were hosting their annual Christmas party. My mother had purchased a little black cocktail dress for me to wear that was completely inappropriate for a teenager.

I was standing alone in the kitchen, trying my best to stay out of the way, when one of the partners at my father's firm, Douglas Harrison, walked in. I'd seen him knocking back scotches all night long, and if his ruddy cheeks were any indication, he was already three sheets to the wind.

He saw me sitting on the bar stool, and the creepy grin that spread across his face sent a chill up my spine.

"Well, don't you look all grown up, Savannah?" he said as he made his way over to me.

I glanced around, hoping that someone else would wander into the kitchen, but no one did. It was just me and Mr. Harrison, who was wearing a too tight suit that showed off his potbelly.

"Good evening, Mr. Harrison. I hope you're enjoying yourself."

He was standing way too close for comfort and I could smell alcohol and cigarettes on his breath. It was enough to make me want to puke.

"I am, dear, and the evening just got even better," he replied as his gaze wandered up my legs and stopped at the low neckline of my dress.

I could have killed my mother right then and there for picking it out.

I tried to get his perverted attention off of me. "Is Mrs. Harrison with you?"

But he didn't take the bait. He didn't even acknowledge the mention of his wife. He just licked his lips, like he was eyeing a steak. The man was at least forty years my senior and looked even older, which just made his attention all the more disgusting. There was nothing even slightly attractive about him. He was fat, bald, and he seemed to always have a sheen of sweat on his pockmarked forehead.

"What are you doing in here all by yourself?" he asked, stepping even closer and officially invading my personal space.

I tried to scoot to the very edge of the bar stool to put some much needed distance between us, but it was pointless. "I'm not really much for parties," I replied, trying to remain polite even though the man was seriously freaking me out.

He caged me in against the island, making me feel trapped. It was a feeling I didn't deal well with.

"I'm not really much for parties either. Why don't we go out back so we can have a little privacy?" At that moment, he ran his sausage fingers along my collarbone and across the edge of my dress.

I shivered and tried in vain to move away from his touch. "I'm sure my father is looking for you."

He placed his hand on my bare knee and gave it a squeeze. "Robert can wait. What do you say we get out of here for a bit?"

That was it. I'd officially had enough. "I suggest you get your pudgy little hand off my leg before you lose it," I said between clenched teeth.

"Oh, come on, honey," he replied as he slipped his hand higher up my thigh beneath my skirt. "You know you—"

He didn't get to finish his sentence before I grabbed a fork off the countertop and stabbed the back of his hand—hard.

He let out a bellow and a string of curses that would have made a sailor blush, drawing the attention of several party guests, including both of my parents. Mr. Harrison tried to play it off as an accident, but I could tell by the look on his wife's face that she knew exactly what had happened. My parents banished me to my bedroom for the remainder of the party with whispered promises to deal with me after the last of the guests left.

After changing out of that god-awful dress, I sat in my room, waiting for my punishment to come. Goose bumps broke out on my arms as I listened to the sound of my father's shoes pounding up the stairs right before he burst through the door, followed by my mother.

"What the fuck were you thinking?" he started, completely red-faced and fuming. "Doug had to have thirteen stitches because of that little stunt you pulled. Have you lost your goddamn mind, Savannah? He's a partner, for Christ's sake!"

My spine stiffened as he spoke. I didn't know why I was surprised. I should have known better than to think either of my parents would take my side in anything. "Well, that partner was practically trying to molest me while his wife was in the other room!" I shouted. "He had his hand up my skirt, and—"

"Well, maybe if you weren't dressed like a two-dollar hooker, he wouldn't have been tempted," my father said. "You were basically asking for it."

I reared back like he'd just slapped me. I felt the tears starting to sting my eyes, but I'd be damned if I let them fall. I wouldn't give my parents the satisfaction of seeing me cry.

"I wasn't asking for anything," I whispered. "And Mother bought that dress for me to wear tonight. If you have a problem with it, take it up with her."

"Don't you dare put this on me, Savannah Morgan. When I bought you that dress, it fit perfectly. How was I to know that you were going to gain too much weight to fit into it?"

That was complete and utter bullshit. I hadn't gained a single pound since she purchased that dress, and she knew it. I didn't have a chance to defend myself before my father spoke again.

"Do you live to humiliate your mother and me, Savannah? Is it your goal in life to embarrass us at every turn?"

At that, my traitorous tears finally escaped, leaking down my cheeks. I was strong, but being called a whore, fat, and an embarrassment in one sitting was too much for even me to handle. They hadn't stuck around long enough to see them fall though. They'd plunged the knife in deep enough to garner a reaction, and then they'd turned and walked away, leaving me lying on my bed, broken once again.

I shook myself from the awful memory of my childhood as my mother started to speak once again.

"Is it too much to ask that you show your father some support for just a few short hours?" she asked, laying the guilt trip on heavily. "It's the least you could do after everything you pulled as a child."

I prided myself on being tough enough to withstand my parents' bullshit, but I was already on guilt overload, and I just couldn't handle any more. That was why I caved to my mother's request. It was yet another mistake to add to all the others I'd been racking up.

"Fine, Mom. I'll be there."

CHAPTER
twenty-three

Walking into the country club was like stepping back into my past that was full of unwanted emotions and memories. I was wearing my little black dress with a delicate lace overlay and lace sleeves from Zara and my favorite Louboutin red platform pumps. My hair was pulled back into a loose chignon, and my makeup was light, but I still felt completely out of place around all of those people. That wasn't my world. I didn't belong there, yet somehow, I was stuck plastering on a fake smile while I associated with people I had no desire to know.

The maître d' walked me over to the table where my parents were sitting with two middle aged men in expensive suits.

"Savannah, darling. We're so glad you could join us," my mother said with a phony smile as she stood to kiss me on the cheek. "You couldn't have put the tiniest bit of effort into your appearance tonight?" she whispered in my ear so that no one else could hear what she was saying.

I straightened and gave a tight-lipped smile to my father as he leaned in for an awkward one-armed hug. I hadn't been there for thirty seconds and I'd already been insulted and made to feel unwanted. That had to be some sort of record.

"Gentlemen," my father exclaimed, "this lovely woman is my daughter, Savannah."

The enthusiasm in his voice turned my stomach because I knew it wasn't real. He would have been more than happy not to have to deal with me. The only reason I was there was to attempt to make him look good.

"Savannah," he said, turning his attention to me, "this is Phillip Waters and Paul Cordova."

I turned to the men and replied politely, "It's nice to meet you both."

The seat next to my mother was pulled out for me, so I took my seat and breathed a small sigh of relief that at least the waiter was already there, taking drink orders.

"She'll have a club soda," my mother informed him when it was my turn to order.

I knew that I should have just smiled and nodded, acting as the good daughter for the evening, but I'd be damned if I was going to be stuck having dinner with my wretched parents without alcohol to relieve my pain.

"Actually," I interrupted, "I'd like a vodka tonic."

I felt the air around me change and I knew that I'd just poked the bear, but it didn't matter. As far as Victoria Morgan was concerned, she was the definition of class. The last thing she would do was make a scene in public. But the look she shot me when no one was paying attention spoke volumes. Clear as day, it said, *Fuck this up, and I'll ruin your life.*

As if she could possibly make it any worse than it already is.

The waiter gave a curt nod and walked off to fill our drink orders.

I spent the next hour and a half in bored silence as my father droned on and on about everything he had to offer. I smiled when it seemed necessary and laughed when everyone else laughed, but I wasn't even paying attention to anything he was saying. I was on my second vodka tonic, and the effects of the alcohol were thankfully starting to work. I was starting to become blissfully numb.

Everyone had just finished their main course and I was beginning to get excited at the prospect of leaving when Mr. Waters asked the one question I knew my parents were dreading.

"So, Savannah, what do you do?"

I picked up my water glass and took a healthy gulp before answering. "I work at Pruett & Carter," I replied truthfully. I wasn't embarrassed about my career, and I couldn't care less if my family was.

"Ah, I see," Mr. Cordova said. "You followed in your father's footsteps and became an attorney. Is there a reason you chose not to work at Morgan & Carls?"

I opened my mouth to speak, but my father cut me off. "She's always been a tenacious girl."

He reached over and gave my hand a loving squeeze. At least, that was what bystanders would think it was, but I knew it was a warning to stay in check.

"She wanted to branch out on her own to prove her worth. I commend her drive."

I couldn't help the snort that escaped me when he said that. I tried my best to play it off as a cough, but there was no doubt my mother knew better. I didn't know if it was the vodka tonics that had given me the unexpected sense of courage or the fact that I'd had absolutely enough of being dumped on to last me the rest of my life, but I could no longer sit idly by and act like the good little girl they expected me to be.

"Actually, I'm not a lawyer," I replied with my first genuine smile of the night. "I'm just a paralegal."

I could see the red creeping up my father's neck from my peripheral vision, and I got a sick little sense of triumph, knowing I'd shaken his cool exterior. For that reason, I decided to continue. "And I always hated the atmosphere at Morgan & Carls. It's so stuffy and pretentious, you know? Pruett & Carter is a wonderful firm." I took that moment to stand and excuse myself to the restroom.

I wasn't in there for fifteen seconds before my feeling of triumph was knocked on its ass by my mother pushing through the restroom door. If the look on her face didn't let me know just how mad she was, the next words out of her mouth did.

"Listen here, you little brat," she hissed out at me. "I know you're used to hanging out with those white trash rednecks you call friends, but while you are in our presence, you will behave like a normal member of society."

I opened my mouth to defend my friends, but she cut me off. "You've been humiliating your father and me your entire life, and it ends tonight. When you walk back to that table, I expect you to act the way we raised you to act."

She took a step closer to me so that I could smell the mint on her breath. "If you don't, I'll make you wish you'd never been born."

She turned on her Jimmy Choos and sauntered out of the restroom like nothing had happened while I stood there with my jaw hanging open in complete shock. As I watched my mom walk out of the restroom, it became clear. No matter what I did or how I acted, I was never going to be accepted by my parents. I'd always known that, but on some deeper level, I'd felt that they still loved me even if they didn't show it. But neither one of my parents was capable of loving anyone but themselves. Why they ever decided to have a child in the first place was beyond me.

The toilet in one of the stalls flushed, and heat began to creep up my neck. Someone had been in there to hear the entire conversation between me and my mother. I ran into the next stall and locked the door until I could get myself in check. I breathed in and out deeply, willing the tears that threatened to fall back down. I refused to cry over my parents. They didn't deserve it.

I sat on the toilet with my eyes squeezed shut as the other person in the restroom went about her business while finishing up at the sink. I finally got my tears under control and opened the stall door to see Charlotte standing at the mirror, reapplying lipstick. A shit eating grin spread across her painted lips when she saw me.

There was no possible way my night could get any worse.

Hoping that she would just finish up and leave, I ignored her and walked to the mirror to fix whatever damage I'd done to my mascara. Seconds later, my luck proved to be absolute shit.

"You're not having a good week, are you?"

I wanted to slap the smug smile off her freshly glossed lips.

"First, your boyfriend, and now your parents? You just can't stop letting people down."

I clenched my fists together until my knuckles were white, my nails breaking the skin on my palms. The last thing I needed was to get into a fight in the women's room of the country club. That would be the cherry on top of the shit sundae that was my life.

I chose not to respond, and I turned to exit the restroom before I did something I truly regretted.

"Oh yeah, don't think I haven't already heard all about you and Jeremy breaking up. Just goes to show what a mistake he made when he left me for you. I'm sure he's regretting his decision right about now. He dumped class for trash. My friends were right. It was only a matter of time before he saw the error of his ways. Don't worry, I won't make him grovel too much when he comes crawling back to me."

I couldn't take it anymore. My stomach was knotted in pain. There was no fight left in me. I just wanted to get out of there. I wanted the comforts of my own home and bed. I felt like I was suffocating. The only chance I had to breathe again was to get out of that place and away from those people. I didn't belong.

I yanked the door open and let my feet carry me to the dinner table. In a complete daze, I reached for my purse. As I began to turn to leave, my father grabbed my wrist to hold me in place.

"Where do you think you're going?" he asked with a silent breath, trying not to draw too much attention to our exchange.

I looked around the table at my parents and their dinner companions. I didn't even bother to address my mother and father. "Mr. Waters, Mr. Cordova, it was lovely meeting you, but I'm afraid I'm going to have to call it a night." I jerked my hand out of my father's grasp.

"Is everything okay, dear?" Mr. Cordova asked with concern written all over his face.

In our brief conversations throughout the evening, it had become obvious that those two men were both decent individuals who had been conned by my mother and father. If it was the last thing I ever did, I was determined to set the record straight before either of the men got tied to something they would eventually regret.

"Forgive me for doing this here, but I think both of you gentlemen should know exactly who you're considering putting your money behind." I turned my full body to face both of the men as I pointed to my father. "Robert Morgan isn't the kind of man you think he is. He's a horrible husband and an even worse father. He's an abuser, a cheater, and an all-around disgusting human being. Backing him for political office would be a bad decision on both your parts. If he's elected as state senator, I suggest you move out of the district."

I turned on my fabulous heels and strode out of the country club with my head held up just a little higher. Everything else might have been falling apart in my life, but I'd finally cut the cord tethering me to my parents. I was done with them, and that felt better than I could have imagined it would.

CHAPTER
twenty-four

Jeremy

I sat alone in my living room with a bottle of whiskey in my hand doing the same thing I'd done every night for the past week and a half—getting drunk. I would wake up with a hangover, down water and aspirin, head to work, and then come home and start the whole damn thing over again. That had been my life since I left Savannah.

Nothing I did made me feel any better or loosened the knot that had taken permanent residence in my chest. Drinking didn't ease the pain. It just allowed me to pass out for a few hours since sleeping wasn't an option. I missed her. Not being with her was like losing a limb, but I couldn't bring myself to forgive her. It wasn't so much the abortion as it was knowing that she would always put me last.

I was about a half hour away from total oblivion when someone started knocking on my front door. I slammed the Jack down on the coffee table, and stood up, instantly staggered to the side, banging my shin on the coffee table. "Sonofabitch!" I muttered as I stumbled to the door, pulling it open without even checking to see who was standing there.

My vision was slightly blurry, but I was still able to make out the sweater set and dark brown hair. Even if I hadn't been able to see, I still would have known who it was strictly from the cloying perfume threatening to suffocate me.

"What are you doing here, Charlotte?" I slurred.

Her brows wrinkled in concern as she took in my haggard appearance. "I wanted to check on you. I heard what happened between you and Savannah, and despite how things ended between us, I still care about you. I just wanted to make sure you were okay."

If I'd been completely in my right mind, I'd like to think that I would have been capable of making smarter decisions. But that wasn't the case. I stepped to the side and let Charlotte into my apartment then proceeded to collapse back onto the couch before taking a healthy swig straight from the bottle I had grabbed off of the coffee table.

"As you can see"—I indicated with a wave of my half-empty whiskey bottle—"I couldn't be better."

Charlotte sat down next to me and placed her hand gently on my knee. "I hate seeing you like this, Jeremy. It isn't you."

I laid my head on the back of the couch, closed my eyes, and pinched the bridge of my nose between my thumb and forefinger. "You shouldn't have come here, Charlotte. I'm not exactly the best company right now."

I kept my eyes shut as I felt her hand begin to travel up my thigh, squeezing slightly. In the back of my foggy brain, I knew it was a mistake not to brush her off right away, but the alcohol was clouding all rational thought, and all I could concentrate on was how damn good it felt to have someone touching me.

I shook my head and tried to stop her, but the effort was halfhearted at best. "Charlotte, you really shouldn't—"

"Shh," she whispered into my ear before kissing my neck.

When did she get so damn close?

All thoughts of pushing her away fled my mind when her hand slid up and started rubbing my dick through the denim of my pants.

Christ, that feels good. I let out a deep moan and thrust my hips up against her hand.

"Let me make you feel good, baby." She ran her tongue along the shell of my ear as she increased the speed of her hand between my legs.

At that very moment, letting her make me feel good seemed like the best idea I'd ever heard. She popped the button of my jeans and began to unzip them. I spread my legs wider to give her better access.

"Do you want that, Jeremy?" she asked in a seductive voice. "Do you want me to make it all better?" She slid off the couch and onto her knees between my spread thighs.

"Yeah, I want that," I panted breathlessly as she took the head of my cock into her mouth and began to suck greedily. "Fuck yeah," I moaned, thrusting up to force her to take even more of me. "Suck it hard, baby." My eyes were still squeezed closed tightly as I felt that telltale tingle in my spine.

Everything except my impending orgasm began to blur, and my grip on reality became even looser as I pumped into the hot mouth surrounding me. All of the bad shit that had happened over the last few weeks finally began to melt away as the image of golden blonde hair filled my head.

"That's so fuckin' good, Savannah," I groaned deeply as I began to come. That was the last thing I recalled until the next morning.

Savannah

It had been three days since my disastrous dinner with my parents, and I hadn't heard a peep out of either of them, not that I'd really expected to. I'd driven the final nail into that particular coffin, and I didn't even regret it. I'd spent the last three days working, running, or obsessively cleaning my house. I did anything and everything to keep my mind off of what needed to be done next.

The box of Jeremy's stuff sat on my dining room table like a beacon shining on every wrong decision I'd made in the past seven years. I couldn't stare at it any longer.

Finally summoning up the courage I needed, I grabbed the box, put it in the back of my car, and made my way to Jeremy's apartment. After I dropped it off, there would officially be nothing left between us. That thought was like a punch to the sternum, but I knew there was no way to really begin moving on unless I cut that last tie.

The ten-minute drive seemed to go by in a flash, and before I knew it, I was parking and turning off my car in front of his building. I sat there, staring up at his bedroom window, trying to loosen the fist that seemed to be squeezing all the air from my lungs. Bolstering as much fake confidence as I could, I stepped out of my car and retrieved the box from the backseat. Each step toward his door caused the anxiety to bubble up in my stomach. I didn't know how I was going to face him, but I knew I had to.

I finally reached his door and gave it a few firm knocks. Then, I waited…and waited…and waited some more. I started to think that he wasn't home, and I bent to place the box on the bench next to the door when I heard the deadbolt disengage. I quickly stood and ran a shaky hand through my hair just as the door swung open.

"Can I help you?"

My head began to swim and the edges of my vision darkened.

Jeremy

My head felt like it was being squeezed in a vise and my stomach rolled as I peeled my eyes open. Sunlight was shining through my bedroom window, bright enough to blind a person, which only caused me to feel worse. It wasn't until I rolled over with a groan, attempting to get away from the light, that I noticed I was lying in bed, stark naked.

What the hell?

Pushing past the pain, I sat up in bed and gently swung my legs over the side. That was when I saw the bra and panties on my bedroom floor…right next to the discarded condom.

Oh fuck! Images from the night before began flashing through my mind, and there was no doubt that I'd completely fucked up.

I stood on shaky legs and reached for a pair of sweatpants that had been thrown over a chair. I couldn't lie and say I didn't hope that Charlotte was already gone, but seeing her underwear on my bedroom floor was kind of an indicator that she was still here somewhere. I had to find her and get her ass out before she grabbed on to some insane notion that a drunken fuck meant we'd gotten back together. I'd just stepped into the hallway when I heard voices coming from the living room area.

Turning the corner, I saw Charlotte standing at the threshold of the front door, wearing one of my white T-shirts, and from the looks of it, nothing else.

What the fuck is going on?

"Can I help you?" she asked in an agitated tone.

"Uh…no. I was…I just wanted to drop this off."

A cold sweat broke out on my skin, and my stomach revolted violently at the sound of Savannah's voice coming from the other side of the door.

Oh Christ. Oh no.

Several emotions ran through me at once—fear that Savannah saw Charlotte in nothing but my shirt at the butt crack of dawn and what she must have been thinking, and then anger at Charlotte for having the nerve to answer my fucking door in the first goddamned place.

"What's going on?" I demanded as I jerked the door out of Charlotte's hand to open it wider.

The pain and unshed tears shining in Savannah's eyes were a direct hit to the gut. Just because we weren't together anymore didn't mean I wanted to cause her unnecessary pain, and seeing a half naked Charlotte in my apartment was absolutely unnecessary.

"I…I'm sorry. I should have called," she stammered. One lone tear escaped, but she batted it away quickly and turned to pick something up off the ground. "I just wanted to return the rest of your stuff. I didn't mean to interrupt."

She refused to meet my eyes as she practically threw the box at me. She turned on her heels and was just about to run down the steps when I stepped out of the door and called her name. I wasn't completely sure why, but I couldn't let her leave, thinking that something more was going on with Charlotte.

"Savannah, wait!"

She paused and partially turned. "It's okay. I'm sorry. I'm sorry for just showing up."

I saw the rise and fall of her chest as she took a deep breath before locking her eyes with mine. The emptiness in her gaze filled my gut with fear.

"Don't worry, Jer. It won't happen again."

Then, she was gone.

I stood in place, frozen to the core.

When I turned back toward my apartment, box in hand, I saw Charlotte standing there with her arms crossed and her eyes narrowed.

"That bitch sure has some nerve, just showing up here," she huffed out.

That one short sentence was enough to send my precarious anger over the edge. "You're the devil, you know that? What the fuck are you still doing here?" I seethed as I pushed past her and back into my apartment, slamming the door behind me.

"What do you mean? I thought we—"

I cut her off with a swipe of my hand, already knowing exactly what she'd thought. "You came over to my place last night, uninvited, while I was shitfaced drunk, and you propositioned me, knowing there wasn't a chance in hell I was in my right mind enough to turn you down. If you think last night was anything other than a drunken fuck, you're seriously out of your head."

She reared back like I'd just hit her. "Are you serious right now?"

She tried to grab a hold of me, but I wrenched my arms out of her grasp.

"As a heart attack, Charlotte. You need to get dressed and get the hell out of my house." I turned and headed to the bathroom.

"You don't mean that, Jeremy," she pleaded.

"Oh, I mean it," I said over my shoulder. "If you're still here by the time I'm done taking a piss, I'll show you *exactly* how much I mean it. Get. Out."

With that, I slammed the bathroom door and stood there until I heard her leave.

That was it. I was done drinking.

CHAPTER
twenty-five

Savannah

I pulled up to my house to see Lizzy's car in my driveway. There was no way I could cover up the fact that I'd been crying my eyes out the whole way home. I walked in and dropped my purse on the table by the door.

"Hey, babe," Lizzy called from my kitchen. "Stacia and I stopped by to discuss Thanksgiving and your birthday."

Oh, fantastic. Now I was going to experience my humiliation in front of *two* of my friends. And I wanted to talk about Thanksgiving and my birthday as much as I wanted a hole in my head.

"I know it's barely noon, but we cracked open a bottle of wine already. Hope you don't—"

Lizzy's words cut off as soon as she and Stacia rounded the corner into my foyer and saw my red-rimmed, puffy eyes and blotchy cheeks. I was a very ugly crier.

"What's wrong?" they asked in unison.

I couldn't speak past the tears clogging my throat, so I just shook my head.

"Jesus," Stacia gasped. "When was the last time you ate, Savvy? You look like you've lost at least ten pounds since the last time I saw you."

She wasn't too far off the mark. I hadn't really eaten all that much in the past two weeks, and with all the running I'd been doing as a stress reliever, the weight had kind of been falling off.

"Why have you been crying?" Lizzy asked.

I couldn't stop the laughter from bubbling up. Every time I thought things couldn't get any worse, they somehow had. What started off as humorless laughter turned into hysterics as I thought about how each day had gotten shittier than the one before. Lizzy and Stacia stood there, staring at me, as I hunched over, laughing so hard that tears were streaming down my face. My abs ached by the time I was finished. They just stayed silent, blinking, while they let me get myself together.

I sucked in a deep breath, still giggling a little, as I filled Stacia and Lizzy in on the latest development. "I made the mistake of dropping off the last of Jeremy's stuff this morning without calling."

They led me into the kitchen, and Stacia poured me a glass of wine. I downed the entire thing in just a few gulps and handed it back to her for a refill.

"Did you guys get into a fight or something?" Lizzy asked.

I let out a sarcastic laugh. "Oh no, nothing like that. We hardly spoke at all after Charlotte answered the door, wearing nothing but his T-shirt."

"WHAT?" they both screeched.

I downed my second glass of wine, and waved the empty glass, indicating I was in need of more. Stacia was right there to fill it.

"Yeah, looks like they're back together. Sure didn't waste any time," I muttered into my glass before I took a big gulp.

"I can't believe that," Lizzy said as she took a seat on a bar stool.

"Well, believe it," I replied. "So you'll have to forgive me if I'm not really in the mood to talk about Thanksgiving or birthdays. Seeing Jeremy post-sex with my archenemy kind of put a damper on things. Not to mention, Emmy's still not talking to me, which probably means Luke isn't talking to me either. And with Jeremy already hating me, plus being back together with Charlotte, I think it's safe to say that I'll be taking a pass on our Thanksgiving dinner plans."

Stacia walked up to me and placed an arm around my shoulders. "You know as well as I do that Emmy will eventually get over this. She just needs a little time. She'll come to her senses, I promise."

"You can't promise that," I said as I shook my head at her. "I screwed up big time. On a scale of one to ten, my mistake ranks up at a billion."

"She was just hurt, Savvy. Losing Ella still affects her, and she handled it badly," Lizzy said.

I couldn't tell who she was trying to convince more—me or herself.

Stacia tried her best to comfort me. "The two of you will make up. You've been best friends since forever. This fight won't end the relationship between y'all."

"How do you know?" I asked. "It's not like there's anything to base that fact on. Emmy and I have never gotten into a fight in our lives. We couldn't stand to be mad at each other for more than a few minutes, let alone days. She's never *not* talked to me before. I don't see her getting over this anytime soon."

"Have a little faith, Savvy," Lizzy told me. "Things can only go up from here."

I appreciated them trying to cheer me up, but it was no use. We chatted for a while longer before I feigned a headache, and they left, so I could lie down and sleep it off.

Trying to rest was a wasted effort. Every time I closed my eyes, all I could picture was Jeremy and Charlotte, together. And every time I pictured them together, my stomach knotted up, so I spent the remainder of the day pacing and chewing my nails down to the quick.

When my own company became too annoying, I pulled on my running clothes and decided I'd go on a much needed run. I still hated exercise, but I couldn't deny the stress relieving aspects of it. And, surprisingly, I'd gotten pretty good at it. I no longer felt like I wanted to die after I finished, and I'd managed to cut time off of each mile. If I wasn't so miserable, I'd be proud of myself.

As I ran, I'd decided to deviate from my original route and I went a different way instead. My iPod was cranked up to help drown out the images of Jeremy and Charlotte that my mind had managed to conjure up.

I'd just finished my second mile when I noticed that the route I'd taken had led me straight to Ben's street. I'd never been to his place, but he'd told me all about it and I knew I was just a few houses away. I knew that the thought that popped into my head at that moment couldn't lead to anything good, but I didn't care anymore. I was so tired of making decisions based on what was best for everyone but me. All I cared about right then was forgetting about the pain I'd been feeling. I wanted to do something for myself for once even if I would regret it later.

I made my way up the path to his front door as the plan took form in my head. I felt a massive sense of determination as I lifted my hand and rapped my knuckles on the heavy wooden door. I hadn't even considered how late it was until he opened the door, wearing nothing but a pair of pajama pants, his hair mussed up from sleep.

"Savannah? What are you doing here? Is everything okay?"

I wrung my hands together nervously, trying to maintain the courage to do what I thought needed to be done. "Sorry if I woke you," I lamely replied. "I was just out for a run and I noticed I was on your street."

He took in my black spandex running pants and tight tank top. "I see that. Any reason you decided to go for a run at nine at night?"

"I just…I guess I was tired of my own company, you know?"

Ben placed his hands on my shoulders and knelt so that he was at eye level with me. "Are you all right, Savannah?"

I was so tired of everyone looking at me with concern or pity. Seeing that in Ben's eyes fortified my nerves. Standing on my tiptoes, I wrapped my arms around his neck and pressed my lips to his. He froze in shock for a few seconds before pulling away.

"Savvy, what are you doing?" he asked.

I reached up and ran my hands through his hair, and down around his shoulders, trying to pull him back down to me. "You asked me out before, but I was still tied to Jeremy. That's done now."

I went in for another kiss, but he grabbed both my wrists in his hands and gently pulled my arms from around his neck.

"Savannah…" he whispered softly with a small shake of his head.

I instantly saw the regret in his eyes. That was enough to rattle me to my core. "Oh my God. You don't want me anymore, do you?" I asked, embarrassment running through my entire body as I took a step away from him.

"I'm so sorry," he responded. And to his credit, he seemed completely sincere. "It's just that…I—"

"Benny, is everything okay out here?" The door next to Ben pulled open wider, revealing a sleepy-eyed, pajama-clad Mickey. "Savannah, sweetie, what's going on?"

Ohmygod, ohmygod, ohmygod.

"Oh shit. Oh God. I'm so sorry." I stood there, staring at the two of them, as tears began running down my cheeks. "I'm so sorry," I repeated, not knowing what else to say.

"Savannah, it's all right," Ben insisted.

"No, it's not!" I ran my hands over my cheeks, swiping at my tears. "As if I wasn't already enough of a fuck-up, I just came to my boss's house in the middle of the night and threw myself at him while one of my closest friends was in his bed."

The hysterical laughter started back up again and combined with the tears I couldn't get to stop.

Mickey stepped past Ben and reached for my arm. "You didn't know we were together, honey. It's okay."

"It's not okay," I demanded. "God, I'm a horrible person," I whispered more to myself than to Ben and Mickey.

"You aren't a bad person," Ben insisted.

"Savvy, babe, why don't you come inside?" Mickey asked, trying to mask her growing concern with a smile.

"I can't. I…I have to go."

Before either of them could say another word, I turned and ran, heading back down the path toward my house. I couldn't stand there with them any longer. I was beyond humiliated.

By the time I made it back to my house, I had three missed calls and voice mails on my cell—two from Mickey and one from Ben. I listened to the first message from Mickey, telling me that she wasn't mad and that she was worried about me before asking me to please call her back. I deleted the rest of the messages without listening to them.

I walked into my bathroom, stripping off my sweaty clothes and dropping them haphazardly along the way. I set the water as hot as I could stand it and stood beneath the spray, wishing the water could wash away my shame.

By the time I got out, my skin was bright pink and pruney, and I didn't feel any better about myself. I needed to do some serious thinking about the direction my life was going in and what I could possibly do to get it back on the right path. I spent the entire night, staring at my ceiling, trying to figure out how to fix everything I'd screwed up.

When my alarm went off the next morning, I was no closer to finding an answer.

CHAPTER
twenty-six

The only good thing that came out of the following week was the fact that Ben spent most of his time in court, so I didn't have to try too hard to avoid him at every turn.

Mickey was a different story though. After a week of avoiding her phone calls, I guess she'd had enough, and she decided to come by the office to talk to me.

"I figured this was my best chance at talking to you," she said from the doorway of my office.

She scared the ever-living hell out of me, and I let out a frightened yelp as I spun around with my hand over my rapidly beating heart.

"Jesus, Mick. Are you trying to give me a heart attack?"

She pushed off the doorframe and walked over to take a seat in the vacant chair. "Well, it's not like you've left me much choice. If I had given you a heads up, you probably would've run on me. What other option did I have?"

I narrowed my eyes at her. "I don't know. Maybe try knocking?"

"Where's the fun in that?" she asked with a wicked grin. The smile quickly faded, and she suddenly became serious. "Why have you been avoiding me, Savvy?"

I let out a frustrated breath and ran my hands through my flat hair. Putting effort into my appearance wasn't something I cared much about nowadays. Most days, I wouldn't bother blow-drying my hair, opting to throw it up into a sloppy ponytail, and I wouldn't even bother with makeup. Most of my clothes sloppily hung off of me since I hadn't been able to eat much, and I'd spent the majority of my free time running.

"I thought that was pretty obvious, Mickey. I showed up at your boyfriend's house in the middle of the night, and I made a pass at him."

She leaned forward, resting a forearm across her knees, and began counting off on her fingers. "First of all, it wasn't the middle of the night. It was, like, nine o'clock. That's still early enough to be okay. Second of all, you had no clue he was my boyfriend. And he's smokin' hot, so I can't really hold that against you, can I?"

She was trying to use humor to lighten the situation, but it wasn't making me feel any better.

"That doesn't matter, Mick. I saw the way he was looking at you that night we were all at Colt's. If I hadn't been so self-involved lately, maybe I would have noticed that my boss and one of my best friends were together."

"You are the least self-involved person I know, Savannah."

I let out a sarcastic snort at that. "Tell that to Emmy and Jeremy. I'm sure they'd both disagree with you."

"I don't care what they'd say," she replied vehemently. "I know the truth. They're just hurting right now. They'll come around."

I started to shake my head, but she cut me off with a wave of her hand.

"And no one knew about Ben and me. We've been keeping the relationship under wraps since it's still in the early stages. We didn't want to have to deal with answering any questions while we're trying to get to know each other."

For the first time in a week, I actually gave the thought of Ben and Mickey being together some serious thought. That put a sincere smile on my face. "And how's that going?"

Her face completely lit up. "It's going great." Her smile spread so wide that I was sure her cheeks had to hurt. "Ben is absolutely perfect," she said. Then, her smile dimmed slightly. "I'm actually a little terrified by just how perfect he is."

"Why are you terrified?"

"It's just that…well, he's amazing," she stated, like one sentence should explain it all.

"Still not seeing how that's a bad thing."

Mickey gave me a look that said it should be obvious. "Look at him, and look at me. He's a suit-and-tie-wearing lawyer, and I'm covered in ink and piercings and tattoo people for a living. It's not like we really fit together."

I reached over and slapped her on the shoulder for being completely insane. "You're ridiculous. Just because you don't look the same doesn't mean you don't fit together. That man has been crazy about you since the first night you met. I bet he's absolutely sprung."

Her uncertainty started to melt away, and it was replaced with hope. "You think?"

I placed my hands over hers and gave them a supportive squeeze. "I know so. You're one of the most amazing people I know, Mickey. And Ben's a smart man. He knows what he has in you, trust me."

She leaned in and wrapped her arms around me, hugging me tight. "He's just so different from what I'm used to dating, you know? He's…"

"Employed?" I offered.

She rolled her eyes and gave a small laugh. "I was going to say, a complete gentleman."

"That too."

She placed her hands on my shoulders and looked me right in the eyes. "You know, maybe your little pep talk there should be directed more toward yourself. You're a pretty amazing person yourself."

I lowered my eyes and let out a deep breath. "I'm not so sure about that. I haven't been feeling all that amazing lately."

"Maybe you should take a little vacation," she suggested. "Get away for a little bit to clear your mind."

Leaving Cloverleaf wasn't something I'd really given much thought to. The town had always been my home, filled with all the people I loved and who loved me. My family.

But I hadn't been feeling that sense of family. To be completely honest, I'd never felt so alone and miserable in my life. I gave Mickey's suggestion some serious thought.

"You know what? I think you're right. Maybe leaving is exactly what I need." I just didn't tell her that I was considering being gone for a lot longer than just a simple vacation.

I'd stuck around the office later than usual. I knew Ben would be coming back after he was done in court, and I needed to talk to him. I knocked on his office door and stepped in just as he turned away from his computer.

"Savannah? I'm surprised you're still here. I thought you would have left a long time ago."

I chewed on my bottom lip as I took a seat in the chair in front of his desk. "I wanted to talk to you without the risk of anyone overhearing."

He looked up at me with a crooked smile. "Well, at least you're talking to me now. I guess that's progress."

I sucked in a deep breath and closed my eyes for a brief second. "Yeah, well, you might not be so happy when you hear what I have to say." I watched his expression as his smile fell away. "I need a favor."

It had been five days since I sprang my unexpected request on Ben, and things were moving along a lot quicker than I'd expected them to. I woke up that morning with a heavy chest as I went about getting ready for work.

It was my birthday. I'd finally made it to twenty-seven. And what did I have to show for it? I was single, my friends were dropping like flies, and I had no relationship with my parents whatsoever. Those facts just made me even more determined to see my plan through.

Happy birthday to me.

It had taken a while, but I finally figured out a way to fix my fucked up life.

I stepped out of the shower, listening hard for a knock on the door. Every year, Emmy would stop by first thing in the morning with a piece of pie and a birthday present. She always wanted to make sure that she was the first person who got to wish me a happy birthday and that hers was the first present I opened.

By the time I was dressed and heading out the door, she still hadn't shown up. I couldn't deny that my heart ached at the fact that she hadn't shown up. I shouldn't have been surprised. Despite Lizzy's and Stacia's incessant pleading, I'd refused to let them throw any sort of party to celebrate. I wasn't in the mood, and there really wasn't anything in my life worth celebrating.

It was just another day.

CHAPTER
twenty-seven

Jeremy

I walked into Virgie May's and took a seat at the counter next to Luke, who was busy reading the paper.

"Morning, Jer," Emmy called from behind the counter. "What can I get for you?"

I looked at Emmy and gave a small smile. "Just a cup of coffee for now, Emmy girl. Thanks."

She sat a mug in front of me and filled it to the top. "How are you doing, honey?" she asked, her voice full of sympathy.

"I'm doing okay, I guess. Did you go by this morning?"

I knew that she would know exactly what I was talking about without having to go into detail.

She lowered her head, refusing to make eye contact, as she began scrubbing the counter. "No, I didn't," she answered quietly.

My stomach dropped a little at her response. A large part of me was still so mad at Savannah that I couldn't see straight, but I hated knowing that she was alone on her birthday. It just didn't seem right. Knowing that Emmy and Savannah weren't on speaking terms didn't sit well with me, but it wasn't like I could say anything to Emmy about it without sounding like a hypocrite.

"I understand," I replied quietly.

Luke had remained silent throughout the entire exchange until that very moment. He let out a humorless snort, and we both turned to look at him. His eyes were still on the paper as he took a sip from his coffee mug.

"Is there something you'd like to say, Mr. Allen? Or are you just going to sit there, making annoying ass noises all damn day?" Emmy asked Luke.

The tension between them was thick enough to let me know that whatever they were currently fighting about wasn't something new.

"You already know what I have to say," Luke replied, never once taking his eyes off the paper.

Emmy reached over, snatched the paper out of his hands, and slapped it down on the countertop. "Why don't you go ahead and share with the rest of the class?"

Luke folded his hands on the counter and shot a sarcastic smile at Emmy. "Fine, if that's what you want, baby girl."

She waved her hand at him, indicating that he should continue. "By all means, go for it."

"All right then. I think both of you are acting ridiculous. You," he said, pointing at me, "are concerned enough about Savannah that you wanted to make sure someone was there this morning to celebrate her birthday with her." He turned to Emmy. "And you are so mad at yourself for not being there for your friend that you can't even look people in the eye when they bring her up. Like I said, ridiculous."

I sat there, stunned speechless at Luke's little rant. *When the hell did that man become so perceptive?*

"Luke, you don't—"

He cut her off with an eye roll. "Know what I'm talking about? I know, I know. You keep saying that over and over again. Doesn't change the fact that you've been miserable ever since you stopped talking to her."

Emmy slammed her hand down in frustration. "What she did—"

Luke cut her off again.

The man was really pushing his luck today. I was certain that interrupting Emmy twice in as many sentences was going to earn him some serious repercussions.

"Wasn't done to you," he replied passionately, causing Emmy to rear back in surprise. "Look"—he turned on the bar stool so that he could address both of us—"I know that what she did was hurtful. I get that. But don't you think the woman has suffered enough? Christ, she's your best friend, Emmy. I see how not talking to her has been eating at you. And, Jeremy, despite what she did, she's still the love of your life."

I opened my mouth to stop him right there, but he wasn't having any of it.

"She was a scared kid. She made a mistake. Trust me, I know *all* about those. But she didn't do it to hurt you, man. It wasn't malicious. Our little group is the only family Savannah has ever had, and she thought she was trying to do right by one of them."

All I could do was sit there and blink, letting Luke continue as he turned back to Emmy.

"Baby, I know you're sensitive about losing Ella, and there isn't a day that goes by where I don't regret not being there for you. But you're a sister to Savannah. The last thing she wanted was to cause you any more pain. You need to get past this. It wasn't done to you, honey. Right or wrong, what she did, she did to spare you."

I saw tears forming in Emmy's eyes as she listened to him speak.

"Jeremy…"

Luke's voice pulled my attention off of Emmy and back to him.

"You have to listen to me when I tell you this. You can't hold on to the past in order to stay angry. All that's gonna do is eat at you until there's nothing left. You have to move on. Forgiveness is tricky, but trust me, it's so worth it in the end."

He reached over and placed a hand on Emmy's, looking at her with a smile full of so much love.

"My mom told me I'd never live a whole life if I didn't have Emmy in it, and she was right. You've gotta ask yourself, will your life ever be whole without Savannah?"

Luke stood and leaned over the counter to plant a kiss on Emmy's lips before leaving for work. Both of us were just silent for a while.

"I think we might have fucked up," Emmy said, breaking the silence.

"Yeah," I replied, feeling my stomach knotting up. "I think we might have."

Savannah

"Savannah?"

I turned around in a daze to find Ben standing at my door.

"You okay? I've been calling your name. Didn't you hear me?"

"Huh?" My brain was foggy, and my energy was shot. "Sorry, I must not have been paying attention."

"Are you feeling okay? You look a little sick."

He wasn't too far off the mark. I wasn't sure if I was coming down with a cold or something, but I definitely wasn't feeling like myself. But I'd be damned if I was going to take a sick day and sit at home, feeling bad for myself.

"I'm fine. Just a little under the weather. I'll be okay."

"You sure?"

"Positive." I tried to give him a reassuring smile.

"Okay. Well, would you mind coming into the conference room? There are some things I'd like to discuss with you."

"Okay," I replied slowly, unsure of what he wanted to talk about.

I stood and followed him into the conference room.

As I walked through the doors, I was greeted by a loud, "SURPRISE!" from all of my coworkers.

On the large mahogany table sat a beautifully decorated two-tiered birthday cake with my name and what appeared to be twenty-seven candles. Surprised didn't begin to cover what I was feeling as everyone began singing "Happy Birthday."

I stood on shaky legs with a fake smile plastered across my face. Being the center of attention was the last thing I wanted in that very moment. I was feeling lightheaded and a little sick to my stomach. All I wanted to do was get back to my desk and work until the day was over, so I could go home and fall into bed. Unfortunately, I wasn't going to get that wish.

"Happy birthday, Savannah," Ben said from somewhere behind me.

I turned my head a little too quickly, and things began to spin. I placed my hands on the back of a chair to try to steady myself. I could feel a cold sweat breaking out on my forehead, and my skin began to feel clammy. Ben was right there to catch me just as my knees went out from under me.

"Savannah? Savannah!" he called frantically.

I could hear him. I just couldn't force my mouth to open and respond. My vision blurred, and the edges started to grow black, darkness creeping closer and closer to the center.

From a distance, I heard an echoed voice calling out for someone to call 911 just before the darkness closed in around me completely, swallowing up anything and everything until there was nothing left.

When I finally awoke, I was lying in a tiny bed in an unfamiliar room. I tried to sit up, but the movement caused my head to pound and my stomach to instantly revolt. I lifted my right hand to touch my forehead, and I felt something catch. When I looked down, I saw an IV needle taped to the top of my hand.

I'm in a hospital?

"You shouldn't be sitting up."

My gaze darted from my hand over to the door where Ben was walking through.

"How did I get here? What happened?"

He walked over to the uncomfortable looking chair sitting next to the hospital bed, and he took a seat, placing an ankle on the opposite knee. "You got here in the back of an ambulance, and what happened was you passed out in the middle of the conference room. You scared the living shit out of us, Savannah."

I vaguely recalled the moment right before everything had gone black. There had been singing and cake.

"I didn't even get a piece of cake." I pouted, remembering how amazing the cake looked. At that image, my stomach let out a loud growl that echoed through the sterile room and my cheeks heated with embarrassment.

"Don't worry. No one got any. You passed out before we even had a chance to cut it. People hadn't even finished singing 'Happy Birthday' before you hit the floor."

My eyes widened. "I hit the floor?" I screeched.

One corner of his mouth quirked up. "Nah, I caught you before you face planted."

I sat back with a huff and narrowed my eyes. "And people say chivalry is dead. You're such a gentleman."

"I do try," he replied.

I laid my head back and rubbed my tired eyes.

"You really scared the hell out of us, Savannah," Ben said softly.

Before I had a chance to respond, the doctor walked into the room. She was a pretty woman in her mid- to late-fifties, if I had to guess. She had her chestnut colored hair with just a hint of gray throughout cut into a sleek bob. "Good afternoon, Ms. Morgan. I'm Dr. Abernathy. Glad to see you're awake. How are you feeling?"

"Um…I'm a little tired, and I have a wicked headache, but other than that, I feel fine. Can you tell me what happened?"

"Ms. Morgan—" she started.

I cut her off. "Savannah, please."

"All right, Savannah. When was the last time you had a proper meal?"

I looked up at the ceiling in concentration. "Uh…I'm not really sure."

"Well, you came in severely dehydrated, underweight, and if I had to guess, completely exhausted. Your body hasn't been getting what it needs in order to function properly, and it seems it reached its limit today."

I rolled my eyes at Ben when he shot me a disapproving look from his chair.

"That's just great. I'm being hospitalized for exhaustion. I'm like a bad celebrity statistic, only without the fame."

"This could have been much worse," Dr. Abernathy continued. "I've hooked you up to an IV that will give you all the nutrients your body needs, and I'm going to go ahead and keep you overnight until your levels are regulated."

"Is that really necessary?" I whined. Yes, I whined. I wasn't happy about that, but I hated hospitals with a passion.

"Yes, it is," Ben interrupted. "You haven't been taking proper care of yourself, so you need to stay until you're better."

I wanted to reach over and smack the knowing look right off of his stupid face.

CHAPTER
twenty-eight

"Savannah? Savannah!"

The doctor, Ben, and I heard a voice calling out my name from the hallway seconds before the door to my room burst open.

Luke stormed in and came right up to my bed before wrapping his arms around me tightly. "Are you okay? Jesus Christ, you scared the shit outta me!"

He was squeezing so tightly that I felt like my lungs were deflating.

"Can't. Breathe," I wheezed out.

"Fuck, I'm sorry." Luke stood and looked around the room frantically, his eyes bouncing between Ben and the doctor. "What happened? Is she going to be okay?" he demanded in an authoritative voice.

"I'm fine, Luke. What are you doing here?"

"I heard the call come through, and I got here as soon as I could. You passed out?"

Dr. Abernathy stepped in to explain the situation to Luke. Ben gave me a what-the-hell look and cut his eyes to Luke. All I could do was shrug my shoulders in confusion. I was flabbergasted that Luke was here.

After the doctor finished explaining to Luke that everything was fine and that they were just keeping me overnight to be on the safe side, she went to go check on her other patients, leaving me alone with Ben and Luke.

Ben cleared his throat uncomfortably and stood from the chair. "I think I'll go get another cup of god awful coffee, so you two can talk."

He headed out the door as Luke took the seat Ben had just vacated.

"What are you doing here, Luke?" I asked once we were alone.

"I told you. I heard the call come in. You really think I *wouldn't* show up?"

"But Emmy will be—"

He held up his hand to stop me. "Emmy will just have to deal with it. Just because the two of you aren't seeing eye-to-eye at the moment doesn't mean that you're any less of a friend to the rest of us. Besides, you don't need to worry about that right now. You need to concentrate on getting better."

There was no stopping the tears welling up in my eyes. His sincerity was too much for me to handle, and before I knew it, I was bawling like a damn baby in front of him.

The discomfort on his face would have been hilarious if I wasn't such an emotional wreck already.

"Come on now, killer, don't cry." He gave me an awkward pat on the back. "The doc said you were dehydrated. Can't have you cryin' all your fluids out."

I let out a deep belly laugh at that. "I don't think that's how it works."

"Well, better safe than sorry."

I got my laughter under control and wiped the tears from my eyes. "It means a lot to me that you're here, Luke. I know we haven't always gotten along, but—"

He reached over and grabbed my hand. "That's in the past, Savvy. No need to get all mushy on me now."

I slugged him on the shoulder and gave him a small smile. "Yeah, well, you know what I mean."

He gave the hand he was holding a reassuring squeeze. "Yeah, I do. You know it can only get better from here, right?"

I did know that, but I couldn't tell him why it was going to get better. I was too exhausted for that conversation.

"I know you're tired. I'll leave to let you get some rest. I just wanted to make sure you were okay."

"I will be," I replied as he walked toward the door. "Oh, Luke?"

He looked over his shoulder. "Yeah?"

"Can you keep me being in the hospital just between us?"

"Don't worry about it, killer. I won't tell everyone."

"Thanks, Luke."

"Anytime." And with that, he was gone.

Jeremy

Luke called early in the morning, asking me to meet him at his and Emmy's house when I was finished at the garage.

By the time I pulled up, the sun had already gone down, and both of their cars were in the driveway. I walked up the stairs to their front porch and through the door, not bothering to knock. None of us ever knocked. We either had a key, or the door would be unlocked.

"Anybody home?" I called out, stepping into the foyer.

Walking in on Emmy and Luke was a running joke with our group of friends. Ever since they had gotten back together, those two couldn't be bothered with making it to their bedroom most evenings before ripping off each other's clothes. Every one of us had walked in on them at some stage of undress at least once. I would think they'd learn to lock the damn door.

"Everyone decent?" I hollered out as I turned toward the living room.

Luke was sitting on the couch next to Emmy with his arm around her shoulders. Her head was bent, and her body was shaking. She sniffled, and I suddenly knew she was crying.

My stomach dropped, and my heart lodged in my throat. "What happened?" I croaked. My mouth went dry as the Sahara.

Emmy kept her eyes down and shook her head.

I walked the rest of the way into the living room and met Luke's eyes.

"Savannah was hospitalized today," he said in a quiet voice.

My knees gave out, and I collapsed back onto the club chair that was thankfully behind me. "What?"

"She's gonna be fine. I went and saw her today. The doc said she was severely dehydrated, and hadn't been eating right. Apparently, she collapsed at work, and they had to call an ambulance. That was the only reason I knew what was going on. I was at the station when the call came in."

It took several seconds for me to catch my breath enough for me to talk. "Why didn't she call anybody?" I finally asked.

The only think I could picture was Savannah lying in a hospital bed, all alone. I knew how much she hated hospitals. The thought of her being there with no one by her side was like a punch straight to the chest.

"She made me promise not to tell, but I kinda found a loophole around that. I said I wouldn't tell *everyone*. I might have left out that I intended to tell the two of you."

I ran my hands through my hair and rested my elbows on my knees. "Jesus," I whispered.

"She looks bad, man. I don't know how much weight she's lost since the last time I saw her, but I'm telling you, it's too much. The girl looks like she hasn't eaten in forever."

Emmy choked on a sob, and Luke turned back to soothingly run a hand over her hair.

"But she's gonna be okay?" I asked, swallowing back a sob of my own.

"Yeah, she's going to be fine," Luke replied. "The doctor wanted to keep her overnight for observation, but she's okay. She's got an IV in, and they're pumping her full of fluids, but she'll get out tomorrow."

At that, Emmy finally said, "God, I've been such a bitch to her. She didn't deserve any of it. I'm a horrible friend."

I was feeling the same way about myself. Yeah, Savannah had messed up and hurt me in the process, but did she really deserve to be treated as horribly as I'd been treating her? I would never forgive myself if something happened to her before I had a chance to make things right. I was a fucking idiot.

I stood as fast as I could and headed to the door. "I have to see her," I said to no one in particular.

Emmy was on her feet the instant I spoke. "Me too. I'm going with you."

She reached for her purse just as Luke caught up.

"Slow down, baby girl," he told her. "I think it's best if Jeremy goes on his own. Why don't you give him time to say what he needs to say? Then, you can go see her tomorrow."

I could have kissed him for that. I understood that Emmy needed to talk to her also, but I needed to speak to Savannah without the risk of any interruptions. I didn't wait for a response from Emmy. I simply pulled the door open and hauled ass to Savannah as fast as I could.

*S*avannah

"Excuse me, sir," a voice said from the hallway. "Visiting hours are over."

The commotion in the hallway had pulled me from my sleep. I was still in a daze when I heard a voice that sounded a lot like Jeremy's.

"I have to go in there. I need to see her."

I closed my eyes, and I was beginning to doze again, convinced I was just hearing things. Then, the door burst open, and I opened my eyes to see Jeremy standing there.

"Jeremy?"

His face morphed from what looked like determination to uncertainty. "Hey," he mumbled, taking a step into the room.

A nurse came rushing in behind him. "Sir, you can't be here," she insisted.

I held up my hand to let her know that everything was all right. "It's okay. Can you just let him stay for a bit?"

Her eyes bounced between me and Jeremy before she let out an aggravated sigh and threw her hands up in resignation. "Fine, but only for a few minutes."

She left, pulling the door closed behind her.

Jeremy made his way to the chair next to my bed and sat down. "What's up with Nurse Ratched?"

I didn't bother responding to his insult of the nurse who had just been doing her job. "Luke told you, didn't he? Jeez, that man is worse than a bunch of gossipy old ladies."

Jeremy chuckled and rubbed the back of his neck. "In his defense, he only promised you that he wouldn't tell *everyone*."

I could just imagine Luke saying something like that. "Got to love his logic, I guess. I didn't think he had it in him to be so clever."

"I was pretty surprised myself."

When his eyes came up and met mine, I wasn't able to maintain contact. Looking down at my hands, I began chewing on my bottom lip.

"That doesn't really explain why you're here," I said to Jeremy.

He reached over the bed railing and placed his hand under my chin, forcing me to meet his eyes. "Did you really think I wouldn't come once I heard what happened?" he asked seriously.

I gave him an awkward smile and shrugged a shoulder. "Honestly? I wasn't sure. You weren't even supposed to know I was in here."

Jeremy pulled the chair closer to the bed and rested his forearms across the rail. "I'm glad Luke told me. And I never want you to doubt that I'll be there for you if you ever need me."

I was so tired of crying. I'd never been that girl who tears up at the drop of a hat, but for the past several weeks, it seemed like that was all I'd been doing. To my dismay, I found myself choked up again. I turned my head away and brushed at the tears staining my cheeks.

"I thought you hated me," I whispered pathetically.

God, who is this woman I've become? I couldn't even recognize myself when I looked in the mirror most mornings. I was growing to hate the reflection staring back at me.

"Sugar, please look at me."

The sorrow in his voice mixed with his nickname for me did me in. The dam burst, and the tears ran down freely.

"Please don't think that. I could never hate you. I was hurt, but I could never hate you." He reached up and brushed a tear away with his thumb. "I still love you, Savvy, always will."

No.

No, no, no, no.

I couldn't hear that. I couldn't handle Jeremy telling me he loved me. I wasn't strong enough. I shook my head frantically. "Jeremy, don't. Please don't say that."

He placed his hands on my cheeks, stopping my head from shaking. "It's true, Savannah. I still love you. I'm still *in love* with you. When Luke told me you were in the hospital, my whole world crashed. All I could think was that I needed to make things right between us, that I couldn't lose you—"

"Jeremy, stop," I demanded.

His sure demeanor faltered the second I spoke.

"I can't do this. I just can't," I pleaded.

I tried pushing away from him, but Jeremy grabbed hold of my hands and wouldn't let go.

"Savannah, we can make this work. I still love you, and you still love me. I know you do."

"No," I said in the strongest voice I could summon up. "It can't work, Jer. Don't you see that? We've tried so many times now, and all we manage to do is hurt each other. Besides, aren't you back together with Charlotte?"

That question gave him pause. "No, I'm not back with Charlotte. It was just that one night, just a stupid, drunken mistake. If I could take it back, I would. I never wanted you to see that."

I let out a sarcastic laugh. "That's exactly what I'm talking about. We keep hurting each other, even when we don't mean to. Our entire relationship was based on mistakes and regrets. People can't function like that, Jeremy. We're toxic."

He stood from the chair so quickly that it went flying into the wall behind it. "We are *not* toxic, Savannah. We made mistakes. Everyone does. There were secrets in our past, but that's all out in the open now. If we try this and are completely honest with each other, we can make this work."

I couldn't listen to him anymore. "I'm leaving, Jeremy," I spit out before he could continue his rant.

"I know. Luke told me they're releasing you tomorrow. Let me pick you up. I'll take you home and we can talk about this."

"No. I mean, I'm leaving Cloverleaf."

Jeremy froze solid for several seconds before looking straight in my eyes. "What?"

"I'm moving. I can't stay here anymore."

I could practically see his sense of calm snap as anger overtook him.

"So...what? Things get a little difficult, and you're just gonna bail out? That's bullshit, Savannah!"

"It's not bullshit!" I screamed. I squeezed my eyes closed and clenched my hands into tight fists, trying to will myself to calm down. "All my life, I've made every one of my decisions based on what's best for other people. That's obviously done nothing but cause problems for everyone around me. I have to do this for me. For the first time in as long as I can remember, I'm making a decision based on what's in my best interest. I hate how my life has been going and who I've become. This is the only thing I can think to do to get back to being that person I actually respect. Because I have to tell you, looking in the mirror has been pretty damn hard lately."

Jeremy moved to sit on the edge, grabbing my hands in his. I could feel his hands shaking just slightly as he squeezed like his life depended on it.

"Savvy, you don't have to do this. You don't have to leave Cloverleaf."

I pulled my hands out of his and folded them loosely in my lap. "It's already done. Ben got in touch with a few of his friends from Austin. I already got a job up there." I tried to smile to let him know that it would all be okay, but I knew it didn't meet my eyes. "My house is already on the market. I'm leaving Sunday."

He stood from the bed and staggered back. Complete shock covered all of his features. "Sunday?"

I couldn't talk, so I just nodded.

"I...you can't...please, Savvy." His eyes grew red as tears welled up. "Please," he whispered.

That one word broke me as he spoke it.

"This is for the best, Jeremy, for both of us. I promise, it might not seem like it right now, but you'll see that this is what we both need. I can't make you happy, not the way you deserve to be. And with me gone, you'll be able to find someone who deserves you." I let out a shuddering breath before I finished. "I never deserved you."

He shook his head and turned to the door. Just as he pulled it open, he looked at me over his shoulder. "You're wrong, sugar. You always deserved me."

CHAPTER
twenty-nine

Jeremy

I spent the entire night trying to come up with ways to convince Savannah that staying was the right choice. But sometime around two in the morning, I finally realized that she was right. She'd spent years trying to please everyone around her. Trying to convince her to stay would be selfish. If leaving is what she needed so that she could feel like herself again, then I needed to learn to be okay with that, no matter how hard it was going to be to lose her.

I woke up and went about my morning in a complete daze. I never stopped to think that there would be a day when I didn't see her even if it was just at a distance. I always assumed that she'd be in Cloverleaf if I ever needed to see her. Knowing she wouldn't be here left a hole in my chest that I was afraid I'd never be able to fill.

My depressing cloud had only gotten darker by the time I made it to the garage that morning. Things were slow, and my guys had everything under control, so I decided to work on the GTO while I had the time.

As I worked on the engine, flashes of my relationship with Savannah played on a constant loop in my head until it finally became too much. Sorrow and anger completely engulfed me. I needed an outlet. Picking up a wrench, I let the weight of the cold metal settle in my hand before I pulled my arm back and let it fly right through the driver side window of the GTO.

It was almost ironic really. My relationship with the only woman I'd ever loved had been destroyed, and now I was destroying my dream car. I grabbed a tire iron off of the tool bench and began to beat the ever-living hell out of the car I'd been working years to restore.

There was no telling how long I had been at it by the time I exhausted myself. Sweat had broken out on my forehead, and I was out of breath from the exertion. Every window and light had been smashed. The driver side door was covered in dents. I dropped the tire iron on the ground with a loud clang and turned to find Luke standing there with his arms crossed over his chest.

"You feel any better?" he asked.

I walked to the mini fridge to get a bottle of water. I downed half of it in just a few gulps. "Maybe a little," I conceded once I'd caught my breath.

"Well, I hope so. You just bashed the hell out of a fine-ass car. Shit like that should just be illegal."

I grabbed a towel and wiped at the sweat on my brow. "You here to give me a hard time? Or do you actually have a reason for interrupting me at work?"

Luke quirked a brow and looked back at the GTO. "This is working? Remind me never to bring my truck in for an oil change."

I started for the office. "Feel free to show yourself out."

I should have known better than to think he'd actually leave. Luke followed me into my office and took a seat, assuming his typical position with his hands crossed behind his head and his feet kicked up on my desk.

"I thought I should stop by this morning and check on you, see how things went between you and Savannah last night."

"Nothing really to tell," I said, falling back in my chair. "I showed up, tried to get her to take me back, and then I left after she informed me that she's moving to Austin."

Luke dropped his feet off the desk and sat up straight. "Uh...what?"

"You heard me."

I yanked open my bottom desk drawer and pulled out the bottle of bourbon I kept in there. I held it up to see if Luke wanted any. He nodded his head, so I grabbed two shot glasses and proceeded to pour. We downed the shots and I refilled both without even asking.

After we each finished our second shot, Luke asked, "You're serious? She's really leaving?"

"Yeah. She's moving Sunday." I said *Sunday* like it was the most disgusting word I'd ever heard.

"Holy shit. No wonder you beat the hell out of the GTO."

"Yep."

He uncomfortably ran a hand through his hair. "I don't know what to say, Jeremy. I'm really sorry."

I was too.

*S*avannah

"I'm still mad at you," a teary-eyed Stacia informed me.

We watched as Luke, Gavin, Brett, and Trevor loaded the last of my boxes into the U-Haul truck I was going to drive to Austin in a matter of minutes.

I wrapped my arms around her and hugged her tightly, feeling a little teary eyed myself. "I told you that nothing's going to change. I'll be back for your wedding in just a few short months. I'm only going to be a couple hours away. We'll still see each other, I promise."

She let out a small sniffle and pulled back slightly. "Yeah, but it won't be the same. You won't be here whenever I need a break from Gavin because he's driving me to contemplate manslaughter."

"Love you too, babe!" Gavin hollered from over by the moving truck.

I ran a hand over her hair and gave her a smile. "You still have Emmy's, Lizzy's, and Mickey's places to escape to whenever you need it. And, anytime you want, you're always welcome to come visit me in Austin for a weekend."

I looked between Stacia, Mickey, and Lizzy, and I felt myself getting choked up. Emmy had apparently shown up at the hospital after I was released, but I still hadn't heard anything from her.

"I'm going to miss you guys so much." I turned and looked at my house—or what was soon to be my old house. "I'm going to miss this place too."

The four of us hugged and sniveled like teenagers as the guys packed the last box away. The latch closed on the trailer with a resounding click before the guys made their way over to us.

Brett wrapped an arm around my shoulder and pulled me in for a side hug. "It's not like you won't be back in a few days for your car. You aren't moving across the country, babe."

I laughed and gave him a playful shove. Then, I turned just in time to see Lizzy completely lose it.

"It's not going to be the same without you," she cried.

Trevor walked up to her and wrapped her in his arms. "It's okay, cher. You've still got me."

She looked up at him with narrowed eyes. "That doesn't help at all," she insisted, earning a laugh from all of us.

I still had my fingers crossed for those two.

Just as I was preparing myself to walk away from everything and everyone I loved, a car came screeching down the street and into my driveway. Seconds later, Emmy jumped from her little Civic and ran at me full speed, barreling into me and wrapping me in a bone-crushing hug. We stood that way for several seconds with her face buried in my neck, tears drenching my white cable knit sweater.

"I'm going to miss you so damn much," she whispered into my hair before finally pulling away and wiping her tears. "But I'm behind you a hundred percent if this is what you need."

I smiled and looked at my oldest friend through blurry eyes. "I'm going to miss you too, Em, more than you'll ever know."

She graced me with a sincere smile, a smile I'd missed so much over the past several weeks. "Are you sure this is what you need?" she asked.

I shrugged my shoulders and answered honestly, "There's only one way to find out."

Luke walked up to us and pulled Emmy against his side. "You know, I really should ticket you for driving like that, baby girl."

"Ticket me, and you're sleeping on the couch for the rest of your life."

We all hugged and cried a little more until it was finally time for me to go. I walked as slowly as possible, keeping an eye on the road the whole time. I couldn't deny that there was a huge part of me that hoped Jeremy would show up to say good-bye. But he never did, and I'd dragged my good-byes out long enough.

With a heavy heart, I climbed into the truck and started the journey to my new life. All I could do was pray that I'd made the right decision this time.

Jeremy

I stepped out of the deli and onto the sidewalk, and the first thing I noticed was Ben walking in my direction. His head was down as he typed away on his phone, so he hadn't noticed me yet. Rage boiled through my bloodstream at the sight of him. That was the man who had helped Savannah leave Cloverleaf, who had helped her leave me. I wanted to rip his pretty boy throat out.

215

I stood in silence until he was just a few feet away from me. "Hey, asshole."

His head shot up, and his eyes narrowed when they met mine. "I'm sorry, I know you can't be talking to me," he replied sarcastically.

"You sure about that?"

He slid his thumb across the screen of his phone and slid it into the back pocket of his sure-to-be designer jeans. "I hope you'd be smarter than to call other people assholes. Kind of hypocritical, don't you think?"

I took a step closer to him. "How the fuck could you help her leave?" I asked, grinding my teeth so hard they hurt. "You were supposed to be her friend!"

He gave me a shove before burrowing his finger in my chest. "I *am* her friend, you son of a bitch!"

"Then, why did you convince her to leave?" I all but yelled.

His eyes widened in shock. "Is that what you think I did?" A sarcastic laugh bubbled up from his throat. "Man, you really are a deluded fuck, aren't you? I didn't convince her to do anything. You should know her better than that."

I couldn't deny his point on that one.

"As a matter of fact, I tried to talk her out of it, but she was adamant that this is what she wanted, so I helped her. Because I'm. Her. Friend."

I'd officially run out of steam on my anger.

"And you might want to check who you call an asshole. You're the one standing here while your girl's packing up her whole life to move to a different city at any minute." He turned and began to walk away but not before delivering one last parting shot. "Looks like you're the one who's the asshole, if you ask me." Then he was gone.

He was right, and that just pissed me off all the more. But this time, that anger was directed to a completely different target. It was directed at me.

CHAPTER
thirty

Three Months Later

Life wasn't exactly as I'd expected it to be. I'd hoped that I would find a way to be happy again and move past the horrible decisions I'd made, and to some extent, I had. I was able to look at myself in the mirror without feeling enormous resentment toward the person looking back at me, but there was still one problem, and it was a huge one. I was terribly lonely. I missed my family.

Work was going well, and I'd managed to make a few friends during my time there, but it wasn't the same. A few men had shown interest, but I had no desire whatsoever to date anyone. I wasn't sure how long it would take me to get over Jeremy—or if I was even capable of doing that. One thing was for sure though—three months was *not* enough time.

I had to admit that I was excited to be going home for Stacia and Gavin's wedding. I missed everyone tremendously. Between wedding plans, work, and life in general, none of us had really had the chance to make a trip to visit. There were phone calls and Skype, but it wasn't the same. I'd even spoken to Emmy quite a few times. Things were still a little strained, but we were getting there, and I was thankful for that. Other than a few inane text messages and emails, I hadn't really talked to Jeremy. We would discuss things like how our days had gone or what the weather was like, but that was about it. Every interaction left me craving something more substantial, but I had no clue how to get us there. I missed him like I was missing a part of myself.

That night was the rehearsal dinner for Gavin and Stacia, and I had just finished packing when my cell phone rang.

"Hello, Lizzy…for the third time today," I answered.

"Are you on the road yet?"

I laughed at her asking the same question she'd asked each time she called. "I would be if you'd stop calling and let me finish packing already."

"God, you're slow," she grumbled pathetically. "Will you please get a move on? Trevor is driving me insane. The guy has stopped by my damn house every single day since you left to, as he puts it, check up on me, which in Trevor-speak just means trying to cop a feel and see if he can get lucky."

I let out a laugh as I grabbed my rolling suitcase and the garment bag containing my bridesmaid dress. "Well, has he?"

"Has he what?" she asked.

"Has he gotten lucky?" I could almost picture her eyes rolling from over the phone.

"*Pfft*, he wishes. The man's slept with every vagina that has crossed his path. I wouldn't touch that with a ten foot pole."

I was willing to put money on her changing her tune eventually, but I kept that to myself.

She changed the direction of our conversation and asked again, "So when are you leaving?"

It was my turn to roll my eyes. "I'm walking out the door now. You sure it's cool if I stay with you?"

"Of course. If you even think about getting a hotel room while you're here, I'll track you down and beat you bloody."

"All right, all right. I'm on my way. I'm excited to finally see everybody."

Lizzy let out a small giggle. "By everybody, you mean Jeremy, right?"

"I mean everybody," I replied.

She got quiet for a few seconds. "You know you don't have to put on a brave face around me, right? You can be honest."

I paused at the front door and rested my head against it. "I know I can, Liz. It's just hard. I miss him so much every damn day. You'd think it would eventually get easier."

"I don't know what to tell you, babe. Maybe things will be a little clearer after this weekend."

God, I really hope so.

I pulled up to Lizzy's house and barely had the chance to get out of my car before Emmy, Mickey, Stacia, and Lizzy came running from the house and up to my car. They were all jerking me into hugs and talking a mile a minute so that I wasn't able to make out anything anyone was saying.

I stepped out of the fray and held my hands up to stop them. "Just slow down. I can't hear what any of you are saying."

None of them missed a beat as they yelled out choruses of, "We missed you," and, "I'm so glad you're home."

I felt the love I hadn't felt since the moment I drove away from Cloverleaf. It felt amazing to be back.

Lizzy and Mickey grabbed my bags to take them inside with Stacia following closely behind them.

Emmy held me back, asking if she could have a minute to talk. As soon as we were alone, she wrapped me in another hug. "God, Savvy, I've missed you so much."

"I've missed you too," I replied, giving her back a pat before pulling away.

"No, I mean, I've missed you. I've missed my best friend. I know things haven't been the same between us, but I just needed you to know that. I've missed you like crazy, and I'd give anything for things to go back to the way they used to be. I need my best friend back. Just tell me what I need to do to make things right again."

I gave her a watery smile. "You just did it. I've missed my best friend too."

"Oh, thank God," she said with a sigh of relief. "Because I need a maid of honor."

My jaw dropped to the ground. Then, my eyes shot down to the beautiful round-cut solitaire adorning her left ring finger. "Oh my God!" I exclaimed, grabbing her hand to examine it closely. "Are you kidding me? Why is this the first I'm hearing of a proposal?"

She was smiling so brightly that my heart couldn't have been filled with any more happiness for her.

"I wanted to tell you in person. Well, I actually wanted to ask you to be my maid of honor in person. I hated the idea of asking you over the phone."

I shook my head, trying to dispel some of my shock. "Yes! Of course I'll be your maid of honor!"

We went back to the whole hugging and crying thing like we were back in high school.

"So when did this happen?"

The happiness was still evident on her face, but something else was there, something I wasn't sure I recognized.

"It was only a week ago. It kind of...came unexpectedly, you could say."

"Well, I hope he didn't spoil the surprise of proposing to you," I replied.

"No, I mean, we weren't really planning on getting engaged just yet."

"Really? What changed?" The minute the question left my mouth, it hit me. Considering the unexpected engagement, I suddenly understood what the strange look on her face was. It was fear. "Holy shit, Emmy. You're pregnant, aren't you?"

A smile spread on her face so wide that it made my own cheeks hurt.

She began to nod her head frantically. "Yeah."

Standing in the middle of Lizzy's driveway, I let out an excited squeal and grabbed a hold of her, jumping up and down with my arms around her. "Oh my God! I can't believe it! This is so fantastic."

I pulled away, holding her at arm's length, so I could look her up and down, just in case there was any way I could notice a little baby bump. Of course, I couldn't. Her stomach was still as flat as always, but I just couldn't help myself.

"I'm so happy for you, Emmy."

That fear crept back into her eyes. "I'm scared, Savvy. What if…" She couldn't even bring herself to finish the sentence.

"Don't think like that, Emmy. This is going to be fine, just focus on that. This baby is going to be a blessing," I told her, placing my hands on her flat stomach and smiling reassuringly. "This one is going to be different. I can feel it."

"You think so?"

I placed my hands on her cheeks and gave a confident nod. "I know so. This is a good thing, babe, a very good thing."

Stacia opened the door and hollered out for us to get our asses inside. I turned to head that way when Emmy grabbed my arm and stopped me.

"No one else knows about this right now. Luke and I kind of want to keep it under wraps until we're in the clear, you know?"

The fact that she'd told me before anyone else showed me exactly how close we were to getting back to the way we used to be.

"Of course. My lips are sealed. And when I promise you that I won't tell everybody, I don't mean that in a Luke Allen sort of way. I mean I promise not to tell *any*body."

We both laughed as we made our way into the house.

Lizzy had been right. Maybe this weekend back in Cloverleaf was what I needed to figure everything out.

CHAPTER
thirty-one

With a few hours to kill before the wedding rehearsal, the girls and I decided on getting manicures and pedicures. The pale pink I'd chosen was going to look great with the pastel yellow of the bridesmaid dresses. I was sitting in the massaging pedicure chair with my head back and eyes closed, feeling more relaxed than I had in months. I was seconds from dozing off when I felt a jab in my side.

"Savvy, wake up."

My eyes popped open, and I glanced over to see Emmy looking in the direction of the door with narrowed eyes and a clenched jaw. When I turned to see what could possibly have her so pissed off, everything in my body froze. My mother was standing at the front counter of the spa with a couple of her country club cronies in tow. She'd spotted me before I saw her, and just stood there staring.

"You want me to toss the bitch out on her ass? I'll totally do it," Emmy whispered in my ear.

I looked at her and smiled without any apprehension. My parents had stopped having an effect on me the moment I'd stopped allowing them to have a hold on me.

"Nah, I'm good. Just let her and her band of bitches get their Botox or whatever it is they're here for." I closed my eyes again and rested my head back against the chair.

"Uh…Savvy? I don't think ignoring her is going to work."

"And why's that?"

Emmy wasn't the one who answered.

"Hello, Savannah."

I opened one eye. I was sure my ears were playing tricks on me. It wasn't that I was surprised that she'd addressed me in public because that was what a classy Southern woman did. She couldn't let her friends know that she and her daughter were estranged. It was what I'd heard in her voice that confused me the most. She sounded nervous, which was something that I wasn't used to at all. She'd always sounded so sure of herself. I didn't even know that she was capable of feeling anything other than superiority.

"Mother," I responded skeptically, waiting to see what she had up her sleeve.

She looked around at my friends, who were eyeing her like they were waiting for her to strike. I'd eventually told them what had happened that night at the country club, and needless to say, they hadn't taken it well.

"You look lovely. Austin must be good for you."

I looked at my friends with wide eyes, each of them shrugging their shoulders as if they were having just as much trouble as I was figuring her out.

"Um...I wasn't aware you knew about the move."

She bit her bottom lip, and then looked down and began to wring her hands in front of her. For the first time, it hit me just how similar our mannerisms were when we were both nervous.

"Yes, well..." She cleared her throat before finally looking back up and meeting my eyes. "I've been kind of keeping up with what's been going on in your life."

I looked at her in astonishment. "You have?"

She gave a slight nod and a small smile. "I have. Look, Savannah, I know that you're busy, but do you think you'd have the time to join me for a cup of coffee? I won't keep you too long. I know the rehearsal is tonight."

She does?

I looked over at Stacia to make sure she was okay with me leaving for a bit. She smiled at me reassuringly and nodded.

"Yeah, okay," I said, turning back to my mother. "I can meet you at Virgie May's in about half an hour, if that works for you." I wasn't sure if she'd ever even been to Emmy's diner, but if I was going to deal with my mother, I wanted to be somewhere comfortable.

"That's perfect. I'll see you there." She turned to walk away but then paused. "And congratulations on the wedding, Stacia. I'm sure you'll be a beautiful bride."

With that, she walked away, leaving me and my friends in shock.

We finished up at the spa, and I headed over to the diner after convincing Emmy that I didn't need her to come with me as backup. When I walked in, I spotted my mother sitting in a high backed booth over by the front window with a cup of coffee and a slice of apple pie in front of her. I'd never in my life seen my mother consume anything with carbohydrates and sugar.

I walked over to the table and took a seat across from her. "Hi," I said when she looked up.

"Hello, darling. Would you like something to eat? The pie here is simply to die for."

I coughed to cover up the laugh that came out. "I know, Mom. This is Emmy's place. The food here is pretty amazing."

Her eyes widened in surprise. "Really? Well, she certainly has an amazing place here. I'm a little disappointed that I've never been in here before now."

I couldn't hold back the snide comment that wanted to come out. "I'm not surprised. You were always above anything having to do with my white trash, redneck friends," I spit out, throwing her words back in her face.

She placed her fork down on the plate and pushed it to the side. She clasped her hands together and placed them on the table. "I deserved that," she admitted.

Um…what?

She let out an exhausted sigh and continued, "I've been a horrible mother to you, and I don't know if I can ever earn your forgiveness for the things I did in the past. But I *can* try to

225

make things right now." Her eyes brimmed with tears as she spoke.

I was completely overwhelmed by her words. I'd waited my whole life for my mother to show me that she loved me. Sitting with her now, having the conversation I'd longed to have for years, was almost too much for me to handle.

She reached across the table and took my hands in hers. "I'm not going to make excuses for how I treated you. I was unhappy with my life, and I took it out on you. When I think about all of the awful things I said to you…"

Seeing her choke up and watching the tears fall down her cheeks put a major crack in the walls I'd worked so hard to put up to protect myself from my parents. I turned my hands over in hers and entwined our fingers.

"I left your father, Savannah."

She couldn't have shocked me more if she'd stripped naked and streaked down Main Street.

"What?"

"After you walked out of that dinner, I couldn't stop thinking of everything you said to those men. It made me stop and take a good long look at myself. Sweetie, you have no idea how awful it is to hate who's looking back at you in the mirror."

"You'd be surprised at just how much I can relate," I mumbled.

"You see? That's what I'm talking about right here. If I'd been the mother you needed, you wouldn't have ever reached the point where you didn't like yourself. It's my fault. I allowed your father to make me miserable for so many years. I was blinded by stupid materialistic things. None of that matters. You're my daughter, and I don't give a damn about any of that if I don't have you in my life."

I didn't know what to say. I wasn't even sure if I could speak. I felt like the wind had just been knocked out of me.

"Mom," I choked out on a sob. I was so thankful to hear her say those things. I hadn't even realized just how much I needed to hear those words until she'd said them.

"I went to your house, but you'd already left. That boyfriend of yours was there, and believe me, he had some pretty harsh words for me."

"Wait—what boyfriend?"

"Jeremy—you know, the boy you've dated since you were a child."

"Mom, Jeremy and I aren't together."

She gave me a knowing grin and asked, "Are you sure about that?"

"I'm absolutely positive. Things didn't end well between us. That was one of the reasons why I moved."

"Well, for someone who's not your boyfriend, he sure is protective of you. For a good five minutes, he laid into me about how I'd failed as a mother and let you down when I should have been protecting you." A tear escaped and ran down her cheek before she lowered her head and wiped it away with a napkin. "He told me about the abortion and why you felt you couldn't be a mother"

I was stunned speechless, but she wasn't finished. I take full blame for the decision you made, Savannah. If you'd grown up in a loving household, you never would have questioned your ability to be a mother."

"Mom, you can't blame yourself—"

"I can and I will," she interrupted. "You listen to me. You are going to be a fantastic mother." Her voice was so full of certainty. "I know this for a fact because I see how much love you have for those around you. Any child would be lucky to call you Mother, and any man blessed to have you."

Who is this woman? The surprises just kept on coming with every word she spoke.

"If you ask me, that Jeremy boy loves you more than life itself. He told me that if I hurt you again, he'd spend the rest of his life making sure I felt the same pain I'd caused you. Then, he slammed the door in my face. It wasn't the easiest lecture call to receive, but if that's the kind of passion he has for you, I have to tell you, I totally approve."

I couldn't believe what I was hearing. "I don't understand. What was he doing at the house?"

"I don't know, honey. He didn't really let me get a word in, so I didn't have the chance to ask."

The whole conversation with my mother was completely surreal. I never thought I'd be sitting where I was right then, the two of us pouring our hearts out to each other, but I was so glad that we were able to get to that place even if it had taken all those years.

I stayed at the diner for as long as I could, catching up and bonding with my mother, before I had to leave to get ready for the rehearsal. We parted with tight hugs and promises to stay in touch.

Things were finally starting to look up. I had my best friend back, and I'd gotten to a place with my mom where I'd never thought I would be. Two large weights had been lifted off my chest. I just wasn't sure I could do anything to ease the weight of the one that remained.

CHAPTER
thirty-two

Jeremy

"You ready for this?" Luke asked as we walked into the venue where the wedding was going to take place.

"I've been ready for this from the moment she moved away," I replied with a confidence I certainly wasn't feeling.

"Then why do you look like you're about to piss yourself?"

"You know, I'm having trouble remembering why we're friends," I told him as I pulled the door open.

We walked into the large open space where Gavin and Stacia were going to say their vows in just less than twenty-four hours.

"Uh…because I contain the awesomeness that you've always striven for but could never quite live up to."

"And modest to boot, huh?"

The truth was that I was absolutely terrified about seeing Savvy again. I'd counted down the hours until she was back in Cloverleaf, and now that she was here, just some feet away from me, I felt the unmistakable need to hurl. I didn't know how I was going to get through the evening or the following day without losing it.

It had taken everything I had not to call her every day and beg her to come home because I knew she needed to come to the decision on her own. She had to decide for herself, not for me. That was what I had told myself every day. That was the reason I had kept our interactions so impersonal. I had to let her do what was right for herself, no matter how badly I wanted her back.

But that didn't mean I hadn't planned for the best possible outcome. Everything was in order. I just had to have faith that it would all work out.

Savannah

Stacia was an evil bitch. There was no question about it. If she wasn't getting married the following day, I might have seriously kicked her ass for putting me in such an awkward situation. She'd sworn up and down that Jeremy and I had been paired together for the wedding procession strictly based on height, but I knew she was full of shit. She'd done it on purpose. If I thought it would do a damn bit of good, I would have pitched a grade-A middle school hissy fit, but I was pretty sure every single one of our so-called friends was in on the little coup.

"I'm disowning you bitches when this weekend is over. You hear me? Dis. Owned."

"Hey, it's not our fault you're a midget and have to stand at the end," Lizzy hissed from next to me, earning a laugh from Emmy and Mickey and an evil glare from Stacia as she and Gavin ran through the motions of what they would be doing at the real ceremony.

I let out a snort and gave an eye roll. Then I turned back to pay attention to the rest of the rehearsal.

Before I knew it, it was time for us to do the practice run of walking back up the aisle. I walked from my perch and met Jeremy at the end of the aisle, looping my hand through his arm. I tried to mask the involuntary shiver that shot through my body at his touch, but it was pointless. I was sure he'd felt it.

We were halfway to our destination when he tilted his head down and whispered in my ear, "You look beautiful, sugar."

God, I missed that name, I missed that voice, I missed his scent. There wasn't anything about him that I didn't miss like crazy.

Clearing my throat, I kept my eyes straight ahead. "Thank you," I whispered.

I was both relieved and sad when we broke apart at the entrance to the venue. Desperately needing a moment alone so that I could collect myself, I parted from Jeremy and headed straight to the restroom. I grabbed a handful of paper towels and held them under the running water before wringing them out and placing them on my forehead.

"You okay?"

I looked up to see Lizzy pushing the restroom door closed behind her to maintain privacy. I placed the cold, damp paper towels on the part of my chest that wasn't covered by my dress in an attempt to cool my flushed skin. Jeremy still had that much of an effect on me.

"Yeah, I'm okay. Just needed a breather."

She narrowed her eyes, really studying my demeanor. "You sure you can handle this?" She walked over to me and took the paper towels out of my hand before tossing them in the trash.

I faked courage that I certainly wasn't feeling at the moment. "Of course. I'm fine, I swear. Let's get back out there before Trevor tracks you down and tries to live out his sex-in-the-women's-restroom fantasy."

Lizzy rolled her eyes and laughed as we went out to join our friends.

Later in the evening Ben showed up to the dinner as Mickey's date, and seeing them together just reaffirmed how perfect they were for each other. While I was happy for them, I also felt a pang of envy at what they had.

As the night progressed, my eyes would unwillingly turn to seek out Jeremy, like I instinctively knew exactly where he was at all times. Every time I looked at him, he would turn to meet my gaze as though he could feel my eyes on him. He would shoot me a little grin, setting my blood on fire every time. It eventually became too much and I decided to call it a night. I hugged everyone good night, including Jeremy, and I left to go back to Lizzy's house.

During the past three months of living in a different city, I knew that I missed Cloverleaf. I just hadn't realized how much until I was back. It was more than just the people that I missed. I missed Virgie May's, I missed my old job, and I missed my perfect little house.

Taking a detour on the way to Lizzy's, I turned and headed toward my old home. Ben had helped take care of the sale, so I wouldn't have to deal with all the small aspects of it from four hours away. He never told me who had bought it, and I'd never wanted to ask.

That house was special to me. I'd purchased it using solely my income from P&C. I had felt so proud of myself when I bought it. I'd spent months painting and decorating it until it was exactly what I wanted it to be. The idea of someone else living in the house I'd poured so much love into killed me, but I'd made my choice. I'd chosen to leave in the hopes of finding a happiness I thought I'd lost. But now that I was back, I wasn't so sure that I'd done the right thing.

I pulled up next to the curb and stepped out of my car. There weren't many lights on my old street, so I wasn't able to see the shiny black GTO sitting in the driveway until I was standing at the end of it.

What were the odds of someone else in this small town owning a car almost identical to the one Jeremy had been restoring for years? I was so lost in thought as I stared at the car that I didn't hear the footsteps coming up behind me.

"Taking a trip down memory lane?"

I let out a startled scream and spun around with years of self defense training kicking in instantly. I pulled my arm back, and with as much power as my little frame could muster, I punched whoever was standing behind me right in the nose.

"Ah! Sonofabitch, Savvy! What the hell did you do that for?"

I looked down at the hunched over form in the driveway and finally registered who it was. "Jeremy?"

"Yeah, Jeremy. Who the hell else did you think it was?"

I felt my defenses rising even though he was the one sporting a bloody nose. "Well, that's what you get for sneaking up on me! You don't just creep up behind a woman in the middle of the night and not expect to get punched in the face. You're lucky I didn't kick you in the balls."

He stood to his full height and tipped his head back, pinching his nose to try to stop the bleeding. "Fuck, I think you broke my damn nose."

I crossed my arms over my chest and cocked a hip. "You deserved worse, scaring me like that. What are you doing here anyway? Did you follow me?"

He turned his head down to look at me, still pinching his nose. "Don't flatter yourself, Ali. I live here. Technically, you're trespassing. Should I call Luke and report that as well as the assault?"

My mind went in a million different directions. I couldn't even form a proper comeback. "What do you mean, you live here?"

He pulled a set of keys from his pocket and made his way to the front stoop. He slid a key into the lock and opened the door. "I mean, I live here—as in, I bought the house. You want to come in, so I can get some ice? Or you want to stay out here all damn night and maybe beat the shit out of anyone else who should accidentally cross your path?"

I made my way into the house in a daze. As soon as I crossed the threshold, the breath in my lungs froze and I came to a dead stop. Nothing had changed at all. I'd rented a small apartment in Austin, so I hadn't been able to take most of my furniture with me. I'd opted to sell the rest of it with the purchase of the house. Everything I hadn't taken with me was still in the exact place where I'd left it. Only now, there were a few other odds and ends that Jeremy added to the mix. He hadn't touched a thing that I left behind. It was almost as if I'd never moved away.

Jeremy stepped around me and made his way to the kitchen. I followed behind him and took a seat on one of my old bar stools at the island as he filled a baggy full of ice and wrapped it in a dish towel.

"You do realize I'm gonna be standing in that wedding tomorrow with two black eyes, don't you?"

"I can't believe you bought my house," I replied, still in shock. "Why didn't Ben tell me it was you?"

Jeremy lowered the ice pack and looked at me. "Because I asked him not to."

"Why would you do that?"

Jeremy leaned against the counter across from me and tossed the pack into the sink. The bleeding had stopped, but he was right about the black eyes. I could already see faint purple marks starting to form. I felt a twinge of guilt, but at the same time, I also kind of felt a sense of pride. I hadn't realized I packed such a mean punch. I was a total badass.

"I asked Ben to keep the sale private. I was hoping to surprise you. I just didn't expect bodily injury to be a part of it."

"Jeremy…"

He let out a breath and continued, "This is your home, Savvy. It's where you belong. I know you said leaving was something you had to do, but I couldn't stop hoping that you'd want to come back one day. I wanted to make sure that if that day ever came, you'd have something to come back to."

I couldn't believe what I was hearing. Jeremy bought my house. He'd bought it for me.

"I don't understand," I said, trying desperately to keep my tears in check.

"You loved this house, sugar. I remember how excited you were when you bought it. It's not right that you had to give all of that up. I want you to have it."

"But you said you live here."

"Yeah, I do." He walked around the island and stopped right next to me, tucking an errant strand of hair behind my ear. "Because I'm your home too."

I dropped my head and squeezed my eyes closed, letting the tears that escaped fall onto my lap.

"I know we didn't always get it right, and I know we caused each other a lot of pain along the way, but that doesn't change the fact that you and I are meant to spend the rest of our lives together. We're meant to start a family and grow old together in this house, so I bought it. I'm just waiting for you to see what's been right in front of you all along, sugar."

I stood from the bar stool and took a step away from Jeremy. I wasn't able to breathe with him standing so close. I couldn't listen to what he was saying. It was too much.

"How can you say that, Jer? Two people who are made to be together shouldn't cause each other pain. I hurt you over and over. That's not how someone is supposed to treat their soul mate."

He took a step closer, causing me to back up again. If I let him touch me, I'd cave. And if I caved, I'd have to admit that there was a possibility I'd been wrong, that leaving wasn't what I was supposed to do. The foundation of my life was already dangerously shaky. A blow like that would cause it to crumble completely, and I didn't know what I would do if that were to happen.

"People make mistakes, Savannah. We're only human. Those mistakes don't define us. It's how we choose to fix them that really matters. I know you felt like leaving is what you had to do, but I want you to know that when you're ready, you can quit running. I'll be here to take care of you. I'll *always* be here, sugar."

That was all I could handle. I couldn't listen to any more. That last sentence terrified me.

"I can't do this, Jeremy. I'm so sorry. I have to go." Without a backward glance, I turned and ran to the door.

I couldn't breathe. No matter how hard I tried, I didn't feel like I could get enough air in my lungs, so I did what I'd always done when I was scared to death.

I ran.

CHAPTER
thirty-three

I woke up the next morning with a splitting headache. I'd spent the majority of the night tossing and turning, replaying Jeremy's words in my head over and over. He'd said he would always be there, but I wasn't sure I could trust that. It wasn't his fault though. It was mine. I wanted to believe him, but a person could only try so hard, could only handle so much.

What if he decided one day that being with me wasn't worth all of the heartache I caused him?

A lifetime of doubt had been ingrained in me from an early age. I just couldn't trust that I was worth it.

One thing I had to be grateful for was the fact that the day was so packed with wedding preparations that I hardly had time to think. We were on the go from the moment we'd woken until the ceremony was going to start. It was a frantic whirlwind of activity up until the very moment I took my place to begin my walk down the aisle.

The doors opened, and I took my first step out, instantly faltering the moment I saw Jeremy standing at the altar in his tux. It should be illegal for a man to look that good. A flush crept up my neck as I walked closer and closer to the altar, unable to take my eyes off of him. If I thought the man looked sexy in jeans and a flannel, it was nothing compared to how he cleaned up in a tuxedo.

Somehow, my feet carried me to my destination without me having to think about it. I turned toward my spot, forced to take my eyes off of Jeremy and the cocky smirk he was giving me, and took my place. The music played as the rest of the bridesmaids made their way down the aisle.

"What the hell happened to Jeremy's face?" Lizzy whispered through the corner of her mouth.

I couldn't contain the snort-laugh that escaped me at her question. Yes, I felt bad for breaking his nose the night before, but there was no denying that the situation was hilarious. My eyes cut in his direction as I tried to suppress my laughter, and he gave me a wink in return as if he knew exactly what I was thinking.

He'd *winked*.

The man had poured his heart out the night before, just to have me run out on him, and he'd *winked* at me. I did *not* deserve him.

"You know you're as easy to read as a book, right? You've got self-doubt written all over your face." Lizzy said with a knowing smile

I leaned over slightly and whisper-yelled back, "Shut up. We're in a wedding, for God's sake."

Emmy leaned over as inconspicuously as possible. "Both of you can it before Stacia comes through those doors. If she sees y'all talking, you're dead."

We all straightened just as the doors opened again and the wedding march began playing. As soon as Stacia began walking down the aisle on her father's arm, I turned to see Gavin's reaction. His face was lit up like a Christmas tree, a huge smile splitting right across the middle. Seeing how happy he was to be marrying the love of his life was so moving.

At that thought, my eyes drifted back to Jeremy. He was staring back at me with so much affection that my heart felt like it was going to beat right through my chest. We spent the rest of the ceremony locked on each other, only turning away to cheer when the minister announced Gavin and Stacia as husband and wife.

The wedding reception was fantastic. Everyone was having a blast. The room was beautifully decorated in white

and soft gold, the food was phenomenal, the DJ was absolutely amazing, and best of all, there was an open bar.

I was sitting at one of the round tables off of the dance floor, watching my friends make fools of themselves while trying to do The Wobble. I couldn't recall the last time I'd laughed so hard.

I picked up my champagne flute and took a sip just as the song changed and "Like a Star" by Corinne Bailey Rae began playing.

"May I have this dance?" Jeremy asked as he came from behind me and held out his hand.

"I don't know, Jer. You know how horrible of a dancer I am. Add three glasses of champagne to that, and you might walk away with more bruises than you've already got."

He took the glass from me and placed it gently on the white covered table. Then, he took my hand, pulled me from the chair, and led me to the dance floor. "I'll take my chances. You just have to promise not to turn into a control freak and let me lead this time."

I threw my head back in laughter. "It's like you don't know me at all."

Jeremy spun me around to face him and placed one arm around my waist, pulling me to him tightly. He grasped my right hand in his left, entwining our fingers, and rested them both on his broad chest. "I know you better than you know yourself, sugar."

Right then, I was sure what he was saying was the truth.

"Are you having a good time?"

I looked up into his gorgeous eyes, not even seeing the bruises I'd caused the night before. "I really am. The wedding was beautiful."

The arm around my waist tightened slightly, and he lowered his face to my shoulder. "You're beautiful," he whispered.

His breath on my bare skin caused goose bumps to break out over my arms. I inhaled deeply, melting further into his strong body as I rested my forehead on his chest. Being in Jeremy's arms felt so right.

"How can you still be so nice to me after everything I've done to you? I don't deserve it."

I felt him press his lips against the top of my head. "Because I love you," he responded simply. "You made a few mistakes, sugar. That doesn't make you a bad person. I know that. I just wish you did too."

I laughed sarcastically and pulled back to look at his face. "A few is putting it lightly, Jeremy."

His smile vanished, and his face grew serious. "It doesn't matter. I'm always going to forgive you. There isn't anything life can throw at us that we can't handle together, babe. One day, you'll see that."

I lowered my head and placed my cheek back on his chest, letting him guide me around the floor.

"Are you happy?" he asked so quietly that I almost didn't hear him.

I stayed silent for a while, putting serious thought into my answer. "I'm not sure," I finally answered honestly.

"Well, let me ask you this—do you still love me?"

That was one question I could answer without hesitation. "Yes. I never stopped."

He leaned down and placed his forehead against mine, keeping his eyes closed, as he said, "Only ever you, Savannah."

"Only ever you," I whispered back.

Jeremy let go of my hand and wrapped his other arm around me, holding on to me like he never wanted to let go. "If you'll just take a chance on us, I promise I'll make sure that you're happy every day for the rest of your life. You can trust me, Savannah."

Every wall I'd put up to guard myself came crumbling down after he said that. There was no way to keep Jeremy out any longer. I didn't even want to.

"You think we can really do this?"

His face lit up just like Gavin's had earlier when he laid eyes on Stacia. "You know what they say—third time's a charm."

I smacked him on the arm. "I'm being serious, Jer."

His joking demeanor faded. "Are there any more secrets between us?" he asked.

I answered with complete certainty, "No more secrets, I swear." Then, I finally faced the one thing that gave me pause. "What about Charlotte?"

"Charlotte stopped being an issue the morning you came to my apartment. She's gone. If I hadn't been drunk out of my mind, that night would *never* have happened."

I had a choice to make, and this time, I was making it completely for myself and no one else. I could either let go of all that hurt and move forward with my life, or I could hold on to that pain and let it prevent me from ever truly being happy. Once I finally got past all my fears and self-doubt, I discovered that the answer was simple.

"I love you, Jeremy. I want to come home."

epilogue

"Wake up, sleepyhead. We've got things to do."

I batted Jeremy away and pulled the comforter over my head.

Gavin and Stacia had left the ceremony around midnight, and Jeremy and I had chosen to leave shortly after. We'd headed back to his house—well, *our* house now—and he'd kept me up for several more hours before I finally passed out from exhaustion.

My man is a sex god. No doubt about it.

"Go away, or die."

"Sorry, sugar. No can do. We've got a plane to catch."

That woke me up. "What do you mean, we've got a plane to catch? Where are we going?"

"That's the surprise. Now, move your sexy ass, or we're gonna be late."

I threw the covers off and jumped out of the bed. I quickly rummaged through my suitcase while arguing, "You can't just spring a last minute trip on me, Jeremy. I only packed for the weekend. When did you have the chance to buy plane tickets anyway?"

"Don't worry about the rest of your things. We'll head to Austin and pack you up when we get back. And I didn't buy these tickets at the last minute. I've had them for a while."

I grabbed my toiletry bag and headed for the bathroom. "Oh, you were that sure of yourself, huh?"

He stepped in my path and wrapped me in a hug. "I had faith. There's a difference." He planted a steamy kiss on me that had my toes curling, and then he pulled away, ending it too soon. "Shake a leg, sexy," he said, giving me a slap on the ass.

By the grace of God, I'd managed to shower and dress in half an hour. We jumped into Jeremy's GTO and booked it to the airport.

"Seriously, where are you taking me?" I asked for the hundredth time.

"You'll see," he said with a smug grin.

As soon as we walked through the glass doors, we turned to check our bags, and I spotted our friends already at the counter. *All* of our friends were there, even Ben was there with his arm around Mickey. Stacia and Gavin were even standing there.

"Uh…babe, what's going on?" I asked as we made our way over to them before hugging everyone hello.

Jeremy ignored my question and kept glancing around, like he was looking for someone.

So I turned my attention to everyone else. "What's going on? Aren't you supposed to be on your honeymoon?" I asked Stacia and Gavin.

"Jer hasn't told you yet?" Emmy asked.

"He hasn't even told me where we're going."

"This has been in the works for a while. We're all going with you. Gavin and I will head out on our honeymoon when we all get back," Stacia said.

I turned to Jeremy, who was still looking around. "In the works for a while, huh? That's a lot of faith."

He looked down at me and pulled me to his side for a kiss. "I'll bet on us every time, sugar. Oh, good, they're here."

"Who's here?" I was so confused.

Everyone we knew was already with us. *Who else could he possibly have been waiting on?*

Just then, three people I never expected came walking up to our group, dragging rolling luggage behind them. One person in particular surprised the hell out of me.

"Mom?"

"Hi, sweetie," she said, running up to give me a huge hug.

I knew that we'd made some serious strides in fixing our relationship, but it was still surreal to have her treat me with so much affection.

"Hi, sunflower!" Burt said, pulling me into a massive bear hug before passing me off to Kathy.

"Will someone please tell me what's going on?" I demanded as my eyes traveled over everyone standing around us.

"We're going to Vegas, baby," Jeremy declared with a shit-eating grin.

"We are?" I squealed, jumping up and down, before throwing myself at him. I'd never been to Vegas and I was beyond excited. "So…what? We're making it a group trip or something?"

"You could say that," Jeremy said, taking a step back and pulling my arms from around his neck.

I suddenly had a feeling that there was more.

"Do you love me, sugar?" he asked, a nervous expression on his face.

I hated seeing him look so unsure. I placed my hands on his cheeks and looked directly in his eyes. "More than life itself, baby. Only ever you."

"So you won't have any problem marrying me?"

What?

"What?"

Right there in the middle of the airport, in front of all of our friends and family, Jeremy dropped down on one knee and pulled a dark blue velvet box from the pocket of his jeans. He lifted the lid to reveal the most beautiful three-stone, oval-cut diamond ring I'd ever seen.

"This is something we should have done a long time ago, sugar. This has been seven years in the making…*at least*. I don't want to wait another day without you as my wife. We have everyone we love with us right now. Marry me, Savannah."

I turned to see my mom and Kathy were both in tears as they looked at us with huge smiles on their faces. Everyone had known. Everyone I ever loved was there with me, standing by me, as I prepared to make the biggest decision of my life. Jeremy couldn't have planned a better proposal.

It was perfect.

He was perfect.

And I couldn't wait to start my life with him.

I got down on my knees right in front of him and wrapped him in a tight hug. "Yes," I whispered into his neck, drenching the collar of his shirt in tears. "It's always been you, Jeremy," I said as I pulled back and looked into my fiancé's eyes. "Only ever you."

The End

acknowledgments

The longer I've been a part of the writing community, the more the list of people I need to thank grows. I absolutely LOVE that.

First and foremost, I have to thank my family. My poor, neglected husband and who supports me day in and day out. Thank you for not complaining—much—when I glue myself to the computer and heavy-sigh at you every time you try to start a conversation while I'm writing. I love you so much, babe! And I have to thank my son for giving me wonderful blackmail-worthy material that I can put into my books and show to future girlfriends for years to come. *Insert evil laugh here*

To some of the best damn friends I could ever ask for: Shea Hoke, Shey (Shannon) Owens, Lynda Ybarra, Amanda Cantu, and Crystal Cantu. I love you ladies so hard, it's not even funny! To L.B. Simmons, Kathryn Perez, Erin Noelle, Syreeta Jennings, Emmy Montes, and Carey Heywood, getting to know you ladies has been absolutely amazing. I adore each and every one of you and am so glad I can call you friends.

Thank you so much to Katherine Peters at Love Words & Books Blog. You've been with me from book one and I appreciate your support more than you'll ever know.

To my editor, Jovana Shirley, and cover artist, Meredith Blair: You ladies are fabulous! Thank you for sticking with me through constant emails and freak-outs.

And last, but surely not least, I need to say a special thank-you to every one of my readers out there. It's because of you that I keep writing. The kind messages I receive from you push me to be the best writer I can be. As long as I have my readers at my back, I'll never stop.

Love to all, and thank you a hundred times over.
~Jess

about the author

Jessica was born and raised in Texas—where she'll stay because she claims the cost of living in Texas excuses the god-awful weather. She is first and foremost a wife and mother. Because of those two things, she's also a self proclaimed wino and coffee addict.

She's always been and avid lover of all types of books, but romances are her main favorites.

Jessica's husband likes to say reading is her obsession, but she likes to call it her passion…there's a difference.

other books by jessica prince

Picking up the Pieces

Nightmares from Within

get to know
jessica prince

Email: authorjessicaprince@gmail.com

www.authorjessicaprince.com

www.facebook.com/#!/AuthorJessicaPrince

Twitter: @JessPrince2013

www.goodreads.com/JessicaLeePrince

Made in the USA
Charleston, SC
23 December 2014